Duty and Deception

Duty and Deception

Roberta Grieve

ROBERT HALE · LONDON

© Roberta Grieve 2015
First published in Great Britain 2015

ISBN 978-0-7198-1698-7

Robert Hale Limited
Clerkenwell House
Clerkenwell Green
London EC1R 0HT

www.halebooks.com

2 4 6 8 10 9 7 5 3 1

Typeset in Sabon
Printed in Great Britain by Beforts Information Press Ltd.

CHAPTER ONE

ANNA GRAYSON PASSED under the stone archway in the Roman city wall, leaving the elegant Georgian squares and streets behind. She found herself in an area of dirt and noise, a warren of poor cottages and small factories which backed onto the river which encircled Midchester.

Although she had visited her father's factory on a few occasions, she wasn't really familiar with this part of town. William Grayson liked to keep his business and family life separate.

She paused to get her bearings, glancing down at the envelope in her hand. It was addressed to William Grayson Esquire at his home, St Martin's House. The messenger who had delivered it had stressed that it was urgent and must be given to Mr Grayson at once.

If it was that urgent, why hadn't he taken it directly to the factory, Anna wondered. He must have known that her father was unlikely to be at home at that hour.

'I'll take it, miss,' her maid, Millie, had offered.

But Anna was glad of the excuse to get out in the June sunshine and she was enjoying the walk. At least she had been until she neared the factory. The noise from the machines was deafening and the smell of dust and hot metal made her reach for a handkerchief. How did her father's employees stand it, shut up here all day?

It was quite a small factory, employing only about twenty people, most of whom were young women. Needle-making, which had been part of the life of Midchester for several hundred years, had started off as a cottage industry. When she was still a child, her father had told her how his great-grandfather had set up in the parlour of his little cottage that backed onto the fast-flowing river.

'It was the machines that did it for the hand-workers,' Father had said. 'Big factories set up in the industrial towns up north. They could produce thousands in the time it took the hand-workers to make a hundred needles. We couldn't make enough to meet the demand. We had to invest in machines or go under. But it was a good thing we did.' He smiled proudly. 'Look at us now – a thriving business giving work to the townspeople, not to mention paying for this fine house, servants, beautiful clothes and jewels for you and your mother.' He had waved an expansive hand to take in the fine drawing room with its rich furnishings and ornaments.

She should be grateful for his hard work and achievements, Anna thought now, but she couldn't help thinking about the factory workers. It seemed somehow wrong that they had to work such long hours just so that she could enjoy an easy life.

As she stepped into the yard, where a shire horse stood patiently waiting for the cart to be loaded, the noise of the machines abruptly stopped. Within seconds of them being switched off, a bevy of young women had spilled out into the yard, laughing and chattering.

They took no notice of Anna as they settled themselves on boxes and crates, some sitting on the bare ground, and opened their packets of sandwiches. She caught a snatch of conversation as she went into the building to look for her father.

'So you will come with me then, Lily?' one of the girls said.

'But, Gracie, Mum will kill us if she finds out,' the other girl replied.

'Please – you promised,' the one called Gracie said.

Lily shrugged. 'All right. I'll come.'

Anna was intrigued but she continued inside and went through to her father's office. As her hand reached for the latch, it was flung open and the factory overseer, Edward Johnson, stormed through, almost knocking her over. He pulled up short with a forced smile.

'Oh, Miss Anna, I'm sorry. What are you doing here?' he asked.

'I've brought a note for Father,' she replied, annoyed with herself for explaining. She had never liked the man and she made to brush past him. But he held out a hand.

'Mr Grayson doesn't wish to be disturbed. Give it to me and I'll take it in to him later,' he said.

'I was instructed to deliver it personally, so if you'll excuse me, Mr Johnson ...'

'Of course, miss. Anything you say, miss.' Johnson stepped aside with obvious reluctance, but he did not walk away.

As Anna went into the office, she could feel his eyes on her and she shuddered inwardly. Despite his good looks, his thick auburn hair and startling blue eyes, she had never taken to him. Why did she dislike him so, she wondered. He had always been very respectful of her but his constant smiling set her teeth on edge. Still, her father thought very highly of him and recently had turned more of the running of the factory over to him.

William was engrossed in some paperwork and didn't look up when she entered.

'What now, Johnson?' he asked irritably.

Anna cleared her throat. 'It's me, Father. I've brought you a note. The messenger said it was urgent and I knew you wouldn't be home till late, so ...'

William's demeanour changed immediately when he saw the envelope in her hand and he leapt up from behind his desk. 'Anna, my dear – you should have sent Millie with it. You didn't have to walk all the way down here.'

'I enjoyed the walk, Father – it's such a fine day.'

'Well, I'm pleased to see you, of course, but I am very busy.' He held out his hand for the note.

She handed it to him and he snatched at it, tearing it open and becoming immediately engrossed in the contents. His face grew red and he muttered something under his breath.

'Is everything all right, Father?' Anna asked.

He waved her away. 'Just business.'

Anna waited, willing him to tell her what it was about. If she'd been a son, he would have shared it with her. She would have been involved in the running of the factory, not stuck at home every day, living the life of a lady of leisure. It was so frustrating. But William was an old-fashioned man who thought the factory was no place for his daughter. Anna could almost have smiled at the irony of him employing so many young women, yet denying his daughter the chance of a career.

'I'll be off then, Father,' she said.

He nodded absently, scarcely looking up from the letter in his hand, but as she turned to leave he said, 'Tell Johnson I want to see him immediately.'

She couldn't help a satisfied smile. Father was obviously annoyed about something. It looked as if the overseer was in for a telling off. He probably deserved it too, she thought, as she delivered the message and saw his face pale.

She walked out into the yard where the factory girls were packing up the remains of their dinner, ready to return to work.

'Back to the grindstone,' one of them grumbled.

'I can think of better things to be doing on a lovely day like this,' the one called Gracie said, looking up into the cloudless blue sky.

As Anna reached the gate, a gust of wind blew a piece of paper across the yard. It came to rest against her skirt and she bent and picked it up, her eyes skimming over the advertisement.

'Meeting on Wednesday evening at the parish hall,' she read. 'Come and listen to the well-known suffragist leader, Lady Beatrice Winslow.'

Anna knew Lady Beatrice slightly. She was a member of the Church Ladies' Guild and served on the board of the local cottage hospital. But she hadn't realized Her Ladyship was involved with the suffrage movement.

She was about to put the leaflet in her pocket when she found herself face to face with the girl called Gracie.

'You one of them suffragettes, then?' she asked, snatching at the leaflet. There was the trace of a sneer on her pretty face.

Anna was taken aback but she kept hold of the leaflet. 'I don't know,' she stammered. 'I hadn't thought about it.'

'Don't know what good it'll do getting the vote – not for the likes of us, anyway.'

'Why do you say that?' Anna asked.

Gracie stared at her. 'Well, it's different for people like you, innit – you being the boss's daughter and all. Even working men don't get to vote so ...'

She made to turn away but Anna grabbed at her arm. 'Wait. Why not?'

'It's only for people like Mr Grayson, factory owners and such – not the ordinary workers like my dad.'

'I didn't realize.'

Gracie gave a sarcastic laugh. 'She didn't realize – huh!'

Before Anna could protest, she took the other girl's arm. 'Come on, Lily. Mr Johnson will be breathing down our necks if we're not back at our machines. Don't want him docking our pay for being late.'

'Wait, please.'

The girls stopped and Anna hesitated, not sure what to say. As Gracie tugged at the other girl's arm, she found her voice. 'I heard you talking earlier. It was about this, wasn't it?' She indicated the paper in her hand.

'So what?'

'Well, I might go to the meeting too. It sounds interesting.'

'Up to you, innit?'

'I'll look out for you both. Tell me your names, please.'

'I'm Grace Mitchell and this is my sister, Lily – not that it's any business of yours, Miss Grayson.'

The two girls walked away and disappeared into the factory. Anna watched them go, wondering if they really would attend the suffrage meeting. She was now determined to go herself and she hoped she would see Grace Mitchell there. For, despite the girl's prickly attitude, she had liked her outspokenness and felt she would like to get to know her better. She had never given much thought to her father's employees but now she wished she had taken more interest in them.

She tucked the leaflet into her pocket and hurried back through the streets to St Martin's House. Would she brave her father's disapproval and go to the suffragist meeting? And he would disapprove, she knew. But perhaps he needn't know.

When Anna came down to breakfast the next day, she was still thinking about her encounter with the Mitchell sisters and trying to decide if she would be brave enough to incur her father's displeasure by attending the meeting.

She could tell he was in a bad mood by the way he huffed and rattled the pages of his newspaper. She had been late coming down because Millie had got flustered while pinning up her hair. She'd dropped the pins and had to start all over again.

As she took her place at the table, Anna patted the smooth bun which always reminded her of a cottage loaf. How she wished the fashion were for something less elaborate. Perhaps she should change to a style she could cope with by herself in the mornings. But Millie had been with them for years and had always dressed her mother's hair. Now, she did the same for Anna and she would be mortified if she felt she was no longer needed. Besides, Anna was too fond of Millie to want to upset her.

'Good morning, Father,' she said, to be answered by a further rustle of the paper. Being late for meals always irritated him but this morning, he didn't comment and she realized that something else had upset him. Perhaps it was the letter she had delivered yesterday. Would he relax his rule and tell her what it had been about?

'What is it, Father?' she asked and waited tensely for his reply. Perhaps it was something trivial, like the bacon not being crisp enough or Millie forgetting something when she laid the table.

'Nothing for you to worry about, my dear,' he said, shuffling the pages of the newspaper again. 'It's these silly women making trouble again. First they chain themselves to the railings outside Downing Street – now this.'

'What have they done now?'

Anna's heart sank. The efforts of the suffragettes to bring attention to their cause had only antagonized people like William Grayson, who had firm ideas about women's place in the scheme of things. He would never agree to her attending Lady Beatrice's meeting.

'Someone called Emily Davison has thrown herself in the path of a horse at the Derby. Completely disrupted the race.' He read a bit more, his face twisted in disgust. 'It says here it was the king's horse. Foolish woman – how does she expect people to take them seriously?' He threw the paper down beside his plate and stood up. 'What did she think it would achieve?'

'The poor woman. Was she badly hurt?' Anna asked.

'Don't tell me you sympathize,' he said, going into the hall.

Anna followed him, saying, 'It was a dreadful thing to happen.'

'Maybe, but I don't want you getting involved in this sort of thing.' He turned to her, wagging a finger in her face. 'If I thought you had anything to do with these people ...'

'Of course not, Father,' Anna said, hoping he wouldn't notice the guilty flush that crept over her face. If she confessed that she was planning to attend a meeting he would certainly forbid it. The news about Emily Davison had given her pause but although she hated the idea of deceiving him, she had made up her mind.

She took William's hat from the hallstand and handed it to him. 'Goodbye, Father. Don't work too hard,' she said, kissing his cheek.

She watched him striding down the front garden path and getting into his motor car. It was only a short distance to the factory but he loved to drive, sitting upright and proud in the Daimler, which had recently replaced the old horse and carriage.

Anna smiled and went back to the breakfast room where she picked up the abandoned newspaper. Father didn't like her reading at table, although he did it himself. But he wasn't here to disapprove, she thought, as she poured herself a cup of tea. Since her mother had died, Anna had been a dutiful daughter, looking after the household and her father. But recently, she had become bored with her narrow existence. Taking an interest in the Votes for Women movement would be anything but boring if the morning paper was anything to go by, she thought.

She read the article which had so upset Father, wondering how badly Miss Davison was hurt. She hoped the lady would survive her injuries. However misguided her action, she'd been really brave. They all were, these militant women. Anna didn't think she'd have the courage to do something like that. Although she admired them, she had often wondered what good it would do for women to have the vote. It would still be the men in Parliament making the laws – laws which kept girls like her virtual prisoners in their own homes, subject to the whim of a man, whether father, husband or brother. Perhaps attending the meeting this evening would convince her.

Anna loved her father dearly but William Grayson had strict ideas about how a dutiful daughter should behave and he'd become stricter since her mother's death.

Lydia Grayson had always supported Anna's ambitions and, in defiance of Father, had insisted that she be allowed to train as a school teacher. But when Anna was fourteen, Mother had become ill and died within a few months. Anna's dreams of becoming a teacher were shattered when Father insisted she left school to take over her mother's role as mistress of the house.

Running the household left her with little to do thanks to Millie, their maid; Cook; Joe, the gardener and a daily cleaning woman. To relieve her boredom, Anna had taken up painting, producing pretty watercolours of flowers. She rarely left the house except to attend church or the meetings of the Ladies' Guild.

But it wasn't enough. She couldn't truly say she was unhappy but there was an underlying core of dissatisfaction. She longed to do something more meaningful with her life. Helping the church ladies with fund-raising for the local orphanage and other worthy causes only filled some of the time. She would have done more, but her father had forbidden her to get actively involved as some of the ladies did, taking food and cast-off clothing to the poorest people of Midchester.

'You could catch something visiting those cottages down by the river,' he'd said. 'I couldn't bear to lose you too.'

Anna thought he was exaggerating and she tried to reassure him. 'Don't worry. I have plenty to keep me busy,' she said.

It wasn't true, of course. But how could she complain? She was fortunate compared to the girls at Father's factory. She didn't have to live in damp, unhygienic conditions, or worry about her next meal, or wear shoes which let in the wet.

She resolved to try and overcome her discontent. Perhaps she ought to brave her father's displeasure, and join the church ladies in their good works.

Marriage seemed to be her only chance of escape, she thought, although that would only be exchanging one form of prison for another. Unless she met the right man, of course. Not much chance of that, though. The only people she saw these days were Mother's old friends, members of the Ladies' Guild, and Mr Collins, the vicar, who was married. The new curate, the Reverend Clarence Higgins, was single but, although he seemed quite pleasant, Anna had scarcely spared him a glance, despite the matchmaking efforts of the church ladies.

The only other man she knew was Edward Johnson, but there was something about him that made her shudder. Sometimes, on her rare visits to the factory, she would catch him staring at her, only to look away quickly when she caught his eye. He had a shifty expression and it puzzled her that Father seemed to trust him so completely. But then, she knew nothing of business and perhaps he was good at his job. As far as her father was concerned, his personality did not come into it. She pitied the factory girls, though. It was obvious from Gracie Mitchell's remark that Johnson was not popular with the workforce.

Thinking about the Mitchell sisters reminded Anna about their conversation and the forthcoming suffragist meeting. She went to her desk in the morning room and retrieved the leaflet. She would go, she decided – just to find out what it was all about. She didn't have to join anything. But how could she slip out of the house without actually lying to her father?

She started as she noticed the time. She should have spoken to Cook about the arrangements for dinner. Shrugging off her guilty thoughts, she put the leaflet away.

A shrill cry came from the direction of the kitchen and she rushed into the hall just as Millie threw open the door.

'Oh, miss, come quick. Cook's hurt bad,' she cried.

'What happened?'

She rushed into the kitchen where Cook was sitting at the table, her right hand supporting her arm. Her face was twisted in pain but she managed to say through gritted teeth, 'It's all right, Miss Anna, just a slight burn. I knocked the pan off the stove.'

Anna pulled Cook's hand away and frowned at the livid red stain which had spread all the way up her forearm. 'It doesn't look slight to me,' she said.

'Put some butter on it,' Millie said. 'That's what my mum does for burns.'

'I'm not sure. Perhaps we ought to let Dr Brown look at it.'

'I don't need no doctor,' Cook protested. 'Besides, I've got work to do.'

'Nonsense. I can see you're in pain.' Anna turned to Millie. 'Run along to Dr Brown's. Let's hope he's at home.' She took Cook's hand, her eyes widening in horror as she saw that the skin on her forearm had begun to pucker and form blisters.

Millie was still standing there, her eyes wide, her mouth open.

'Well, run along, Millie – get the doctor,' Anna snapped.

After she'd gone, Anna fetched a clean tea cloth from the drawer and gently laid it over the livid burn. She had read somewhere that warm sweet tea was good for shock and she busied herself at the kitchen range, wincing as Cook groaned in pain.

She turned from the stove as Millie burst into the kitchen. 'Doctor's here, miss,' she gasped.

The tall young man who followed Millie into the room was a stranger and Anna found herself looking up into a pair of grey eyes and a clean-shaven face with a slight cleft in his chin.

Confused, she stammered, 'Where's Dr Brown?'

'He's gone away for a few days. I'm Dr Peters – I'm standing in for him.' He smiled at her and glanced across at Cook. 'Is this the patient?' he asked, placing his bag on the table and crouching down beside her.

'What seems to be the trouble?'

'I spilled hot water on myself – a silly accident,' Cook mumbled.

'Let me take a look.' He gently removed the cloth from her arm and examined the burn.

Anna looked away, swallowing when she saw how large the blisters now were. Millie was staring in horror so Anna said, 'Go and set the table, Millie.' It was better for her to be busy, she thought.

Forcing her gaze to return to the injured woman, she watched as Dr Peters dressed the burn, admiring his deft and gentle fingers as they fastened the bandage.

He sat back on his heels. 'There, that should feel more comfortable,' he said. He took a small bottle from his bag and shook two pills into his hand. 'Take these now and two more this evening. I'll leave the bottle.'

'Thank you, Doctor,' Cook said. 'It feels better already.' She struggled from the chair and said, 'Sorry to be so much bother, miss. Better get on. I'm all behind.'

The doctor put a hand on her shoulder, pushing her back into the chair. 'You need to rest.' He turned to Anna. 'It's quite a serious burn. We mustn't let it become infected. No cooking until it starts to heal,' he said firmly. 'I'm sure your maid can cope for a couple of days.'

Something in his tone made her hackles rise. 'I do know how to cook, Doctor. We'll manage.'

He snapped his bag shut. 'Call me again if necessary.'

'I'll show you out,' Anna said.

As she watched him walk briskly down the front path, her heart was beating faster than usual and her cheeks were flushed. She certainly wouldn't call him again. If Cook needed a doctor she would just have to wait till Dr Brown got back. How dare he insinuate that she was one of these frivolous society women who needed servants to do everything?

CHAPTER TWO

ANNA WENT SLOWLY back to the kitchen where Millie was handing Cook a cup of tea and urging her to stay in her chair.

'Millie's right,' she said. 'You heard what the doctor said.'

'But the pie, miss – it's only half done,' Cook protested.

'Never mind that. As I told Dr Peters, I can cook. Why don't you go to your room and lie down? You're looking a bit pale. You've had quite a shock, you know.'

After a token protest, Cook relented and Anna took an apron off the hook behind the door. She covered her fine wool dress, before rolling out the pastry which Cook had already prepared.

While Millie peeled potatoes, chattering all the while, Anna carried on with the preparations for their meal. She took great care to crimp the edges of the pie exactly as Cook had shown her when she was a small child and it was with a sense of satisfaction that she placed it in the oven and sat down at the kitchen table.

'I've done the vegetables, Miss Anna. Why don't you go into the morning room and I'll bring you some tea,' Millie said, wiping her hands.

'Very well. I'll just look in on Cook and make sure she's all right. And call me if you need any help. I don't expect you to do everything.'

Anna quietly opened the door to Cook's bedroom at the top of the house and was pleased to see that she was dozing on her narrow bed. It must be very painful for her to agree to abandon her work, Anna thought. She could not remember Cook ever having a day of illness. She had served the family devotedly for years and she deserved to be well looked after. For the first time, Anna noticed the lines in the woman's face, the silver-grey hair, and it occurred to her that Cook should have retired long since. But what would they do without her? She, like Millie, was part of the family – more so since Lydia Grayson had died seven years ago.

Anna crept down the back stairs and went into the morning room where she paced up and down restlessly until Millie brought the tea. Only an hour or so ago, she had been complaining to herself that her life was dull and she did not have enough to fill her time. Now it seemed her unspoken wish had been granted but she would have given anything for it to have happened in any other way. Poor Cook should not have to suffer just so that she, Anna, could feel more fulfilled in her life.

She stood at the window, sipping her tea and watched Joe, their part-time gardener and handyman, trimming the hedge. The garden was a riot of colour on this bright June day but the roses were almost finished. Perhaps she would go outside and deadhead them later on. She could have cut the hedge too but Father said it was no job for a lady. She sighed. If she told him she had done the cooking today he would probably insist that they employed someone until Cook was able to work again. Perhaps it would be easier to let him think Millie had done it.

He would be home for his dinner soon, she thought, suddenly remembering that she ought to be back in the kitchen.

'The pie,' she gasped, rushing out of the room.

Millie was straining the vegetables and there was a delicious aroma emanating from the range oven.

'I've laid the table, Miss Anna,' she said.

'Thank you, Millie.'

The pie was done perfectly, its crust golden brown, a little gravy seeping out at the edges.

'Will you go and see if Cook wants anything? I'll finish off here.'

As she busied herself with mashing the potatoes and decanting the vegetables into their tureens, her thoughts turned to the young doctor and she wished she had not been so sharp with him. Perhaps she could make amends if he called again, she thought, blushing slightly at the memory of his finely chiselled features and warm grey eyes. But it wasn't just his good looks that appealed to her. It was the compassionate way he had dealt with Cook's injury. Then she remembered that he was only in Midchester until Dr Brown's return. She would probably never see him again.

*

William Grayson put his knife and fork down, and wiped his mouth with his napkin. 'Very nice, my dear. You must compliment Cook for me.'

Anna hadn't had a chance to tell him about Cook's injury but Millie spoke up before she could stop her. 'Miss Anna made the pie, sir,' she said.

His eyebrows rose. 'You – why?'

Anna quickly told him about the accident and, as she had predicted, he immediately suggested getting a temporary cook.

'But it will only be for a couple of days, Father,' she protested. 'The doctor said she must rest today and tomorrow but she should be able to get back to work after that.'

'Well, if you think so, my dear. But I really don't want you slaving away in the kitchen. You have enough to do with your church and charity work.'

If only he knew, Anna thought, smiling inwardly. Hadn't she recently been chafing at the way time hung so heavily on her hands?

'I can manage – and Millie is a great help. Everything is under control,' she said.

'Very well,' he said.

Anna was surprised he had given in so easily but to forestall any further discussion on the subject she asked if he'd had a good day.

Although he didn't usually like discussing the factory with her, he smiled and said, 'Very good indeed – another big order. The Worcester factory has let someone down and they came to us for an urgent supply.'

'That's good, isn't it, Father?' she said, pleased that he seemed more cheerful today. Lately he'd been looking tired and she had feared that it was business worries weighing him down. 'Can you cope with such a big order?' she asked.

He nodded, concentrating on his pudding, and when he didn't say anything else, Anna knew the discussion was over. He had often told her that factory business was not a topic for the dinner table – not that he talked about business much anyway. The meal continued in silence, for her own life was so mundane that she had nothing of interest to say to him. Perhaps she would tell him about the meeting after all. But no, he had made his feelings on the subject quite plain at breakfast that morning. Still, she was determined to go, even if it meant deceiving him.

Millie came in to clear the table and Anna asked how Cook was.

'I took her up some broth and she seemed to enjoy it,' Millie said. 'She's sure she'll be fit by tomorrow but I told her to make the most of the rest.'

Anna smiled, excusing the familiarity which was born out of the maid's long service with the family.

'Quite right, Millie. I'll go and speak to her,' she said, excusing herself from the table.

The following day, Cook was a little better but Anna persuaded her to rest. She was kept busy in the kitchen for most of the day and the time passed so quickly that it was with a start she remembered the suffragist meeting was that evening.

She hadn't left the house for the past two days and she decided to tell her father that she was going out to a Church Ladies' Guild meeting. She hated lying but she knew that if she told him the true object of the meeting he would certainly forbid her to go. During their meal he had once more railed against 'these misguided women' as he called them, having read in the evening paper that Miss Davison had died from her injuries.

When they'd finished eating, she rang for Millie to clear away and was about to tell her father she was going out when he said, 'I'm off to the club. Don't wait up for me. And tell Millie not to wait either. I have my key.'

Anna was relieved that she hadn't had to lie after all. Perhaps he need never even know she'd gone out. She debated whether to confide in Millie but decided it was better not to. Fond as she was of the woman who had cared for her so devotedly all these years, she knew that Millie was a gossip and might blurt something out in Father's hearing.

She got up from the table and went through to the kitchen where Millie was eating her own meal. Cook was already in bed.

'The master's gone out and might be late back so he said not to wait up,' Anna told the maid. She put a hand to her forehead. 'I'll just go and check on Cook and then I'm going to bed too. I have a bit of a headache.'

'Shall I bring you a hot drink, miss?' Millie asked.

'No, thank you, Millie. I'll take a glass of milk up with me. Then you won't need to disturb me.'

'Very well, miss. Sleep well.'

Feeling a little guilty at the deception, Anna went up to her room where she changed into her best dress – a dark green wool with a matching fur-trimmed jacket and hat. She wondered how many there would be at the meeting and what sort of people they would be. She didn't want to stand out in the crowd. Would they all be upper class ladies like Lady Beatrice Winslow? Or would there be some working girls like the Mitchell sisters there too?

She crept downstairs and out of the side door into the Square and walked through the streets of elegant Georgian townhouses, passing Dr Brown's house on the way. She wondered if he was back yet or if Dr Peters was still standing in for him. She resolutely put the young man from her mind, telling herself she had no interest in him. But a picture of his serious face as he tended to Cook's injury would persist in invading her thoughts at the most inconvenient moments. She resisted the urge to look up at the windows and walked briskly on until she came to the cathedral.

She turned into the High Street, past the medieval market cross and hurried down a side street to the parish hall. Although it was still light, it was unusual for Anna to be out alone in the evenings and she was relieved that there were still quite a few people about. She felt quite daring walking through the streets, unaccompanied. On the rare occasions that she and her father attended a dinner or a charity ball, they always travelled in the motor car, however short the distance.

As she neared the hall, which the newly-formed Sussex Women's Suffrage Society had hired for the evening, she saw the two girls from the factory walking along in front of her.

The older one, Gracie, turned, smiling when she spotted Anna. 'So, you came then? I didn't think you'd have the nerve to turn up,' she said. 'Lily, say good evening to Miss Grayson.'

Lily smiled shyly. 'Good evening, Miss Anna,' she whispered.

'You don't have to call me "miss" – it's just Anna if we're going to be friends.'

Gracie tapped her foot on the pavement. 'Well, *Anna*, we'd better hurry. Don't want to miss the fun.'

'Have you been to any of these meetings before?' Anna asked.

'Only one. We went along for a laugh, didn't we, Lil? Didn't know what all the fuss was about. But it was interesting what the speaker said.'

'We thought it would just be posh ladies with nothing better to do but it made sense,' Lily said.

'Yes. Why shouldn't we vote like the men?' her sister said.

'But you said you didn't think it would do any good – us having the vote, I mean.'

'We won't know till we've got it, will we?' Gracie laughed. 'I hope there's a good turnout,' she said as they reached the hall. 'We're very lucky to get Lady Beatrice. She's been so much in demand since she started the society. Everyone wants to hear her speak.'

'What do you mean by "we"? You two haven't joined the movement, have you?' Anna was horrified. She hoped her father never got to hear of it. He would certainly disapprove of any of his workers getting involved in politics. They might even be dismissed.

'We haven't joined yet. But Lily and I have talked about it and after this evening we probably will. We must show our support in a practical way.'

There was that 'we' again, as if Gracie was quite confident that Anna agreed with everything she said. And she did – in principle.

Even at the beginning of this new century, women were still second-class citizens with very few rights. There was always someone – father, brother or uncle to tell them what they could or could not do, even if they never married. Anna recalled her earlier rebellious thoughts. But however much she wanted to rebel, one thing was sure. She couldn't possibly join any sort of political organization. Her father would be very angry and would no doubt forbid her to attend any more meetings if he found out what she was up to.

She followed the girls into the hall where rows of chairs had been arranged facing a low platform and they managed to find seats quite near the front. The room was filling up and Gracie looked round with a smile of satisfaction.

'You see – there are lots of people who think like us,' she said. 'Even a few men. That's a good sign.'

Anna looked around and noticed a group of young men standing at the back of the hall. There were plenty of seats left and she wondered why they didn't sit down. Then she saw them nudging one another and grinning. Their smirks sent a shiver down her back. She was sure they hadn't come to hear Lady Beatrice speak. They were out to make mischief.

She tugged at Gracie's arm.

'I don't think I want to stay after all,' she whispered. 'It looks as if there's going to be trouble.'

'Don't be so silly. There's always a few hecklers at these meetings.' Gracie giggled. 'It makes it more exciting.'

Anna felt it was the kind of excitement she could do without. She didn't get the chance to say so as a ripple of anticipation went through the room and someone began to clap. The applause was taken up by the rest of the audience as a group of ladies filed onto the platform.

Anna recognized the tall, imposing figure of Lady Beatrice immediately. She had spoken at the church guild some months ago, trying to raise money to help the homeless. Her companions seated themselves in a row on the platform and the chairman introduced, 'Our very distinguished guest, Lady Beatrice Winslow.'

There was another spatter of applause and when it had died down, Her Ladyship started to speak. As her voice gathered momentum, filling the furthest corners of the large room, Anna found herself listening attentively and even nodding agreement occasionally. Lady Beatrice was clearly passionate about her subject and the sacrifices they would have to make to get anybody to take notice of their demands.

Anna hoped that would not entail joining the agitators she'd heard about, who threw things at prominent politicians or chained themselves to railings. She could just picture Father's face if she did anything like that.

But to her surprise Lady Beatrice went on to say that, although she understood why such things went on, she did not agree with their tactics. 'That is the difference between the suffragettes and ourselves,' she said. 'I am a suffra*gist* – and I believe in using constitutional persuasion to achieve our aim. Militant tactics will not work in the long run.' She went on. 'It has been suggested by some medical men that we who desire the vote for ourselves and our sisters must be suffering from some sort of mental condition,' she said. 'That is utter nonsense ...'

Before she could continue, the young men at the back began to catcall and laugh. Some of their remarks made Anna flush with embarrassment, but Lady Beatrice ignored them and tried to carry on with her speech.

But it was no good. Every time she opened her mouth, the catcalls began again.

'I knew they meant trouble,' Anna whispered to Gracie.

'And trouble is what they'll get,' Gracie said, leaving her seat and running up the aisle, brandishing her umbrella.

'Gracie, no, you'll get hurt,' Anna shouted, going after her.

The chairman banged on the table but no one took any notice. Several other women now stood up, shouting, 'Let her speak.'

One of the audience, her face pale and strained, was clearly frightened by the commotion. She tried to get to the door, but a well-built youth gave her a shove.

'Hey, stop that,' Gracie yelled, lashing out with her umbrella.

Anna grabbed her arm. 'Please, Gracie, leave him alone. You're just as bad as they are. Violence is not the way.'

'Quite right, miss,' a voice said in her ear. 'You young ladies should go home and leave this to us.'

She turned to see a large, ruddy-faced policeman, truncheon at the ready. He tried to pull Gracie away from the heckler. 'If you don't stop that, I shall have to arrest you, miss,' he said.

The heckler snatched at Gracie's umbrella, trying to wrest it away from her. But instead of going to her aid, the policeman pinned her arms to her side. 'I did warn you, miss.'

Suddenly the hall was full of more policemen. But they weren't arresting the troublemakers. It was the women who were being lined up along one wall, those who were too timid to join in the melee, submitting meekly to having their names taken.

But a few like Gracie were protesting violently and Anna saw that the threat of arrest was very real. She turned to Lily, who was watching her sister's struggles but making no attempt to help.

'What shall we do?' she asked.

Lily cowered back, shaking her head. 'I just want to go home,' she whispered. 'I told Gracie we shouldn't come.'

But Anna couldn't desert her new friend. As the policeman fumbled for his handcuffs, her temper erupted. This was so unjust.

'How dare you?' she screamed, pummelling the policeman's back. 'We didn't start this ...'

As he turned towards her, Gracie managed to escape his clutches. She pushed a chair over, laughing when he tripped and fell. She grabbed Anna's hand.

'Come on, let's get out of here,' she said, pulling her towards the back of the hall.

'Wait, what about Lily?'

Although the hall was emptying fast they could not see her at first.

'Don't say she's been arrested,' Gracie gasped.

Then Anna heard whimpering and looked round to see the younger girl cowering behind an overturned chair, blood pouring from a cut over her right eye. One of the policemen crouched over her, holding a handkerchief to the wound.

'Leave my sister alone. We'll take care of her,' Gracie said.

The man looked up at her. 'She needs a doctor,' he said. 'She'll be attended to at the police station.'

'But she hasn't done anything wrong,' Anna protested.

'Maybe so, miss. But I'm only doing my job.'

Gracie changed her tactics and smiled at the policeman, who was younger and better-looking than the one who'd tried to arrest her earlier. 'Please, mister. Let us look after her. There's a cloakroom out the back. I can bathe that cut and then we'll see that she gets home safely, won't we, Anna?'

'All right,' he said reluctantly, helping Lily to her feet. Holding firmly to her arm, he led her towards a door behind the stage. Anna and Gracie followed him into the little room.

'You can leave us now,' Anna said. 'We won't cause any more trouble.'

The policeman ignored her and turned on the tap, wetting his handkerchief and proceeding to bathe Lily's forehead.

'There,' he said. 'It's not as bad as it looks. Perhaps she doesn't need a doctor after all. Better get her home, though. She looks ready to pass out.'

'Why are you helping us?' Anna asked.

'Happen I don't agree with arresting women for speaking their minds,' he said. 'It was those hecklers started it. I was standing at the back of the hall as we'd been told there was going to be trouble.'

'So why didn't you arrest the troublemakers?' Anna asked, staring at him defiantly.

'Orders, miss. There's people at the top don't like the idea of women stirring up trouble. There's been all that business in London with that Mrs Pankhurst. And then that society lady throwing herself under the king's horse. A shame she died. But my bosses don't want that sort of thing happening down here in Sussex.'

Lily was starting to revive and Gracie helped her up.

'Perhaps we should go now – that's if you're sure we're not under arrest,' she said, smiling up at the policeman again.

'I'll let you off this time,' he said with a twinkle in his eye.

'We'll have to make sure you're around next time we decide to hold a meeting, Constable...?' Gracie said.

Anna grabbed her arm. 'Gracie, don't be so forward,' she said. She couldn't believe her new friend was actually flirting with him – after all, he could still change his mind and arrest them.

The policeman grinned and pointed to the stripes on his uniform. 'It's Sergeant – not Constable – Sam Hawker at your service.' He gave a mock bow. 'And next time you see me I won't be in uniform. I've been promoted to Detective Constable.'

'Congratulations, Detective,' Anna said. 'But if we don't leave now, you'll be under arrest for helping us. I can hear someone calling you.'

There were footsteps outside the door and Sam Hawker motioned to the girls to step to one side before he opened it.

'All clear, sir,' he said. 'I was just checking that no one was hiding in here.' He left the room, pulling the door closed behind him.

CHAPTER THREE

THE THREE GIRLS held their breath until the voices and footsteps faded away. When all was quiet, Anna opened another door which led on to an alley running down the side of the hall. They crept to the end and peered round the corner. The young men who had started the riot were still milling about on the pavement and Anna ducked back into the alley as they began to jeer loudly. Had she and her friends been spotted? She ventured a peep once more and was dismayed to see some of those who'd been in the audience being led to a Black Maria parked in the street.

She motioned to Gracie and Lily to stay quiet as the door to the hall opened again. Then a loud cheer went up from the women as Lady Beatrice and her fellow speakers were led out and escorted to another vehicle. With great dignity, Her Ladyship stood and waited until one of the policemen opened the door for her. With a gracious incline of her head, she stepped up into the back of the Black Maria.

Gracie clutched Anna's hand. 'What a heroine,' she whispered.

Until tonight, Anna wouldn't have agreed. Her heroines were Grace Darling and Florence Nightingale, women whose bravery had been more practical. But to stand up for something in which she passionately believed and keep her dignity in the face of such foul abuse took a certain kind of heroism. And, Anna thought, squeezing her friend's hand, Gracie had been pretty heroic too, even if she didn't really approve of her flirtatious ways.

The three young women hid in the alley, waiting until the vans had driven away and the onlookers had dispersed. Anna's thoughts were in turmoil as she realized that this evening's farce would be written up in the local paper. Her father was bound to see it and his prejudices would be confirmed. She wondered how biased that report would be. Sergeant Hawker had told them that the police knew there was likely to be trouble. But instead of removing the hecklers they had blamed the women for the riot.

The newspaper was bound to portray the events as a victory for law and order, the gallant police force quelling a riot of unruly women bent on trying to change what many saw as the natural order of things.

The injustice of it made Anna's blood boil. But then she smiled, recalling Gracie's assault with the umbrella. She wasn't afraid to stand up for what she believed in either. Her admiration for her new friend grew along with a burgeoning sympathy for the new movement. Hadn't she been feeling rebellious herself earlier on, fretting about having to wear the clothes that convention demanded and not being allowed to do the things she wanted to do? Change had to start somewhere – and why not here, now?

She peeped round the corner again, and seeing that the coast was clear, said, 'I must get home before Father gets back from his club. He'll be furious if he finds out where I've been.' She might be feeling rebellious but she wasn't quite ready to defy her father – yet.

The new friends linked arms and walked down the road, talking over the exciting events of the evening. When they reached the corner of St Martin's Street, Anna paused. 'You will let me know when the next meeting is, won't you?'

'You haven't been put off?' Gracie asked.

'Well, it wasn't quite what I was expecting,' Anna said. 'But I think it was most unfair, the way the police behaved. I think we should do what we can to fight injustice.'

'Hear, hear,' Gracie said, but she was smiling. 'I must say there was one policeman who behaved very well. He can arrest me any time.'

'Really, Gracie, you shouldn't carry on like that. It's not ladylike,' Anna protested.

'Well, I'm not a lady, am I?' Gracie turned away sharply. 'Come on, Lily, let's get you home.'

Lily, who had been lagging behind, didn't reply and Gracie turned to her in alarm. Her sister looked pale and shaken, leaning against a wall and holding a hand to her forehead.

Gracie shook her arm. 'Lily, are you all right?' She called to Anna, 'Help me, please. I think she's going to faint.'

Anna had reached her front gate but she hurried back and put her arm round the younger girl. 'We must get her home. She should see a doctor.'

'We can't afford a doctor,' Gracie snapped.

'Let me worry about that,' Anna said, ignoring Gracie's tone.

'I can take care of my sister. Perhaps you should go home in case *Daddy* finds out where you've been.' Her earlier friendly manner had been replaced by bitterness.

'Don't be like that, Gracie. I want to help. It's Lily you should be thinking of.'

Gracie muttered something which Anna took to be agreement and they set off across town, supporting Lily between them.

When they reached the row of cottages beyond the city wall where the girls lived, Gracie said, 'We'll be all right now.' She pushed open the front door and helped Lily inside.

'Don't let Lily go to work tomorrow. I'll make sure it's all right with Mr Johnson,' Anna said. 'And I'll ask Dr Brown to call.'

'I said we can't afford a doctor, and Lily can't afford a day off work either,' Gracie snapped.

'Stop being so stubborn, Gracie. Can't you see your sister's ill? Don't let your stupid pride get in the way of helping her.'

In reply, Gracie shut the door in Anna's face.

As she walked away, Anna wondered what she had done to make Gracie so angry. But then, she knew from her church work that, far from being grateful, those in need were often resentful of any help offered. Perhaps she should have been a bit more diplomatic, she thought.

As she passed the doctor's house, she hesitated. Gracie had been adamant that her sister would be all right, but Lily had looked really ill. Anna was concerned that the blow to her head might be more serious than they'd thought.

She really didn't want to offend Gracie for, apart from her tendency to quickly take offence, there was something about her spirit that appealed to Anna. But she had to do what she thought was right. No matter if Gracie was annoyed, she decided – her sister would be seen by a doctor.

It wasn't until she was standing on Dr Brown's doorstep and her hand was poised over the knocker that she began to have second thoughts. If the doctor – a family friend who had known Anna since she was born – was back, he would surely wonder why she was asking him to call on one of her father's workers at this time of night. And he was bound to speak to William about it too.

On the other hand, if Dr Peters answered the door ...

Her thoughts were in turmoil, but even as she hesitated, she knew she couldn't walk away. She would never sleep for worrying if Lily was all right.

She knocked firmly on the door and waited with bated breath, rehearsing what she would say. When the door opened, she stood speechless for a moment, as a tide of heat flooded her face and she confronted Dr Peters once more.

He had obviously been in the middle of his supper, wiping his mouth with a linen napkin while running a hand through his wavy brown hair.

'What can I do for you?' he asked, peering at her in the dim light which spilled out from the hallway.

'I'm sorry to interrupt your meal but I need a doctor,' Anna said, stammering a little.

He smiled down at her, his grey eyes twinkling. 'It's Miss Grayson, isn't it?' he said, then continued without waiting for an answer. 'What seems to be the trouble this time? Is it your Cook – is she worse?'

Anna shook her head. 'No, the burn is healing nicely. It's ...' she choked back a sob as the shocking events of the evening began to catch up with her.

'What's happened? Are you hurt?' He looked at her in concern, taking in her dishevelled state.

Embarrassed by his scrutiny, she put a hand up to straighten her hat, realizing that her hair was falling out of its pins. And in the light spilling from the open door, she noticed that there was a bloodstain on her jacket – Lily's blood.

The doctor noticed it too.

'You *are* hurt,' he said. 'Come in and let me look at you properly.' He took her arm and drew her into the spacious hall, making her stand under the gas lamp and scrutinizing her face.

She pushed him away. 'I'm perfectly all right, thank you. It's my friend. She got hit on the head. She didn't seem to be too badly hurt but I'm worried about her.'

Dr Peters looked grave. 'A blow to the head can be serious.' He stuck his head out of the front door and looked up and down the street. 'Where is she?'

'We took her home but I thought Dr Brown should take a look at her.'

'Well, since the good doctor is still not back from his travels, you'll have to make do with me. Wait here while I get my bag.' He disappeared into a room off the hall.

While he was gone, Anna looked at herself in the mirror and tried to tidy her hair. She bundled it up, not bothering with the pins, and tucked it under her hat. No wonder he had looked so shocked at her appearance, she thought, jumping as the grandfather clock in the corner began to chime.

Ten o'clock. Would Father be back from the club yet, she wondered. And would he realize she was not at home? Well, she couldn't worry about that now. Concern for Lily came first.

Dr Peters returned, carrying his bag. He took his hat from the hall-stand and said, 'Where does your friend live? Should I get the pony and trap out?'

'No. She lives in Chapel Lane. It's only a few minutes' walk away.'

'You'll have to show me. As you know, I'm new to Midchester and I haven't learned my way around yet.'

When he took her arm, she tried to pull away but he held on to her firmly, saying, 'You've had a bit of a shock by the look of you.'

As they passed under the arch that had once supported the city gate and entered the maze of narrow streets beyond the city wall, his grip on her arm tightened.

She was very conscious of his closeness and she started when he asked, 'How did your friend come to be hurt?'

Anna hesitantly told him about the suffragist meeting, leaving out the moment when they'd almost been arrested. 'We were trying to get away from the riot when Lily was hit,' she said.

'What were you doing there?' he asked.

'We were curious, wondering what it was all about,' she said.

She looked up, expecting to see disapproval on his face but instead he smiled. 'So you're one of these votes for women types, are you? I wouldn't have expected you to be interested in such things.'

She thought he was laughing at her and she pulled away from him. 'And why not?' she said, furiously. 'You men seem to have had it all your own way up to now ...' She started to march away, head held high.

'Wait, Miss Grayson – please.' He caught up with her and stepped in front, barring her way. He spread his hands and shrugged his shoulders. 'Look, it's none of my business so let's drop the subject. But I have a patient to attend to and – I confess – I am hopelessly lost. I've never been in this part of town before.'

He looked so helpless that she couldn't help smiling. 'Doctors don't get called to this part of town very often – the people who live here can't afford it,' she told him. He looked dismayed and she hastened to add, 'Don't worry, you'll be paid.'

'That doesn't concern me,' he said. 'What surprised me was that a young lady like yourself had friends in this part of town.'

Stung by his superior tone, she snapped at him. 'There's nothing wrong with this part of town. The people who live here may be poor but they are respectable working people.'

'I did not mean to give offence,' he said.

Anna didn't reply, merely indicating the cottage where the girls lived – the only one with a lamp still burning in the window.

Gracie opened the door at her knock, peering out hesitantly. 'Oh, it's you, Miss Anna. What are you doing back here?'

'I've brought Dr Peters. Is Lily all right?'

'I think so. You needn't have bothered.' The sharp tone was back in her voice.

The doctor stepped forwards. 'Well, I'm here now. I might as well take a look at her.'

'You'd better come in then. But be quiet. I don't want to wake Mum and Dad.' Gracie opened the door reluctantly and they stepped straight into a tiny front room, crammed with furniture. Lily lay on the horse-hair sofa, a blanket covering her. She stirred when the doctor crouched down beside her, placing a hand on her forehead.

Gracie stood in the doorway and, seeming to forget that she was annoyed with Anna, clutched at her arm, an anxious expression on her face.

Dr Peters straightened up from his examination. 'I don't think it's too serious,' he said. 'She just needs to rest. But if she feels faint or her speech starts to slur, or if she's sick at all, don't hesitate to call me again.'

Gracie nodded. 'You do realize we can't pay you?' she said, that edge of belligerence in her voice once more.

'I told you not to worry about that,' Anna said. She touched Gracie's arm. 'I'd better go. You'll be all right now?'

Gracie nodded. 'I'm sorry I was so ratty with you. I do appreciate your help.'

'I understand,' Anna replied. 'So, are we friends then?'

'I suppose so. Perhaps we'll see each other at the next meeting – if this evening hasn't put you off.'

'I'll be there. Take care of Lily, won't you – and make sure she doesn't try to go in to work tomorrow. You don't have to tell anyone what happened – just say she's sick. Father will see to the doctor's expenses.' Anna turned to the doctor. 'I really must be going home now. Thank you for coming out so late.'

'Wait – you can't walk home alone.' He smiled down at her. 'And you can make sure I don't get lost again.'

They walked through the dark streets in silence, their footsteps echoing on the pavement. As they reached the corner of St Martin's Square, Anna stopped.

'I'll be all right from here. Thank you for helping Lily.'

'It was no trouble at all.' He hesitated. 'I'm sorry if I made assumptions about you and your friends. But I'm curious – how did you come to know those girls?'

'They work for my father. You know he owns the needle-making factory just outside town?'

Dr Peters did not answer for a moment and Anna began to turn away.

'Wait,' he said. 'I'm still curious – and not just about your unlikely friendship with your father's employees. I'd really like to get to know you better, Miss Grayson.'

Anna felt herself blushing and she could not deny that she had felt an immediate attraction to the handsome young doctor. Indeed, she had thought of him constantly since he had come to the house to attend to Cook. But she daren't encourage him, sure that her father would not approve. Until now, every man who had shown an interest in her had been warned off. Anna wasn't sure if it was because he wanted to keep her at home as an unpaid housekeeper and companion in his lonely widowhood, or because he was aiming for a more ambitious match for his daughter. It wasn't something they'd discussed.

She was silent for so long that he reached out and grasped her hand. 'Please say that I may call on you.'

She nodded and whispered, 'Yes, you may.' She pulled her hand away and with a return to her usual spirited manner said, 'You'd better go home and finish your supper.'

He laughed. 'Yes, I must. But I look forward to seeing you very soon so that you can enlighten me about the women's suffrage movement.'

She smiled and said, 'Goodnight, Doctor.'

'Please – if we're going to be friends, you must call me Daniel,' he said.

'Goodnight, Daniel,' she whispered.

She watched as he walked away, conscious that her heart was beating much faster than usual and that her usually pale cheeks were a little flushed.

When she turned in at her front gate, the house was in darkness so she guessed that her father had come home and was now safely in bed. She walked round to the side-door, hoping that it was still unlocked. All was quiet and she turned the handle, sighing with relief. She felt her way through the scullery and kitchen to the front hall. Holding tightly to the banister rail, she mounted the stairs and entered her room. She lit the lamp, glancing with dismay at the state of her clothing. How would she explain the blood on her jacket? She would have to take Millie into her confidence, for she had no idea how to remove the stain herself.

As she slowly undressed and got into bed, she went over the events of the evening. Altogether it had been one of the most exciting times of her life. Sneaking out of the house and attending a meeting which she knew her father would definitely have disapproved of, as well as listening to Lady Beatrice's impassioned speech would have been exciting enough, not to mention the riotous ending to the meeting.

The walk through the city streets with Daniel Peters, the consciousness of her arm in his, the warmth of his hand as he took hers to wish her goodnight had been more exciting still. Would she get the chance to meet him again or would her father spoil things for her as he had so often in the past?

CHAPTER FOUR

THE NEXT MORNING, as Anna was seeing her father off to work as usual, helping him on with his coat and handing him his hat, he paused at the front door.

'Oh, Anna, my dear, I almost forgot to tell you. I have invited Edward Johnson to dinner tonight. We have some business to discuss which is better dealt with outside the factory. See that Cook provides something a bit special for our meal.'

Anna could not hold back her exclamation of surprise. 'Johnson? You mean your overseer?'

'You were not brought up to be a snob, Anna,' her father said severely. 'Edward Johnson is a fine upstanding man and a credit to the works. I am thinking of promoting him to manager.'

Before Anna could reply, Millie came through from the back of the house, holding the jacket she had worn the night before.

'Are you going out somewhere, my dear?' William asked.

'No, Father. I have no plans to go out today.' She turned to Millie and said, 'Thank you, Millie, I see that you've found the coat that needs cleaning.'

William smiled. 'I'll leave you to your domestic duties then, my dear.' He kissed her cheek and walked briskly down the front path.

She closed the front door and took a deep breath. How could her father even think of promoting that odious man? And as for inviting him to dinner ...

Trying to collect her thoughts, she turned at Millie's shocked exclamation. 'That's blood on the lapel there, miss. Whatever happened to you? Did you hurt yourself?'

'Don't make such a fuss, Millie. It's not my blood. Someone had an accident while I was out yesterday and I stooped down to see if the person was all right. It must be her blood. Can you get the stain out?'

Millie frowned. 'I don't know. It seems to have dried on. You should have given it to me straight away.'

'Well, do your best with it.'

'Yes, Miss Anna.' The maid hesitated and Anna knew she was curious about what had happened. Sometimes, having few real friends to talk to, Anna had confided in her. But she was wary of saying too much now for fear of her blurting something out in front of Father.

She went back into the dining room and picked up the discarded newspaper. But today there were no reports concerning the women's suffrage movement. *The Midchester Gazette* did not come out until the following day and Anna couldn't wait to see what the paper would say about last night's meeting.

She ought to let Cook know about their expected guest, she thought, putting the paper down. Although her arm had almost healed, it was still bandaged and she was still in a little pain. Perhaps she would offer to cook tonight as Father had asked for something special. But, although Anna had urged her to rest more, Cook preferred to keep busy and had insisted on resuming her duties. She would be extremely hurt at the implication that she could not manage one extra for dinner.

Anna went into the kitchen, feeling a little guilty for wishing Cook had been out of action for just a bit longer. She had so enjoyed planning and cooking the meals, not to mention the pleasure of having some-thing useful to do with her time. Now, she would have to return to a life of idleness and boredom, broken only by the weekly Ladies' Guild meetings and helping with the church flowers. But perhaps her life wouldn't be so boring from now on. She had woken this morning feeling doubtful about her future involvement with the suffrage movement. But now she thought perhaps it would be good to have an outside interest even if it meant deceiving her father in order to attend the meetings.

Cook interrupted her thoughts. 'Mr Johnson? Do you mean the overseer at the factory?' Disapproval was etched on her plump face but she smiled grimly. 'Something special, the master said, eh?'

Anna nodded. 'What do you suggest, Cook?'

'Well, I had decided on steak and kidney pie – you know it's the master's favourite and he's been looking a little peaky lately. I thought it would cheer him up. You know how he likes his pies, Miss Anna.'

'I'm sure that will do nicely. Thank you.'

Cook turned towards the stove and began banging pots about.

Anna hid a smile as she heard the older woman's muttered words, 'The overseer, invited to dinner? Never heard the like.'

It echoed her own thoughts exactly.

'Are you sure you can manage, Cook?' she asked.

'Don't worry about me, miss. Millie will help me,' she replied.

'Well, let me know if you need me. I don't want you overdoing it,' Anna said.

'I'll be all right.' Cook plonked herself down at the kitchen table and began checking off the delivery from the greengrocer.

Anna left her to it and went into the morning room. She sat down by the window, which looked out onto the walled garden, wondering why her father had invited Johnson to the house. Surely any business they had to discuss could be done in the office. Thinking about Cook's remark concerning her father, she suddenly realized that he did indeed look a little 'peaky'. He had not been himself for some time now and she chided herself for not taking more notice. Was he ill, or just worried about the business? Perhaps that was the reason for promoting Johnson. Anyway, she doubted if she would be told. There would be polite, boring conversation at dinner and then the two men would retire to Father's study to talk about the real reason for their meeting.

Well, it was no use speculating, she thought, getting up and pacing the room. Now, she must find something to fill the empty hours until Father came home, since it seemed that she was not wanted in the kitchen.

Most young women of her age might envy her the freedom to pursue their own interests. But she wasn't free, was she? Father had to know where she was and what she was doing, and he wasn't slow to express his disapproval if she embarked on anything he thought unsuitable.

Then she thought about Gracie Mitchell and her sister Lily, chiding herself for railing against her privileged life when girls like them were forced to spend long hours at the factory bench. It was hard, dirty work, she knew. Still, as Father would say, they were lucky to have jobs with regular pay and two weeks holiday a year. And he treated them well, providing overalls and hairnets to protect their clothing and hair from the ever-present dust. And, if any of them became ill through their work, he paid for a doctor and sent baskets of fruit to their families.

But how would he feel about paying Lily for time off from an injury sustained out of working hours, Anna wondered. She hoped Gracie hadn't said too much when she explained why her sister wasn't at work that day.

Still, it had been an exciting evening and she resolved to defy her father and attend any future meetings. She sat down at her writing desk, deciding to make a note of the points Lady Beatrice had made in her speech so that next time she would have some idea of what it was all about. As she wrote, several questions occurred to her and she wrote them down too. She wasn't sure if she'd be confident enough to stand up and ask them in a crowded hall but perhaps she'd get a chance to find the answers somehow.

She hadn't recognized anybody last night but she'd been too worried about being recognized herself to really take note of the others present. And, afterwards, in her desire to escape undetected, she had tried to avoid drawing attention to herself. But the hall had been crowded and she was sure there must have been some of her acquaintances present. She would make some discreet inquiries at tomorrow's meeting of the Ladies' Guild.

She had just finished writing when Millie tapped on the door and announced that luncheon was served. The morning had gone by quickly for a change and it hardly seemed any time since breakfast.

'I managed to get that bloodstain out,' Millie said, a note of curiosity in her voice. 'Are you sure you weren't hurt, Miss Anna?'

'No. It was my friend. She hit her head when she fell.' Anna spoke without thinking, covering her mouth as she realized she had said too much.

'I thought you said it happened when you were at the factory the other day.'

'I'm sorry, Millie. I didn't mean to deceive you but I didn't want Father to hear.'

'Oh, dear, Miss Anna. What have you been up to?' Millie spoke with the familiarity of long service to the family.

'I went to a meeting and there was a bit of trouble. Some hecklers barged in and broke things up. My friend got knocked over and hit her head.' Anna smiled at Millie's shocked expression. She'd be even more shocked if she realized that the 'friend' she spoke of was one of the factory workers.

'It could have been you,' Millie exclaimed. 'Oh, Miss Anna, how did you get mixed up in something like that?'

'I went to hear Lady Beatrice Winslow speaking,' Anna said, hoping that Millie would not ask what the meeting had been about. She did not think the maid would understand her interest in votes for women.

'Well, thank goodness you weren't hurt. I don't know what the master would say if he knew ...'

'He doesn't know and I don't want to worry him. So let's forget it, shall we?' Anna followed Millie into the dining room and sat down. 'By the way, thank you for managing to get the stain out.'

Millie smiled and left the room, returning a few moments later with a laden tray.

Anna wasn't at all hungry and, as she picked at the food, she wondered what she was going to do with herself for the rest of the day. She felt a little flat after the excitement of yesterday. Reading the latest Marie Corelli novel or struggling with her embroidery seemed a bit pointless now that she had more serious things to think about.

Her thoughts turned once more to the Mitchell sisters and she hoped that Lily had obeyed the doctor's instructions to stay at home today. Perhaps she would call on her and see how she was. She also needed to speak to Father and make sure that Lily got paid for being absent from work. How could she manage that without letting him know that she was acquainted with two of his workers? It was not a friendship he would approve of.

In fact, Anna thought, with a sigh, there was very little that Father *did* approve of. Most of the time he treated her as little more than a housekeeper and, as long as she behaved decorously, limiting her activities to her church work, he gave her a modicum of affection. But if she so much as expressed an opinion, his attitude would change and he would make his feelings plain.

Well, she thought, getting up from the table and ringing the bell for Millie, she would just have to brave his displeasure. A promise was a promise. Perhaps when he got home this evening she could nudge his conscience about paying sick workers without actually mentioning Lily directly, although he would probably say that paying their doctor's bills was enough. She had to try, though. From what Gracie had told her, the family depended on the girls' wages. Their father had a very low-paid job at the tannery on the other side of town and their mother did not go out to work.

When Millie came in to clear the table, she said. 'Please tell Cook it was a delicious meal – I'm just not very hungry today,' she said

Millie loaded the tray and paused with it balanced against her hip. 'Are you feeling well, miss? You look a bit pale, if you don't mind me saying so.'

'I do mind. I'm perfectly well,' Anna snapped, still thinking about the hard life the Mitchells had.

'Sorry, miss.' Millie turned towards the door.

'No, Millie, I'm the one who's sorry. I shouldn't have spoken so sharply. It's just – I'm a little tired, that's all.'

'I expect seeing your friend hurt yesterday upset you.'

Anna nodded. 'Yes, it was upsetting. In fact, I might call on her this afternoon to see how she is.'

It was a spur of the moment decision, although Anna had no idea what she would say when she got there. She'd think of something on the walk through town.

'Is my jacket dry?'

'Yes, miss. I'll fetch it for you.'

As she waited for Millie to comply, there came a peal of the front door bell.

'Now, who's that calling unannounced?' she muttered.

Millie came into the hall, brushing past her and opening the door before Anna had a chance to say that she wasn't at home to visitors.

Hurriedly, she slipped into the morning room and sat down, trying to compose herself. She didn't want to explain to any of the church ladies that she had been about to go out, or where she was going.

She had hardly drawn breath when Millie tapped on the door. 'Dr Peters to see you, miss. Are you at home?'

Anna nodded and clasped her hands in her lap, trying to control her breathing. I knew I shouldn't have given him permission to call, she thought, as a tide of heat rose up her cheeks.

'I knew you weren't well,' Millie whispered. 'What were you thinking of, getting ready to go out when the doctor was about to call?'

'I'm not ill, I tell you,' Anna said irritably. 'Besides, I expect he's come to inquire about Cook. Now, will you show my visitor in, please?'

'Very well, miss.'

Anna made a valiant attempt to compose herself as the young doctor entered the room, putting on her best hostess voice. 'Good afternoon, Doctor. How kind of you to call. I'm sure you'll be relieved to hear that

Cook's arm is much better.' She turned to the maid, who was hovering in the doorway, agog with curiosity. 'Millie, tea, please – at once.'

When the maid had left the room, he said, 'I am, of course, very relieved that your cook is on the mend. But that's not why I'm here. You did say I might call on you, didn't you?'

'Yes, Doctor.'

He approached her chair and took her hand. 'I thought we had agreed that you were going to call me Daniel,' he said.

'Yes – Daniel. Please sit down.' She realized she was stammering and she relapsed into silence. She had never felt so confused in a man's presence before. But then, she had never met someone like Daniel Peters before. He was nothing like the vicar and his curate, or the business friends her father sometimes invited to dinner, who were the only other men of her acquaintance.

The silence was broken by Millie, who came in carrying the tea tray. Anna busied herself with the cups and saucers, all the while taking deep breaths and telling herself not to be so foolish.

As she handed him his tea, Daniel smiled and said, 'You must be wondering why I've called.'

She had been wondering – and hoping. Hoping that he felt the same attraction to her as she felt for him. But when he answered her nod, he said, 'I called on your friend this morning while I was on my rounds. I thought you might be worried about her. I was very relieved that she had taken my advice and stayed at home.'

Anna swallowed her disappointment that his concern seemed to be more for Lily than a desire to further their acquaintance. 'That was most kind of you. Is she recovering?' she asked.

'She'll be back at work tomorrow, none the worse for her little escapade.'

'It wasn't exactly a little escapade,' Anna said hotly. 'It was an important political meeting. It was those thugs who turned it into a riot.' How dare he belittle what had happened?

'I understand that you might feel committed to the cause, however misguided,' he said.

'Misguided.' Anna banged her cup down in its saucer, slopping the tea onto the white tablecloth. 'How else will we ever get things changed? I'm not just talking about the vote. I'm thinking of people like Lily and Gracie having to work long hours in a factory and still not being able to afford a doctor ...'

'Well, getting hit over the head or worse, is hardly likely to help, is it?' The doctor drained his cup and stood up. 'Perhaps I'd better leave since I appear to have upset you. It was not my intention, I assure you.'

Anna stood up too, her face flushed. 'Well, don't go before I've paid you for your attendance last night.' She reached down beside her chair for her handbag but he was already at the door.

'I don't charge those who can't afford to pay. Besides, I'm sure Miss Mitchell would be extremely upset if she thought she was accepting charity from you.' And with that, he left the house before she could ring for Millie to show him out.

The crash of the front door slamming was still ringing in her ears when Millie rushed in.

'What was that noise?' she asked. 'And where is the doctor?'

'Dr Peters has just left. The wind caught the front door – that's what you heard.' Anna was proud that she managed to keep her voice so steady.

Millie looked sceptical but she did not comment. Instead she began to gather up the tea things. At the door she turned and said, 'So, miss, if you aren't ill and he hadn't come to see Cook, what was the doctor doing here?'

'It's none of your business, Millie. And I'll thank you not to be so impertinent.'

Millie looked a little abashed and stammered an apology.

Anna relented. 'He attended the young lady who was injured in the accident yesterday and called to reassure me of her progress.'

'That was kind of him, miss,' Millie said. 'Still, I'm pleased it wasn't a professional call. I was quite worried about you, miss. You looked so pale this morning and now you're all flushed. And you hardly touched your breakfast or your luncheon. I really thought you were sickening for something.'

She picked up the tray and left the room.

Perhaps I am sickening for something, Anna thought, when she was alone again. She had certainly never felt like this before. She put a hand to her cheeks, which were still burning. Both her encounters with the young doctor had left her in a state of confusion. How was it that he could make her so angry and yet leave her with this longing to see him again?

For she couldn't deny that she did want to see him again. She was sure she could make him revise his hasty judgement of her as a rich girl dispensing charity to her father's workers and getting involved in politics on a whim. And maybe she had judged him too hastily too. After all, she had seen his caring side, the way he had tended to Lily and his thoughtfulness in coming to reassure her about the girl's recovery. Perhaps she should not have reacted so impetuously to his comments.

She hoped she would have the opportunity to put things right, to start all over again as if they were meeting for the first time – that's if they ever did meet again. Midchester was a small town but Anna did not have much of a social life. Her father disapproved of dances and balls, visits to the theatre or concerts or anything else where she might meet people of her own age and with common interests. It was unlikely that their paths would cross again.

Anna sighed and picked up her book but the over-blown romantic prose of Marie Corelli's *The Treasures of Heaven* did nothing to improve her mood.

Daniel Peters slammed the front gate behind him and strode off down the street, cursing under his breath. He certainly wouldn't be calling on Miss Anna Grayson again if that was all the thanks he got. Perhaps he could have chosen his words more carefully, he supposed, but surely it hadn't been necessary to react so hotly.

He'd been acting kindly, anxious to reassure her that her friend had suffered no ill effects from the blow to her head. It had nothing whatsoever to do with the way those brown eyes lit up when she smiled, transforming her rather serious expression into something approaching beauty, especially when her cheeks flushed that delicious rosy pink. At least that's what he tried to tell himself.

He shook his head, trying to rid himself of the image. Miss Anna Grayson wasn't for him. Even if she forgave him for his tactlessness, she would never entertain a relationship with a poor country doctor who could not even afford his own practice.

And, if by some miracle, she did, her father would put a stop to it.

When he turned the corner, Dr Brown's carriage was just coming to a halt outside his house. Daniel hadn't been expecting him home till later in the day. He hurried to take the older man's bag and preceded him to the front door.

'Did you have a good trip, sir?' he asked.

'Glad to be home,' Dr Brown replied. 'A little of my sister's company goes a long way. She introduced me to a friend and hinted that I should marry again.'

Daniel smiled but didn't reply. He knew his colleague still mourned the loss of his wife several years ago, but now he'd settled into the life of a confirmed bachelor. His work and the occasional fishing trip were his only interests.

There was already a queue at the side door and Dr Brown said, 'No rest for the wicked. I'd better get unpacked and back to work.'

'I can take surgery for you tonight, sir,' Daniel offered.

'If you would, Daniel. I must confess I am a little tired after the journey.'

Daniel went through to the ante room which housed the surgery and, as he examined patients and dispensed medicines, he tried to push thoughts of Anna to one side. As the last patient left he thought he had been successful, although a mental image of her flushed cheeks and sparkling eyes still lingered at the back of his mind.

Surgery over, he joined Dr Brown, who was just sitting down to his supper in the dining room.

'Thank you, my boy. Not too many tonight?' he asked.

'The usual,' Daniel replied.

'So what's been happening in sleepy Midchester while I've been away?'

'It's been pretty quiet as usual – visits to a few ladies, a couple of minor ailments.' Daniel hoped Dr Brown wouldn't ask for details. He didn't want to mention his attendance on the factory girl and the circumstances of her injury. It would mean explaining his meeting with Anna Grayson and he was reluctant to speak of her, given the way he felt. But then it occurred to him that as his colleague was friendly with William Grayson, he might get to hear about it from him.

He cleared his throat and said, 'I was called out last night actually. A young girl was injured at one of those women's suffrage meetings.'

'Did they arrest her? Did you have to go to the police station?'

'No, I went to her home.'

Dr Brown speared a piece of beef and chewed thoroughly before asking, 'Anyone I know?'

'It was one of Grayson's factory employees.' Daniel felt himself blushing just at the mention of Anna's surname and hoped the doctor wouldn't notice.

But Brown gave a hearty laugh. 'Pretty, was she?' He took a swig from his wine glass. 'Be careful, my boy. You don't want to get mixed up with factory girls.'

'I can assure you, it's nothing like that, sir,' Daniel said.

'Good.' He was silent for a moment, concentrating on his food. Then he looked up, waving his fork. 'I wonder why a factory girl was there. I thought it was upper class ladies with nothing better to do who were making such a fuss about the vote.'

'I didn't ask, sir. I think the girls went out of curiosity and they just got caught up in the mayhem. The police treated them pretty roughly by all accounts – and it wasn't them who started the trouble.'

'It sounds as if you have some sympathy for these women,' Dr Brown said. 'It wouldn't have anything to do with the pretty girl you treated last night, I suppose?'

'No, sir, not at all.' Daniel was denying an interest in Lily Mitchell, not in the women's suffrage cause, but he did not say so. He wasn't sure if the older doctor would approve and, since he entertained hopes of one day being taken on in the practice permanently, he didn't want anything to jeopardize his chances.

CHAPTER FIVE

ANNA WAS STILL seething at Daniel Peters's description of her as 'misguided' but she couldn't help smiling a little at the expression on his face when she had answered back. He obviously wasn't used to people – especially young ladies – speaking their mind. She had to admit she had enjoyed the exchange and hoped he would call again. She doubted it, after the way she had dismissed him.

If only it were Daniel coming to dinner tonight, though, she thought. She would enjoy carrying on their discussion about the suffrage movement and the place of women in society. At least it would be a more interesting conversation than the one she was anticipating this evening. Why, oh why, had Father invited Johnson to the house? Couldn't they talk business at the factory?

Anna went into the kitchen to see how Cook was managing. A delicious smell wafted from the big range oven and pans were bubbling on the hob.

'Do you need any help?' she asked.

'It's kind of you to offer, Miss Anna, but I'm managing. That young doctor knows his stuff. My arm feels much better now.'

'I don't want you to overdo it though, Cook. I'm a bit cross that my father invited a guest while you are not yet fit. You don't need any extra work at the moment.'

'It's no trouble, miss. You said not to do anything special and I'm sure my pie will be good enough for Edward Johnson,' Cook said with a sniff.

Anna did not reprimand her for her outspoken remark.

'I'm sure you're right,' she said. 'But you must ask if you need help.'

'Well, you could take that saucepan off the heat for me. It *is* a little heavy. I'd ask Millie but she's busy laying the table.'

Anna lifted the pan and took it over to the sink. It *was* heavy. Cook had peeled enough potatoes to feed an army. She drained them into a colander and then tipped them back into the pan. 'Would you like me to mash them for you?' she asked.

Cook nodded a little reluctantly. 'You shouldn't have to do this,' she said.

'You know I don't mind helping. It's better to keep busy,' Anna replied.

'The master wouldn't like it if he knew how much time you spent in the kitchen.'

'He's so old-fashioned,' Anna said, getting out the butter, salt and pepper and attacking the potatoes with the wooden masher. Pounding them into a smooth, creamy mass helped to dissipate her feelings.

'He just doesn't understand how bored I get. Besides, what he doesn't know can't hurt him,' she said.

Cook did not comment and seemed to be concentrating on inspecting the pie. Anna finished mashing the potatoes and decanted them into a tureen.

'There, that's done,' she said. 'Now what else would you like me to do?'

'I'd like you to go upstairs and change. You've done quite enough.'

Millie burst through the door, stopping short when she saw Anna carrying the tureen. 'Oh, miss, I could have done that.'

'You have plenty to do, Millie. Have you put out the best china?'

'Yes, miss.'

'Thank you.' Anna would have considered the everyday crockery quite good enough for their unwanted guest but she knew Father would expect her to make an effort.

'Now, if you're sure there's nothing else I can do to help, I'm going upstairs to dress,' she said with a smile in Cook's direction.

In her room, she looked in the mirror, realizing why Cook had suggested she change. There was a greasy mark on her bodice and tendrils of hair had escaped from its bun. She went to the wardrobe, trying to decide what to wear. She did not normally change for dinner and she was reluctant to make an effort just for the factory overseer. But she was unwilling to face her father's disapproval and finally she selected a dress that she knew he liked, reflecting that if only it were Daniel coming to call she would have chosen something more becoming. Seated at her dressing table, she tidied her hair, making sure that the pins were firmly in place.

The thought of Daniel had brought a flush to her cheeks but, as she held a cold flannel to her face, she told herself the heat from the kitchen was responsible. She must not think of Dr Peters again. He had let her know in no uncertain terms what he thought of young ladies getting themselves embroiled in riots at public meetings.

A knock on the door startled her out of her thoughts and she called to Millie to come in.

'Oh, you're ready, miss. I came to see if you wanted your hair done.'

'Thank you, but as you see, I managed.'

'Everything's ready downstairs. I expect the master will be home soon – with his guest.' Millie sounded disapproving, as Cook had earlier.

Anna could not say anything. After all, she agreed with them. But Father's word was law. She would just have to bite her tongue and be agreeable to Edward Johnson for as long as dinner lasted. Despite her curiosity as to the purpose of the invitation, she did not think she could bear too much time in the man's company and she hoped they would disappear into the study as soon as the meal was over.

The peal of the front doorbell sent Millie hurrying downstairs. Anna followed slowly, her stomach churning at the prospect of being polite to the overseer. The two men were still in the hall as Millie took their coats and hats, and Anna pasted a smile on her face.

'Hello, Father.' She kissed his cheek, then turned to the overseer. 'Good evening, Mr Johnson.' Usually she referred to him by his surname alone, but as a guest she felt she should use his title.

'Miss Anna – so kind of you to invite me,' he said, taking her hand.

She pulled away and opened the door to the dining room. 'Do go through and take a seat.'

'Yes, Johnson, come along in,' said William. He pulled out a chair and gestured to the other man to sit. 'And what has our wonderful cook prepared for us tonight?' he asked, turning to Anna.

'Your favourite, Father – and yours too, I hope, Mr Johnson. Steak and kidney pie.'

'Excellent,' said William. 'Cook's pastry is out of this world.'

'I'm sure I shall enjoy it, sir.'

Anna sat down and rang the bell. Millie answered its summons immediately and Anna told her she could begin to serve.

The meal progressed pleasantly enough. Johnson ate with obvious enjoyment and William encouraged him to second helpings. Anna observed him closely, noting that his manners were better than she had expected. But he was obviously making an effort to impress his employer – and her too, she realized with an uncomfortable shiver. She hoped there would not be too many of these invitations. It was an effort to remain polite, for despite Johnson's efforts she still could not take to the man.

They spoke of neutral topics at first – the fine June weather which had brought a riot of rambling roses into bloom just outside the dining room window, the work being done on the cathedral tower. Then the conversation turned to the plans for the church fête and Anna squirmed as her father said, 'My daughter works very hard for the church, you know.'

'It's not just me, Father,' she said, blushing.

'But your flower stall raised a lot of money for the orphanage last year, my dear,' William said proudly.

'And will you be doing the same this year, Miss Anna?' Johnson asked.

'I expect so,' she murmured. 'More vegetables, Mr Johnson?'

'I think I will, thank you. An excellent meal – you must compliment your cook.'

'Well, Johnson, my daughter had a hand in it too, you know. Our cook had an accident and was laid up for a few days. Anna has been helping out and is proving very adept in the kitchen.'

'I'm pleased I was able to help,' Anna said, handing him the tureen and trying to smile. Why had Father felt it necessary to mention this, especially since he had always frowned on her spending time in the kitchen? Not a suitable occupation for a 'lady', he always said.

Johnson was smiling at her. 'Well if this pie is anything to go by ...'

'Oh, no, Mr Johnson. Cook made the pie.'

'Nevertheless, Mr Grayson, you have a very accomplished daughter,' Johnson said.

Anna looked down at her plate, trying to hide her embarrassment and annoyance, a feeling which intensified when the overseer continued, '... and a very modest one, too.'

Why didn't Father say something, chide the man for his familiarity? Her ears were buzzing and she only just caught the end of William's next remark. 'I don't know what I'd do without her,' he was saying. 'Still, I suppose I will lose her one day. She is bound to marry ...'

This was too much. To forestall any further personal remarks, Anna laid down her knife and fork and picked up the bell from beside her plate. Millie came in straight away, and Anna suspected she had been hovering outside the door.

She asked her to clear the dishes and bring in dessert, and when she returned carrying a bowl of trifle, Anna said, 'Will you serve, please, Millie?' She stood up. 'I'm sorry Father, I don't want any. I have a dreadful headache – spent too long in the sun, I think. Will you excuse me, please?'

'But, Anna – our guest ...'

She turned to Johnson. 'Please forgive me. I really do feel quite ill. I'm sure you and Father can manage without me – you have plenty to talk about.' Before her father could protest further, she kissed his cheek and said goodnight.

She closed the door behind her and leaned against the wall, taking deep breaths. What an odious man. Oh, please, Father, do not invite him here again, she thought. She could not endure another evening like this and she would not always be able to plead a headache.

Millie came out of the dining room and looked at her in concern. 'You should go to bed, Miss Anna. I'll bring you up some warm milk and aspirin.'

Anna nodded and went slowly upstairs, undressed and got into bed. She had not lied when she said she felt ill. Her head was really pounding as her thoughts churned. What on earth was Father thinking, encouraging that man's familiarity? And why on earth would he even think of promoting him to manager of the factory? Until a couple of years ago, Johnson had just been one of the workers, maintaining the machines that the girls worked at. Then the overseer had been dismissed and Johnson had taken his place. Now he had wormed his way into Father's good graces and yet another promotion.

A knock came at the door and Millie came in with a tray, laden with milk and a plate of biscuits. 'I noticed you did not eat much at dinner, miss,' she said, helping Anna to sit up and placing a pillow behind her.

'I'm not hungry, Millie.'

'Well, I'll leave the tray here in case you want something later. Now, take two of these pills and a sip of milk.'

'Has he gone yet?' Anna asked, swallowing the pills and drinking the milk.

'No, they're in the study. Talking business, I expect.' Millie took the glass and put it on the tray.

'I'm afraid Johnson will think me very rude and I know Father is cross with me, but I could not bear another moment in his company.'

'I don't blame you, miss,' Millie said. 'Now, stop fretting and try to sleep.'

Anna said goodnight and lay down, trying not to think about the overseer and her father's motives in inviting him to the house. She had a dreadful suspicion that it had something to do with her but she dared not let the thought take form. It was just as she was drifting off to sleep that she remembered the name of Johnson's predecessor.

It was Len Mitchell. Could he be related to Gracie and Lily? Gracie had told her their father worked at the tannery but perhaps he had originally worked for Grayson's. If Johnson had taken her father's place it was no wonder that she had expressed her dislike for the overseer so vehemently.

The next morning Anna got up late, hoping her father had already left for the factory. She was still thinking about the Mitchell family and wondering why Mr Mitchell had lost his job. Father would just fob her off if she asked him and it wasn't something she could broach with the sisters either.

Deep in thought, she started when she saw William still seated at the breakfast table.

'I see you have recovered from your headache,' he said, looking up from his newspaper and frowning. 'Really, Anna, I'm disappointed in you, rushing off to bed like that. You were very rude to our guest.'

'I'm sorry, Father. I really did feel ill. Besides, Mr Johnson came to talk business with you and, as you so often remind me, it is not a subject for young ladies.'

'Do not use that tone with me, miss. I don't know what has come over you lately.' He rustled the pages of the paper. 'I trust you are not being influenced by what you read in the paper – young women have too much freedom these days.'

'I don't know what you mean, Father.' Anna helped herself to scrambled eggs from the dish on the sideboard and sat down, although she didn't think she would be able to eat.

William folded the paper and stood up. 'Perhaps it's time you got married, settled down, had children.'

'That's all very well, Father, but unfortunately I don't know any young men – at least any that you would deem suitable.'

William smiled. 'I'm not so sure about that, my dear. Not that I want to lose you, of course. As I said to Johnson last night, I don't know what I'd do without you.'

Anna's face flamed but she did not reply. How dare he discuss her with his employee? As she handed him his hat and briefcase, a cold feeling settled in the pit of her stomach. Surely he was not implying that Johnson ... No. It was impossible.

CHAPTER SIX

A FEW DAYS later, Anna was getting ready to go to the meeting of the Church Ladies' Guild and she wasn't looking forward to it. But if she didn't turn up, Mrs Collins, the vicar's wife, would call wanting to know why. Anna didn't dislike her and accepted that the woman was kind, rather than nosy, but she resented her interference and her constant attempts at matchmaking. However desperate she was to get away from her role as unpaid housekeeper to her father, Anna had no intention of exchanging her situation for that as the wife of someone like the Reverend Clarence Higgins, or Edward Johnson for that matter.

Since that disastrous dinner her father had only referred to the overseer once, saying that now he was manager of the factory, his increased salary and enhanced status would make him a suitable match.

'I hope you will give it your earnest consideration, my dear,' he said. 'It would set my mind at rest about your future.'

And that of the factory, Anna had thought, giving a non-committal reply. Since then, she had dreaded William's return from work in case he brought the subject up. But he had not mentioned it again and she hoped that meant that Johnson wasn't prepared to fall in with her father's plans.

She opened the door to the kitchen where Millie was washing up the luncheon things and told her that she would be back around five o'clock. Cook, despite her arm still being bandaged, was stirring the stew. She looked up and said, 'Take an umbrella, Miss Anna. Looks like rain.'

Anna smiled affectionately. 'I will, Cook. You take care of that arm and stop worrying about me.'

As she went into the hall and got her coat, Millie followed her and helped her on with it, then closed the door behind her. She went down the front path smiling. Sometimes it was irksome to have the servants fussing around her but she knew it was out of affection. Since the death of her mother, Cook had taken on an almost motherly role and Millie, who had been with the family since Anna was a baby, had always been fond of her.

Having no relatives, apart from her father and an aunt who lived in London and seldom visited, Anna accepted their affection and the familiarity that went with it. It was comforting to know that when she got home, Millie would greet her with a hot drink and a blazing fire, eager to hear the latest gossip from the guild ladies.

She passed the cathedral and turned down the narrow lane to St Peter's Church, entering the parish room at the side. She took her coat off and sat down, greeting the other members. They were a rather staid-looking group of middle-aged and older ladies, and Anna wished there were some younger members to chat to. She couldn't help comparing this group with the passionate women at the meeting the other evening. She smiled, remembering Gracie wielding her umbrella. She certainly wouldn't fit in here, she thought.

When Mrs Collins, a large imposing figure, entered the hall, she was accompanied by another woman. Anna recognized her companion with a start of surprise. It was Lady Beatrice Winslow, whom she had last seen being ushered into a Black Maria by a burly policeman.

The meeting was called to order and the vicar's wife introduced Her Ladyship, saying that the scheduled speaker was indisposed.

'Lady Beatrice was kind enough to step in at the last minute,' she said.

There were gasps from some of the audience and a murmur of protest but Mrs Collins held up her hand for silence. 'I know some of you may not agree with Her Ladyship's views but I think she deserves a hearing. Who knows, she may convince some of you to rally to her cause. There will be time for questions afterwards.'

Anna sat up straighter and smiled. It looked as if this week's meeting wasn't going to be as boring. How she wished Gracie could be here to listen to her heroine again. And this time, she hoped, there would be no interruptions from the rabble of discontented youths who had brought the previous meeting to an untimely close.

Much of Lady Beatrice's talk was a repetition of what she had said at that earlier meeting and Anna's thoughts were beginning to drift when her next words made her sit up straight and pay attention.

'Our opponents think that we are privileged women with little better to do than stir up trouble. But it is not only the titled and well to do that should be agitating for the vote,' Lady Beatrice said. 'There are women working long hours in factories up and down the land, struggling to feed and clothe their families, and earning a fraction of what the men are paid.'

She paused dramatically and Anna squirmed uncomfortably, conscious that her own father was one of those factory owners. But, she reassured herself, Father looks after his workers, not like those who exploit people in order to make a fortune.

She listened intently as Lady Beatrice went on.

'You may ask what having the vote will do for these women. It is true that, even if our demands are met, working people will still not have that privilege.'

Anna nodded, remembering that Gracie had said her father had never been allowed to vote as he was not a householder.

'Rest assured, the day will come when everyone in Britain will have a say in who governs them. That day may be far off, but we have to start somewhere. And the first step is to allow us to vote. Our rallying cry must be "Votes for Women".' Lady Beatrice finished to a storm of applause and then submitted to a barrage of questions.

As she had expected there were dissenters among the more conservative members, but Anna was surprised – and pleased – that there were more supporters than opposition. She herself had been half-convinced at that first meeting but now Lady Beatrice's passionate conviction had completely won her over.

Later, as tea was served, Anna found herself sitting next to Lady Beatrice. She was burning to ask more questions but she was wary of drawing attention to herself. But, as she leaned forwards to replace her cup on the table, Her Ladyship caught her eye and smiled.

'Didn't I see you at the meeting the other evening?' she asked.

Anna nodded, feeling Mrs Collins's eyes boring into her.

'It was such a shame things got out of hand. I do hope you weren't caught up in the mayhem,' Lady Beatrice said.

'I managed to get away,' Anna replied. Then, taking a deep breath, she said, 'I'm so sorry you were taken away.' She could not bring herself to say the word arrested.

'I was prepared for that – and, as you see, I was not detained for long.' She paused. 'In fact, it was a good thing in a way.'

'What do you mean – how could it be?'

'Have you not seen the *Midchester Gazette*? They gave us a splendid write-up. I'm sure it will bring more people to the cause when they see how we were treated.'

'I thought the newspapers would be unsympathetic. The police seemed to blame you for the riot – not those hooligans who started it.'

'I'm sure the editor wanted to report it that way,' Lady Beatrice said with a tight smile. 'Fortunately his wife is a supporter of the movement, and she persuaded him that a good newspaper should be impartial and present both sides of the story.'

Anna hadn't had a chance to read the local paper that day as Father had taken it with him when he left for the factory. So that was what he'd been huffing about over breakfast, she thought, recalling his annoyance when she had seemed to sympathize with Miss Emily Davison the other day. He had sternly warned her not to become interested in the subject of women's suffrage and now she suspected he had taken the paper to prevent her from reading the offending article.

'Do you think people are beginning to listen?' Anna asked.

'Oh, yes. We've been campaigning for a long time but it will come. Every day more people rally to the cause – men as well as women,' Lady Beatrice said, her eyes alight with fervour.

Anna could not imagine her father or the Reverend Higgins ever agreeing that women should have the vote. Unbidden, a picture of Daniel Peters surfaced and she recalled his slightly mocking smile when he had referred to her little escapade. When he had told her he wanted to learn more about the movement, she had believed him but their argument when he had called at her home had shown her that he had only been mocking her.

Despite her attraction to him, she knew that she could never fall in love with a man who held such old-fashioned views about the place of women in society. Wasn't that why she had so resolutely refused to entertain Mrs Collins's determined match-making efforts?

Anna brought her attention back to what Lady Beatrice was saying and nodded enthusiastically when she realized that she was being asked to join the Sussex Association of Women Suffragists.

'Of course I'll join,' she said. 'When is the next meeting?' Fired by Lady Beatrice's fervour in that moment, she didn't care what her father might think – or Daniel Peters for that matter.

Lady Beatrice told her that the association was holding a rally in Brighton the following weekend and asked if Anna would like to join them. 'There are several of us going from Midchester and there will be delegates from all the surrounding towns and villages.'

'I don't know if my father will allow me to come,' Anna said, hating the idea that, as a grown woman, she had to ask permission.

'Well, there's plenty of time to decide. You must come to tea and I can tell you more about the movement. Are you free next Wednesday?'

Anna was a little flustered at the unexpected invitation but, as she hesitated, Lady Beatrice continued, 'Your father can't object to after-noon tea, surely?'

'Of course not. I'd love to come,' Anna said.

'I'll send my chauffeur to pick you up then.' Lady Beatrice stood up and glanced towards the door. 'My car's here now. I must go but I look forward to our next meeting, Miss Grayson.'

As Her Ladyship turned and thanked Mrs Collins and the church ladies' committee for inviting her, Anna looked up to see a maid ushering in a tall, fashionably-dressed young man. He strode confidently across the room, taking Mrs Collins's hand and bowing over it.

'I am so sorry to take Her Ladyship away from this delightful gathering,' he said. 'Come long, Bea.'

Lady Beatrice took his arm. 'Alfred, there's no rush.'

The young man smiled. 'Then we have time for you to introduce me to your friends,' he said.

'Very well. Ladies, this is my cousin, Mr Ponsonby-Smythe. He is staying at the Manor for a while.' She introduced him to each of them, leaving Anna to the last. 'And this is Miss Anna Grayson.'

'Ah, any connection with Grayson's, the needlemaker?' he asked, stroking his moustache. His eyes were alight with interest.

Anna was surprised, knowing as she did how the upper classes usually looked down on those in trade. Lady Beatrice, in her fervour for 'the cause', had been a notable exception.

'Mr Grayson is my father,' she said, somewhat stiffly.

Alfred nodded and was about to say more when Lady Beatrice tapped his wrist.

'Alfred, I thought you were in a hurry,' she said.

'Of course. My apologies. I do hope we meet again, Miss Grayson,' he said, bowing over her hand and smiling into her eyes.

When they had gone the meeting broke up and, as Anna said goodbye to Mrs Collins, the vicar's wife gave her a conspiratorial smile.

'I do believe that young man was quite taken with you,' she said. 'A relative of Her Ladyship would be a good catch.'

Anna blushed and smiled. 'Nonsense, Mrs Collins.' She donned her gloves and departed hastily, smiling inwardly at the older woman's matchmaking attempts. While Mr Ponsonby-Smythe was rich and charming, and in Mrs Collins's words, a 'good catch', Anna had not been impressed with the young man at all. There was something too smooth in his manner as if the charm were all an act. Besides, she thought it unlikely that she'd see him again. Lady Beatrice had not mentioned the invitation to tea again and had probably already forgotten her impulsive gesture.

Despite that, excitement warred with apprehension as Anna hurried through the streets towards St Martin's Square, feeling more alive than she had for years. At last she had something to fire her interest, to drag her out of the routine and boredom of her everyday life. For she had decided that she would defy her father if necessary and attend the rally in Brighton the following week. She would find a way.

She turned the corner and, as she passed Dr Brown's house, she could not resist a glance up at the windows, wondering if Daniel was there.

She spotted a carriage in the yard at the side of the house and her steps slowed. So, Dr Brown had returned from his travels. Did that mean that Daniel had already left Midchester? After all, he was only here as a stand-in while the doctor was away. Well, what did it matter if he had gone, she asked herself, shaking her head and walking briskly away. She had no interest in Daniel Peters.

But she knew that she was deceiving herself. She had seen him three times within the past week and, despite their heated exchanges on the subject of women's suffrage, she found herself longing for a glimpse of him. She couldn't suppress the faint hope that, now that the old doctor was nearing retirement, Daniel would be taking over the practice.

At the corner, she glanced back just once and then, pushing him firmly to the back of her mind, she hurried on, her thoughts returning to Lady Beatrice and the Brighton rally. If anything could distract her from the disturbing image of Daniel's devastating smile, it was the heady prospect of taking part in something she was beginning to think was far more important than anything she had done in her life so far.

CHAPTER SEVEN

FOR THE NEXT few days, Anna was very careful to behave as her father expected of her. She had no excuse to leave the house so that when he arrived home from the factory each day, she was able to say truthfully that she'd spent her time in domestic pursuits. She attended church with him on the Sunday and, to onlookers, gave every appearance of being the dutiful daughter he demanded.

But, even as she made the automatic responses during the service, and sang the hymns as enthusiastically as she always had, her heart was thumping with excitement at the prospect of attending the rally the following week with Lady Beatrice.

During Mr Collins's sermon, Anna found her attention wandering and she glanced around furtively at the other members of the congregation. Mrs Collins was at the front, the feathers on her hat nodding as if in agreement with her husband's words.

Clarence Higgins, from his place near the altar, caught her eye and smiled. Anna looked quickly away, pretending she hadn't noticed. As she turned her head she saw Dr Brown in his usual pew but he was alone. Had Daniel left Midchester? Despite her oft repeated admonition to herself that she had no interest in him, she couldn't quell the little stab of disappointment she felt. She had to admit she'd hoped to have the chance to force him to reverse his earlier impression of her.

The service over at last, Anna followed her father out into the warm sunshine of a glorious summer day. It was Millie's day off and she was impatient to get home and make sure that Cook was managing the roast dinner by herself. Although her arm was almost healed, it was still painful and Anna worried about her lifting the heavy pots off the stove.

Father liked to linger and chat to their friends and neighbours, and she had to wait till he was ready to move on. When Dr Brown came up, he mentioned Cook's accident.

'Your locum did a very good job. She's mending nicely, Anna tells me,' William said.

'He's a good man. I shall miss him when he leaves,' Dr Brown said.

Anna's heart leapt. So he was still here – but not for long apparently.

'He won't be taking over your practice then?' William inquired.

'I'm not ready to retire yet, Grayson,' the doctor protested. 'Besides, it'll be a long time before that young feller can afford to buy into his own practice. He's taken a position at the cottage hospital for the time being.'

They went on to talk about other things, leaving Anna to digest the information. Her mind was in turmoil – she just couldn't make up her mind whether she was pleased or sorry that Daniel was staying in Midchester, and that their paths were sure to cross again.

The next day, a liveried servant knocked at the door of St Martin's House, bearing a note from Lady Beatrice. Anna was in a fever of excitement as she tore open the invitation. She had almost convinced herself that Her Ladyship had forgotten about her.

'What is it, my dear?' William looked up from his own letters and smiled.

'It's from Lady Beatrice Winslow. I'm invited to tea at the Manor.'

'Lady Beatrice? I was not aware that you were acquainted with Her Ladyship.'

'I met her at the Church Ladies' Guild,' Anna said, hoping her father had not heard of her new friend's suffragist activities.

'She does a lot of charitable work, I hear.' He paused and Anna waited with bated breath. 'It seems you are starting to move in different circles, my dear. I'm pleased for you.' He turned back to his newspaper and Anna sighed with relief.

She hadn't been sure whether he'd approve of her new friendship. At one time he'd encouraged her to make friends but on the few occasions anyone had taken an interest in her, he'd found reasons to discourage her. She'd always thought he wanted her to stay at home acting as his housekeeper, until he had invited Johnson into their home and hinted strongly that he would not object to a match.

Until now she'd been content – keeping house for her father was infinitely preferable to marrying someone like Johnson. Could it be that now that she'd become acquainted with Lady Beatrice, Father had changed his mind, hoping she'd meet a more suitable man among her circle? Anna smiled at the thought. If only he knew where Her Ladyship's real interest lay. Besides, she wasn't ready for marriage, she told herself. She tried to ignore the flush on her cheeks at the thought of Daniel Peters and rang for Millie to clear the breakfast things.

As she was about to leave the room, her father gasped and she turned quickly. He was clutching one of the letters he had just opened. His face was ashen and a sheen of sweat glistened on his brow.

'What is it, Father?' She rushed across the room and took his hand. 'Are you ill? Shall I fetch Dr Brown?'

He shook her off. 'Don't be silly, Anna. There's nothing wrong – a touch of indigestion, that's all.'

'Are you sure? I thought it was the letter that upset you.'

William seemed to recover quickly and he gave a little laugh. 'Of course not. I was just surprised at one of our suppliers writing to me here instead of to the factory.'

'Why would he do that?'

'I have no idea. There's probably a simple explanation and it's nothing for you to worry about, my dear.'

'But I thought Johnson dealt with the suppliers,' Anna said.

'He does usually. I'll have to have a word with him.' He stood up and gathered the letters together, folding them into the inside pocket of his jacket. 'I must be off then.' He kissed her cheek. 'Don't forget to acknowledge Lady Beatrice's invitation.'

'I'll do it right away,' Anna said, seeing him to the door.

After he'd driven off, she closed the door and went into the morning room. She sat at her desk, frowning as she wondered if there was some problem at the factory. She recalled the messenger who'd brought a note to the house a couple of weeks ago. But Father had brushed off her inquiries, saying there'd been a misunderstanding over an order. But this letter seemed to have really upset him. She sighed. There was no way her father would ever confide in her – a mere woman. And, despite her dislike of Johnson, she knew that her father thought highly of him. They would sort it out between them, she thought, whatever the problem was.

Getting out notepaper and pen, she dismissed the matter from her mind and wrote, accepting Lady Beatrice's invitation. She sealed the envelope and decided to walk to the post box on the corner. Her Ladyship should get her note this afternoon.

Outside in the warm June sunshine, she strolled along slowly, nodding to neighbours and acquaintances who were also taking advantage of the fine weather. She posted the letter and stood for a moment, looking around her. Across the square, Dr Brown was just getting into his carriage. He gave her a nod of acknowledgement and she smiled back, wishing it were his young locum greeting her.

A foolish thought, given the way they'd parted after their last meeting. She thrust the thought away and turned her mind to her visit to the Manor.

It wasn't until she was home that she thought again about her father's reaction to the letter her father had received. Despite his dismissal of her concern, she knew he'd been upset by it. And why had it come here instead of to the factory?

Usually, William carelessly left any correspondence beside his plate for her to put away. It mostly consisted of invitations and charitable requests, seldom anything important. Anna couldn't help being curious, especially as he had so hastily thrust the letter into his pocket as if he did not want her to see it. She resolved to mention it again when he came home, although he would certainly brush off her concern. He never talked business to her and was unlikely to start now. But she had to try. She did not like to see him looking so drawn and worried.

When Millie came in to announce that luncheon was served, she smiled and said, 'I shall want your help this afternoon, if Cook can spare you.'

'What for, miss?'

Anna abandoned formality and leapt up from her chair. 'Oh, Millie. I'm so excited. Lady Beatrice Winslow has invited me to tea at the Manor on Wednesday.'

'That's nice, miss.'

'You must help me choose something suitable to wear.'

'Yes, miss. You must look your best among those fine ladies.'

Millie seemed to think that Anna's excitement was due to her new friendship. She couldn't tell her the real reason – that at last she'd found something to relieve the tedium of her narrow existence. It wasn't just the purpose of the visit which had got her pulses racing. So much had happened in the past couple of weeks – befriending the Mitchell sisters, meeting Lady Beatrice and getting involved with the suffragist cause. And meeting Daniel Peters too. But she wasn't going to think about him.

Anna flopped down on her bed with a sigh. 'It's no use, Millie. I can't wear any of these.' The room was strewn with the discarded contents of her wardrobe. If only she'd taken more interest in the new fashions. Whatever she wore, she was sure she'd feel out of place at the Manor.

'What about this one, miss?' The maid held up an afternoon gown of pale lilac sprigged with flowers. 'This is so pretty – just right for summer,' she said.

'I don't think so. It's out of style, Millie. I've had that one for years.' She sighed. 'I don't want to let Lady Beatrice down.'

'It's important to you, isn't it, Miss Anna?'

'Yes, Millie. As you know, I don't go out much in society and I want to create a good impression.' It sounded rather frivolous to Anna but she couldn't tell her maid the real reason why this meeting meant so much to her.

'Is there time to get a new gown made?' Millie asked.

'Maybe, but I've used up all my allowance this month. Oh, well – this will have to do.' She jumped up from the bed. 'Can you put these away for me, please?'

She went downstairs, leaving Millie to tidy the room. She sighed. What was wrong with her – worrying about what to wear? She'd never been interested in fashion before.

She should be thinking about the reason she was visiting Lady Beatrice – the cause. What was more important than that? Thinking about it served to take her mind off Father's strange reaction to the letter he had received that morning. But when he arrived home that evening, she couldn't help noticing that he looked more tired than usual and when she asked him how his day had gone, he answered absentmindedly and then shut himself in his study until dinner was announced.

Knowing that he didn't like conversation at the table, Anna held her peace until the dessert dishes were cleared away and coffee was served. She stood up and said to Millie, 'I think I'll take mine in the drawing room.' She turned to William. 'You look a little tired, Father. Why don't you join me? I'll play some music for you.'

'I'm sorry, my dear. I have some letters to write – business, you know.'

'Oh, can't you forget business for one evening?' Anna hoped that by the time she had played some of his favourite tunes he would be sufficiently relaxed to talk about whatever was worrying him.

To her surprise he answered sharply. 'Please, Anna, stop bothering me. Haven't I told you countless times that the business is nothing to do with you? Let me deal with things in my own way.'

She blinked back tears. He very seldom raised his voice to her. 'Father, I'm worried about you. I don't like to see you so tired and stressed.'

'I'm perfectly all right. Now, let me attend to my business and you stick to your domestic duties.'

Chastened, she answered in a small voice. 'Very well, Father.' But inside, she was seething.

He seemed to sense that he'd upset her, for he paused on his way out of the room and touched her arm. 'I'm sorry I was so brusque with you, my dear. But there really is nothing you need concern yourself with.' He smiled down at her and asked if she had accepted Lady Beatrice's invitation.

'I posted a reply this morning.'

'Good, good,' he answered absent-mindedly and, without waiting for a reply, he left the room, closing the door firmly behind him.

Anna gazed after him, a worried frown on her face. She felt sure he was worried about the business. Had they lost an order, or had a supplier let them down?

As she sipped her coffee alone in the drawing room, she couldn't stop going over things in her mind. She sighed. There was nothing she could do about it if he refused to confide in her. But she couldn't sit here brooding.

Despite the interesting turn her life had taken recently, there were still long, lonely hours to fill. It was still fairly light and she went to the window and looked out at the long shadows which swept across the lawn as the sun went down. It was too late to go for a stroll around the garden, and she thought she might as well go to her room.

At the foot of the stairs, she paused and quietly opened the study door. Her father was not at his desk as she expected. Perhaps he had retired early, although it was unlike him to go up without saying goodnight to her. But he *had* been looking especially tired tonight.

As she passed through the hall, she noticed that his hat and coat were gone from their usual place. She had not heard him go out but he often spent the evenings at his club. She went slowly upstairs, feeling a little hurt that he had done so without wishing her goodnight. He probably preferred talking to his cronies at the club than to her, she thought bitterly. There he could talk business to his heart's content.

CHAPTER EIGHT

'MILLIE, DON'T FUSS.' Anna twisted away from the maid's fluttering hands. 'My hair looks perfectly all right.'

'Just one more pin, miss.' Millie pushed the hairpin into the piled up mass and stepped back, surveying her efforts with satisfaction. 'There – that won't fall down in a hurry,' she said, holding up the hand mirror so that Anna could see the back.

'Yes. That will do. Thank you, Millie.' Anna stood up and smoothed the skirt of the lilac dress. She had to admit that, out of style or not, it was a very pretty gown and showed off her figure to perfection. She thought she would pass muster among any of Lady Beatrice's upper class friends who happened to be there.

Millie had wandered over to the window and she turned excitedly. 'The car's here, miss. Hurry up.' She crossed the room and thrust a folded parasol into her mistress's hands.

Anna reached the foot of the stairs just as a knock came at the front door and Millie hurried past her to open it.

The chauffeur handed Anna into the open-topped Lanchester and made sure she was comfortable before closing the door and getting into the driving seat. Anna tried to look as if she was used to such treatment, although in truth she would have been quite happy to walk to the Manor on such a fine summer's day. The large country house was just on the outskirts of Midchester, along a pleasant country lane. But Lady Beatrice had insisted on sending the car.

It was only a few minutes before they were turning into the drive, a long avenue of elm trees leading up to a large house with an impressive Georgian frontage. Originally, it had been quite a modest, timbered, Elizabethan manor house but subsequent generations of Winslows had added to it so that now it was one of the most substantial mansions in the county.

The car halted in front of the porticoed entrance and the chauffeur leapt out to open the door for her. A maid ushered her into a drawing room with several long windows giving a view to the distant Downs.

'Miss Grayson, Your Ladyship,' the maid said, standing back to allow Anna to enter the room.

Anna bit back a gasp of surprise as a tall, gaunt figure rose from a chair by the fireplace. Leaning heavily on a silver-topped cane, the elderly woman took a few steps towards her.

'Come on in, Miss Grayson. My daughter will join us shortly,' she said, indicating a chair opposite her own.

'Good afternoon, Lady Winslow,' Anna replied, pleased that she had managed to get her voice under control. It had not occurred to her that Lady Beatrice's mother would be present. She waited until Lady Winslow was seated again before taking her own chair.

She looked round, hoping that her friend would join them soon. As she struggled to think of something to say, the old lady leaned forwards and scrutinized her.

'So you are another one of Bea's waifs and strays, are you?'

What on earth did she mean, Anna thought, blushing violently. Fortunately, she was saved from having to reply by a voice from the doorway.

'Don't talk such nonsense, Mother. Miss Grayson is a member of the suffragist movement.' She turned to Anna with a smile. 'At least I do hope you will join us formally.'

'I have been seriously thinking about it,' she said.

'Good, good. Mother, have you rung for tea?'

'I was waiting for you to join us.' Lady Winslow tugged at the bell pull beside her chair and turned to Anna. 'So, you are another of these modern women, agitating for the vote? It's all nonsense of course. It will never happen. I had hoped my daughter would have got it all out of her head by now and be ready to settle down. There is a perfectly suitable young man asking for her hand. And by the way, where *is* Alfred? I thought he was joining us for tea.'

'Alfred would rather be out riding than taking tea with us ladies,' Beatrice said with a laugh.

'Not true, my dear. He dotes on you.'

'Mother, please, you are embarrassing Miss Grayson.' Lady Beatrice turned to Anna with a little laugh. 'I'm afraid my mother is of that generation which believes marriage and a family is the only course open for women but I am not ready for it yet – if I ever will be.'

Lady Winslow gave a short laugh and turned her piercing gaze on Anna, saying, 'And what about you, Miss Grayson? Are you of the same opinion as my daughter?'

Until recently, Anna would have agreed with her new friend. She had always thought that, apart from the possibility of having children of her own, marriage would not change her life very much. She would still be an unpaid housekeeper, subject to the control of her husband, just as she was now, living at home with her father. But now her cheeks grew warm as she thought of the young doctor who had recently come into her life. However hard she tried, she just could not stop thinking about him.

'I – I haven't thought about it,' she stammered.

'Nonsense. I am sure a pretty girl like you must have suitors queuing up for your hand.'

That might be true, Anna thought, trying not to think of the Reverend Higgins and his gauche compliments or Edward Johnson, with his obsequious flattery. She gave a definite shake of her head but before she could speak, Lady Beatrice interrupted.

'Mother, will you please stop interrogating Miss Grayson. She is not here to talk about her marriage prospects.'

'I suppose you are going to discuss the *cause* and your part in it. A complete waste of time, but have it your own way. But please, I beg you, defer your discussion until after tea. Let us talk of civilized subjects.'

Anna, conscious of her unsuitable dress, and hoping that ladies' fashions would not be deemed a suitable subject for conversation, tried to think of something to say.

But at that moment the maid came in with a tea trolley laden with tiny sandwiches, toasted muffins and fairy cakes. Conversation lapsed while she busied herself serving the tea.

Lady Winslow waved an impatient hand. 'That will do, Ada.'

The maid deposited a cup and saucer on the small table beside Anna and scurried away.

Anna was surprised that she was the only guest. She had imagined that there would be several suffragist supporters present. At least she was spared the embarrassment of feeling out of place. After a short silence during which she attempted to pick up her tea without rattling the cup in its saucer, Lady Beatrice said, 'Have you asked your father if you might attend the rally on Saturday?'

Anna shook her head.

'Would it help if I wrote and asked if you could accompany me?' asked Lady Beatrice.

'If he's got any sense, he'll refuse,' Lady Winslow said. 'I can't stop you doing what you want, Bea. You're of age. But if your poor father were still alive, he would have something to say about it.' She put down her cup and leaned forwards, touching Anna's knee. 'I'm sure Mr Grayson would not want you to get mixed up in this business. Look at what almost happened to my daughter at the last meeting she spoke at.'

'Mother, it was just a few unruly youths – nothing to worry about at all.'

'But some of you were hurt,' said Lady Winslow.

'The police were rougher than the hecklers,' Bea replied. She grinned and turned to Anna. 'None of them dared to harm me – but I wish they'd tried. I would have given as good as I got.'

'Beatrice, please. I do not like to hear you talking in such a manner,' Lady Winslow protested.

'But, Mother, surely it is better to be able to defend myself if necessary. All women should have the means to do so.'

'But how...?' Anna could not imagine defending herself against a burly policeman, although she had to admit that the sight of Gracie wielding her umbrella had brought out something in her that she scarcely dared to acknowledge.

'I have been taking lessons,' Beatrice said. 'You know, I am not in favour of Mrs Pankhurst's militant methods – they do more harm than good to the cause. That's only my opinion of course.'

'I agree,' said Anna. 'So why...?'

'Well, I heard that she and her followers have been learning jiu jitsu. Have you heard of it?'

'It's like wrestling, isn't it? I don't think I'd be able to do something like that.'

Beatrice explained that it was a Japanese form of self-defence. 'We do not initiate these violent encounters – as you know, I always counsel my followers that peaceful protest wins hearts and minds in the long run. But when we are faced with violence we must be able to fight back.'

'I suppose so,' Anna said doubtfully.

'I hope you will not follow my daughter's lead and get involved in these brawls,' Lady Winslow said. 'You seem like a nicely brought up girl.'

Anna had been feeling rather nervous of the old lady, blushing and stammering under her scrutiny, but now she found her voice. 'I agree with Lady Beatrice and I think she is very brave to stand up for what she believes in,' she said.

'That's as may be,' Lady Winslow replied. 'And now, let us change the subject, please. Do you ride, Miss Grayson?'

The rest of the meal passed uncomfortably for Anna as Lady Winslow quizzed her about her leisure pursuits – those she deemed suitable for a young lady – while Lady Beatrice tried to put her at her ease. At last, the maid came to clear the tea things and Lady Winslow stopped talking and leaned back in her chair.

As her eyes closed and she began to snore softly, Lady Beatrice winked at Anna and whispered, 'Let us take a turn in the garden.'

Anna nodded eagerly and stood up. They stepped through the open French windows onto a terrace and descended the stone steps to the lawn which stretched away to a gleaming lake.

As they strolled across the grass, Lady Beatrice took Anna's arm. 'You must not mind my mother. She is rather old-fashioned in her outlook. Nothing would make her happier than to see me married.'

'Do you mind me asking – the young man Lady Winslow mentioned...?'

'Oh, you mean Alfred – my cousin.' Lady Beatrice laughed. 'He wants to marry me, it is true, but ...' She gave a delicate shudder. 'Besides, it's my money he wants – not me.'

Anna couldn't think of what to say. Although she was shocked at Lady Beatrice's frankness, she remembered meeting Mr Ponsonby-Smythe at the vicarage. She had taken an instant dislike to the man and didn't blame her new friend for rejecting him.

Beatrice squeezed her arm. 'What about you? Do you have a beau?'

Anna stopped walking and said, 'Lady Beatrice, I thought you wanted to talk about the suffrage movement – not my personal life.'

'You're quite right. I'm sorry, Anna – I may call you Anna?'

'Of course.'

'And you must call me Bea – all my friends do.'

They walked on towards the lake and Beatrice told Anna how she had become involved in the suffrage cause. 'At first it was just a bit of fun – a relief from the boredom of hunt balls, tea parties and shopping trips up to town. But then I began to see that it was really important.' She turned to Anna, her face aglow with enthusiasm. 'I do hope you can come on Saturday. I'll write to Mr Grayson and ask.'

'I'm sure Father will refuse his permission. He has no sympathy for the cause.'

'Does he have to know? We could say we're going to the races.' Beatrice's eyes gleamed with mischief.

'I don't think I could lie to him,' Anna said doubtfully.

'I do see that, but you wouldn't have to lie – not directly. I'll write to him asking if you may join my party at the Brighton Races on Saturday. He can't object to that, surely.'

Anna still wasn't sure if it would be right to deceive him but she desperately wanted to attend the rally, so she nodded acceptance.

'That's settled then.'

Although Anna was really keen to go, she couldn't help feeling a little apprehensive, especially after their earlier conversation about the need to defend themselves, should any rioting occur.

But as she made to voice her misgivings, a man appeared on the terrace waving to them.

'Oh, dear. It's Alfred,' Beatrice said in a resigned tone.

He came down the steps and greeted them. 'Why, if it isn't the lovely Miss Grayson. How nice to meet you again,' he said.

'Miss Grayson is just leaving. Could you ask George to bring the car round?'

'No need, dear cousin. My motor is parked in the drive. I can run Miss Grayson home.'

'Oh, please, that's not necessary,' Anna protested, turning to Beatrice. 'It isn't far. I would prefer to walk on such a lovely day.'

'Nonsense, Anna. Let Alfred take you. He loves showing off his new motor.'

There was nothing Anna could do without appearing rude so she accepted. They walked round to the front of the house where Alfred's sporty, maroon two-seater Hispano-Suiza was parked.

'I hope to see you on Saturday then. Goodbye, Anna.'

Beatrice waved them off as Alfred shot off down the drive, with Anna holding onto her hat. She was used to riding in motor cars, but she found that being driven somewhat recklessly by Beatrice's cousin was a different experience to sitting upright beside her father in the Daimler. In truth, she found it rather exhilarating. Still, although she was secretly enjoying the experience, she was relieved when they pulled up outside St Martin's House. She was finding Mr Ponsonby-Smythe's personal remarks rather embarrassing.

He jumped down and ran round to open the passenger door for her before she could do so herself. As he helped her down, he raised his hat.

'Goodbye, Miss Grayson. I do hope we meet again soon. It would be such a pleasure to further our acquaintance.'

'Mr Ponsonby-Smythe, I think your remarks are inappropriate, especially since I understand you are practically engaged to Lady Beatrice.' It wasn't quite true but Anna hoped it would put him off.

His laugh was mocking. 'You are quite wrong. In spite of anything Lady Winslow may have told you, my dear cousin has turned me down flat. So ...'

'Goodbye, Mr Ponsonby-Smythe.' Anna turned on her heel and marched up the short front path, waiting until she heard the car drive away before ringing the bell.

Millie was waiting behind the door to take Anna's coat and hat, obviously agog to hear about tea at the Manor.

'Not now, Millie. I must speak to Cook about dinner and then go and change.'

'Very well, miss.'

Anna smiled and relented. 'I'll tell you about it while you're helping me to dress,' she promised.

She was still smiling as she entered the kitchen. Dear Millie was always so pleased when Anna got to enjoy a treat or a special outing.

As the maid helped her off with her tea gown and retrieved a dinner dress from the wardrobe, Anna told her about meeting Lady Beatrice's mother and described the house and grounds.

'And what about the young man who brought you home?' Millie asked, confirming Anna's suspicion that she had been watching from the window.

'Millie, it's really not your place to ask such questions but I'll tell you anyway. It was Lady Beatrice's cousin.'

'He's very handsome,' Millie said.

'That's quite enough, Millie.'

'Sorry, miss.' The maid accepted the rebuke and concentrated on helping her mistress with the hooks on her dress.

As she descended the stairs to the dining room, Anna couldn't help agreeing with Millie. Alfred Ponsonby-Smythe *was* handsome but he was a little too smooth for her liking. She hoped that if her friendship with Beatrice progressed, it would not mean coming into contact with him too often. There was something about his rather cynical smile that made her feel uncomfortable.

Later, at dinner, Anna expected her father to be as curious as Millie about how she had spent her afternoon but he seemed even more preoccupied than usual as he picked at his food.

'Is the meal not to your liking, Father?' she asked.

He glanced up and shook his head. 'It's fine – I'm just not very hungry.'

Anna was now convinced there must be a problem at the factory but she knew that further probing would just irritate him. As far as he was concerned, she wouldn't understand. Running the factory was men's work. She continued her dinner in silence, reflecting on the irony that although he employed so many women, trusting them to handle dangerous machinery, he didn't think his daughter capable of understanding the complexities of managing orders and finances.

CHAPTER NINE

AT BREAKFAST THE next day, Anna looked up eagerly when Millie entered the room holding a bundle of letters. She held her breath as her father opened them, perusing each one slowly. Had Lady Beatrice kept her promise to write and ask Anna to go to Brighton with her? She took a bite of her toast, swallowing nervously as she saw that he was frowning.

'Is something wrong, Father?'

'I don't know what to make of this,' he said. 'It's from Lady Beatrice Winslow.'

'Is it one of her charities?' Anna knew it wasn't but she could not say so.

'No, it's an invitation – for you, my dear.' He looked at her keenly. 'She is asking my permission to allow you to accompany her to the Brighton races.'

His frown told her that he thought the racecourse a most unsuitable destination for his daughter. She held her breath. Would he consent? She very much doubted it and she was trying to think of ways to persuade him when he shook his head and said, 'I'm not sure I approve. You could come into contact with all sorts of undesirable people.' He paused and her heart sank, but then he went on, 'although I understand the Royal family is fond of horse racing so perhaps ...'

'Oh, please, Father, may I go?'

'Do you really mean to tell me you'd enjoy such an outing?'

'Oh, I would, Father.'

'Well, if it's acceptable for Her Ladyship ...' He perused the note again. 'She does say she will take proper care of you and you will be chaperoned. Two other ladies will be accompanying her, as well as her cousin, Mr Ponsonby-Smythe.'

Anna was a little piqued that Beatrice's cousin would be in the party.

She had thought from his remarks yesterday that he had no time for the "Votes for Women brigade" as he called them. But she smiled appealingly at her father.

'Please, do say I may go – it could be a nice change to experience something different.'

'I suppose so. If your poor mother was still with us, I'm sure she would have been arranging all sorts of outings and parties so that you might meet the right sort of people. She had such plans for you, my dear. I'm afraid you find life very dull stuck at home, housekeeping for your poor old father.'

'Not at all, Father,' Anna said, smiling. Not for anything would she let him guess how much she had been chafing against the narrowness of her life. 'Do you mean you'll allow me to go then?'

'I suppose so.'

'Oh, thank you, Father.' Anna was tempted to jump up and throw her arms round his neck but she resisted, knowing how he hated any outward displays of affection.

As soon as the meal was finished and Millie had cleared away, she hurried to the morning room to write a note accepting Lady Beatrice's kind invitation. She could hardly contain her excitement and remained in a fever of impatience mixed with apprehension for the next few days. She dreaded that something would happen to prevent her accompanying Lady Beatrice to Brighton. Her father could change his mind, or discover the true nature of the outing, or Cook might have another accident necessitating her staying at home to take care of the household.

She hardly slept for imagining the various scenarios that would put a stop to her escapade. Perhaps she shouldn't go after all. But she couldn't back out now. Besides, it was so exciting to have something to look forward to. She would just have to make sure her father never discovered the truth about her reason for going to Brighton.

Anna rose early on Saturday morning, scarcely able to contain her excitement, although she tried to appear calm as she went down to breakfast. She was wearing a plain gown in dove grey silk with darker trimmings and her father smiled as he looked up from his newspaper.

'You look charming as usual, my dear,' he said. 'But are you sure that dress is suitable for the races? I am sure Lady Beatrice will be decked out in her finery.'

It was unlike Father to notice what she was wearing but Anna realized that, although he did not wholeheartedly approve of her visiting a racecourse, he was impressed by the interest being shown to her by Her Ladyship. He did not want her to be outshone by the other ladies in the party.

She could not tell him that she was wearing her plainest dress on the instructions of Lady Beatrice. Unlike their suffragette rivals with their purple and green colours, the suffragist movement had not designed a uniform for their supporters but had decided on red, green and white for their sashes and banners. It was felt that a dress in plain grey or navy blue would be a perfect background for the movement's colours.

'I think it is going to be a very hot day, Father,' she said now. 'I will be cooler in this dress. Besides, my hat is sure to impress the other ladies.' She hoped that he would not realize the significance of the brightly coloured ribbons and rosette which trimmed her straw bonnet, and which loudly proclaimed her allegiance to the suffragists.

Fortunately, she was spared further questioning about the outing as he declared himself late and hurriedly left for the factory.

A little later, Lady Beatrice's chauffeur knocked on the door of St Martin's House and, holding onto her hat, Anna ran down the path in a most unladylike manner. Without waiting for the chauffeur to open the door for her, she climbed up into the big, open-topped Lanchester. Lady Beatrice patted the seat beside her.

'Good morning, Anna. Lovely morning for a drive in the country-side,' she said. 'You've already met my cousin. And this is Miss Spencer and, her friend, Mrs Hughes.'

Anna recognized both of them from the earlier meeting. They had been among the suffragists arrested at the same time as Her Ladyship.

She smiled a greeting and settled back into the seat between Lady Beatrice and her cousin, barely able to contain her excitement at the prospect of attending the rally.

'I had not thought you were interested in the suffragist movement, Mr Ponsonby-Smythe.' she said.

He gave a rather sarcastic laugh and winked at her. It was just the way he had behaved the other day and she felt herself blushing.

'My cousin has tried to convince me of the worthiness of the cause,' he said. 'But I am not entirely persuaded. Besides, I think my time would be better spent at the races.'

'I thought you would have driven there yourself in that little motor car of yours,' Anna said.

Alfred sighed. 'Unfortunately, she's developed a fault in the engine and she is with the mechanic at the moment. He's promised she'll be ready to collect later in the day.' He smiled. 'I had to use all my charms to persuade Bea to let me travel with her.'

'You are not attending the rally then?' Anna asked.

Lady Beatrice turned towards him and said, 'You might do better to join us, Alfred. You know how my mother feels about your gambling.'

'Stop preaching, Bea,' Alfred said. 'I don't try to tell you what to do. You stick to your little hobbies and I'll stick to mine.' He turned to Anna. 'I can't believe a pretty young thing like you wants to get mixed up in all this nonsense. Why don't you come to the races with me – much more fun.'

Before Anna could reply, Lady Beatrice said, 'Really Alfred, you do talk such nonsense. Miss Grayson is a well brought up young lady. You can't possibly expect her to accept such an invitation.'

He gave that rather unpleasant laugh again. 'Just teasing, dear cousin.'

Anna felt very uncomfortable during this exchange and didn't know what to say but she was saved from having to respond when Mrs Hughes leaned over from the back seat and tapped Alfred on the shoulder. 'Your teasing will get you into trouble one day, Mr Ponsonby-Smythe. And remember, you are in the minority here. Be careful we women don't gang up on you.' It was said in a light-hearted teasing way and everyone, including Alfred, laughed.

But Anna still felt a little embarrassed and she turned her head to look at the passing countryside, hoping that they would soon be nearing Brighton. Although she already looked on Beatrice as a friend, she did not like her cousin at all and resolved that, on the return journey, she would try to sit in the back seat with one of the other ladies.

Soon they were driving along the road which ran parallel to the sea. They passed the West Pier and proceeded a little further, stopping at the entrance to the Palace Pier. The pier and promenade were thronged with day trippers as well as local residents out to enjoy the summer sunshine. Families sat in groups on the shingle facing the sea, and several intrepid bathers were descending the steps of the bathing machines along the shore, shrieking as their bare toes met the cold water.

The open space in front of the pier was crowded with visitors of another kind, however. A platform had been set up with a row of chairs and in front of it were the suffragist supporters, many of them holding banners aloft.

As the chauffeur brought the Lanchester to a stop, Beatrice stood up in her seat.

'A perfect spot,' she declared, 'and a wonderful turnout.'

She stepped down from the motor car unaided, turning to the other passengers. 'Come along, ladies, there's work to be done.' Her face was alight with zeal.

The chauffeur unloaded a pile of placards and banners from the boot of the car and Beatrice instructed him to continue on to the race-course with her cousin.

'You must return here for us at four o'clock. If Alfred wants to stay later than that, he can find his own way home,' she said.

'Very well, Lady Beatrice,' the chauffeur said.

'Don't worry about me, Bea. My own car should be ready to collect by then,' Alfred said.

'Well, if it's not, don't expect us to wait for you.' Bea handed a leather case to him and, ignoring his groan of protest, she said, 'And don't forget to hand out these leaflets at the races. I know you don't sympathize with the cause but you did promise.'

'Anything for you, dear cousin.'

Lady Beatrice smiled and kissed his cheek. 'Thank you. Enjoy the races – and try not to lose too much this time.'

Anna hoped her friend had not seen the cynical look on Ponsonby-Smythe's face as he turned away. She had a sneaking suspicion that the leaflets would be thrown away as soon as he reached the racecourse.

As they made their way to the platform, Miss Spencer said, 'No hecklers today, thank goodness.'

'Not so far,' Lady Beatrice answered. 'But, although we intend this to be a peaceful rally, we must be ready for anything.'

The ladies ranged themselves on the platform, Lady Beatrice in the front row with representatives of various local societies in the county. Anna recognized Mrs Betty Corbett, a well-known suffragist from the Bellingfield Society, who had been one of the speakers at the Midchester meeting.

Anna looked down from the platform across a sea of faces, some of them holding the banners that Beatrice's helpers had handed out. Several of them were also decked out in the suffragist colours of red, white and green. It was a huge crowd, far more supporters present than she had imagined, including a good number of men too. Fortunately, they looked respectable types, not like the rowdy youths who had crowded the back of the church hall at the previous meeting.

The rally was proceeding very peacefully and Anna was pleased that there would probably be little need for the policemen who were standing at the back of the platform, their truncheons at the ready. She really hoped there would be no trouble today but she remembered Bea telling her about the jiu jitsu lessons, and she couldn't help a sneaking feeling that it might be rather fun to see her friend in action.

She thrust the thought aside and turned her attention to the speakers, listening to them with rapt attention.

When a pause came in the proceedings, she scanned the faces among the crowds in front of the platform. Some looked like working girls enjoying a day off from their factories and offices. Many of them had made an attempt to show their support of the suffragist movement with red and green ribbons in their hats and sashes across their bodices.

They certainly seemed very supportive – a mixed crowd from all walks of life. She thought some of the faces looked familiar and wondered if the Mitchell sisters were among the crowd. One man caught her eye but he turned away and she wasn't sure if she had really recognized him. There were plenty of men around with auburn hair after all. And what would Johnson be doing at a suffragist rally? From the way Gracie had said he treated the factory girls, it seemed unlikely that he would be a supporter of the cause.

Anna hoped that if it had been Johnson, he hadn't spotted her. He'd be sure to mention it to her father and she didn't want him finding out where she had been today. She pushed the thought aside and concentrated on the next speaker. Mrs Betty Corbett put the case for women's suffrage extremely well and, as she listened, Anna finally began to understand what it was really all about. What had started off as an adventure, something to brighten up her rather humdrum life, had developed into a cause she was beginning to embrace with the same fervour as her new friend.

The rally ended with a rousing song and the speakers descended from the platform, lingering to chat with some of their supporters.

As the onlookers began to disperse, Anna saw someone waving from across the road. The tall young woman stood out from the crowd and to her delight, she recognized Gracie Mitchell and her sister, Lily. They were both dressed in their Sunday best and Gracie had a sash in the suffragist colours across her bodice, and a pretty straw hat decorated with red ribbons.

Anna responded to their waves and crossed the road to greet them. 'I'm so pleased to see you both. How did you manage to get here?' she asked.

'We came on the train,' said Gracie. 'What about you?'

'I'm with Lady Beatrice and her friends.' Anna pointed to the group standing at the pier entrance. 'You must come and be introduced.'

'She won't want to speak to the likes of us,' Gracie said.

'Oh, please, Gracie. There's plenty of time before our train,' Lily said before Anna could speak. She put a hand up to her head and giggled. 'Do you think she'll like my hat, Anna?' she asked.

Anna smiled. 'It is a lovely hat,' she agreed.

'When I saw Lady Beatrice's at that meeting, I knew I had to have one just like it. I was saving up for a new winter coat but I spent the money on this,' Lily said.

It was indeed exactly like Lady Beatrice's hat, a smart navy blue felt, prettied up with a scalloped edge. Red, white and green ribbons were twisted into a rope-like effect around the brim and fastened at the front with a silk rosette in the same colours. Anna hoped that her ladyship would be flattered rather than offended when she saw it.

'Come on then,' she said.

Gracie hung back. 'Are you sure?'

'Of course – she welcomes the opportunity to thank her supporters,' Anna said. 'There she is.' She took Gracie's arm and started back across the road to where Lady Beatrice was still surrounded by her well-wishers.

They had just reached the other side of the road when a group of youths ran past, shouting insults at the ladies. Two policemen started off after them, truncheons at the ready.

Some of the suffragist supporters began to murmur in protest and one shouted after the youths, 'Shame on you.'

At that, more policemen appeared.

'Now then, ladies, let's not have any trouble,' said a burly sergeant.

'It's them causing the trouble,' Mrs Hughes protested.

The crowd surged this way and that, and Anna began to be seriously concerned. It was just like the other evening when the police seemed to be sympathizing with the troublemakers. At one point, a policeman grasped Mrs Hughes by the arm and it seemed that Bea might be called on to demonstrate her fighting prowess to help her friend. But Mrs Hughes kicked him on the shin and broke away.

The lads who had started it all had disappeared at the appearance of the police but there were still a few hecklers refusing to be moved on. It looked as if a full-scale riot was about to erupt but at that moment, a hired charabanc appeared round the corner. The representatives from Haywards Heath scrambled to get on the bus and, as the crowds began to disperse, Gracie pulled at Anna's sleeve.

'We ought to be getting back to the station,' she said. 'Mum thinks we've come for a day at the seaside and we promised we wouldn't be late home.'

'Oh, please, I haven't met Her Ladyship yet,' Lily begged.

Gracie shook her head but before she could reply, a voice spoke from behind them.

'Who wants to meet me? Friends of yours, Anna?'

Anna nodded and explained to Lady Beatrice that Gracie and Lily had been at the meeting in Midchester the previous week.

'They were really impressed with your speech and are keen to support the movement,' she said.

Lady Beatrice smiled and shook hands with the sisters. 'I do hope you weren't caught up in all that trouble the other evening,' she said, her manner as gracious as if she were meeting ladies of her own class.

'We were more concerned about you, Your Ladyship,' Gracie said. 'I think it's disgraceful the way they treated you.'

'Well, at least there have been no arrests today.'

They continued to chat for a few minutes until Gracie said apologetically, 'We must go. We don't want to miss our train.'

'I wish I could offer you both a lift back to Midchester but there's no room. I have other passengers already,' Lady Beatrice said.

'Thanks all the same. We've got return tickets anyhow,' Gracie said.

As the loaded charabanc pulled away, more cars arrived to pick up those who had come from all over Sussex to attend the rally. Lily and Gracie said goodbye and Lady Beatrice shook hands with them, thanking them for their support.

They started to walk away, pushing their way across the still crowded pavement. Lily shook off her sister's arm and turned back to where Anna and the other ladies were waiting for the chauffeur to return with the Lanchester.

Anna was talking to Miss Spencer when she heard Lily call out. She turned just as her friend reached the group, smiling at the girl's enthusiasm. There was no time to speak as a motor car swooped down on the group and she stepped back in alarm. She heard a loud thud above the sound of the engine. The car didn't stop and there followed a moment of silence as it pulled away. Then the air was rent with a high-pitched screaming which seemed to go on and on.

Anna stood rooted to the spot, only gradually becoming aware of the screams, which now turned to a long, drawn out wail. At first she wasn't sure what had happened. Then she looked down and saw what looked like a bundle of old rags lying in the gutter. She took a step forwards and her eyes were drawn to a navy blue hat, its ribbons bedraggled and torn, lying a few feet away from what she now realized was a body.

The crowd surged forwards, obscuring the dreadful sight. It seemed that minutes passed but it could only have been a few seconds before she pulled herself together and pushed between two of the horrified bystanders. She could not take her eyes off the hat, which still sported its gaily-coloured rosette.

'Lady Beatrice – Bea,' she murmured, stepping forwards and reaching out.

But Gracie pushed her roughly aside and sank to the ground, her high-pitched wails turning to an anguished sobbing.

'Lily, Lily, speak to me.' She smoothed her sister's hair back, gasping as her hand came away covered in blood. She turned a sheet-white face to Anna. 'She's not dead? She can't be.'

She started to wail again as Anna pulled her gently to her feet and put her arms around her. She could not find any words so she stroked Gracie's back, guiding her away from the scene. She glanced back to where a man knelt by the body, looking up and speaking to one of the policeman.

'Come and sit down, Gracie,' Anna said, leading her to a nearby bench. Gracie's wailing turned to hiccupping sobs and she was shaking violently but when Anna looked into her eyes, it was not grief but anger she saw there.

'That bloody car. It was driving too fast,' she said.

'But there were so many cars pulling up and such a crowd, Gracie. It was an accident.'

But she wasn't so sure. Had someone pushed Lily into the road? Anna shook her head. No, it must have been an accident. There were so many people anxious to catch Lady Beatrice's attention. She put the idea out of her head and was trying to comfort Gracie when the man who'd been attending to Lily stood up and approached them. A flush stained her cheeks as she recognized Dr Peters. What was he doing here?

He ignored Anna and crouched in front of Gracie, taking her hand in his. 'I am so sorry, Miss Mitchell. I couldn't save her.'

Gracie's shoulders heaved as a great wrenching sob escaped her. 'What am I going to tell Mum and Dad?'

'If you like, I'll come with you and break it to them,' Anna offered but Gracie ignored her.

'How could someone do that to my poor sister?' she sobbed. 'I saw it. Someone pushed her into the road just as that car appeared from nowhere.'

'It was an accident,' Dr Peters said. 'If she was pushed it was because they were all crowding round, trying to speak to Lady Beatrice. And then there were the hecklers.'

So she hadn't been mistaken, Anna thought. Gracie had seen something too.

She turned to Daniel but he shook his head.

'Let the police deal with it,' he said. 'It must have been an accident – the crowds, the confusion ...'

Anna tried to remember exactly what had happened, but it was all so muddled. She was almost sure that someone had pushed Lily, though. But was it deliberate? Surely if it had truly been an accident, the car would have stopped? The driver must have realized he'd hit someone. With a surge of anger, she recalled the sporty little car – the same colour as Alfred Ponsonby-Smythe's. Cars like that were hardly common on the roads of Sussex. No – it must be a coincidence.

Still, perhaps she should tell someone. But what if she was wrong? She resolved to say nothing unless she was questioned.

She bit back a sob. What an ending to what had been such a wonderful day. Poor sweet Lily, so full of life, so proud of her new hat. When Anna had seen it lying in the gutter, she'd been sure it belonged to Lady Beatrice. Her first fleeting thought had been to wonder what effect the incident would have on the future of the movement. More bad publicity had been her instant reaction. Now she felt a wave of hot shame.

What did that matter compared to the loss of a friend and, in Gracie's case, the loss of a sister?

CHAPTER TEN

ANOTHER POLICEMAN HAD appeared on the scene, red-faced and breathless from chasing the hecklers. Notebook in hand, he was trying to take down details of the accident. The supporters who remained were speaking at once.

'Ladies, please. One at a time,' he said.

Anna hoped she wouldn't be questioned. There were plenty of witnesses and she didn't think she'd be able to speak without breaking down. Besides, what had she really seen? It had all happened so quickly that now she couldn't really be sure.

She still had her arm round Gracie's shoulders while Daniel sat on her friend's other side, speaking in a low voice. Gracie, still white-faced and silent, listened as the doctor explained there would be an inquiry into the accident.

'I'll call on you after I've spoken to the authorities on your behalf.' He turned to Anna. 'You'll look after her, won't you, Miss Grayson?'

Anna nodded and patted Gracie's shoulder.

A horse-drawn ambulance pulled up beside them and two men got out carrying a stretcher, lifting Lily's body into the back of the vehicle. Gracie's sobs broke out afresh and she leapt up.

'No, you can't take her away,' she protested.

'They must move her,' Daniel said.

'Where are they taking her?'

The doctor gently explained and said to Anna, 'Can you see her home, Miss Grayson?'

'Of course,' she replied.

'I'll make the necessary arrangements and let you know.'

'Thank you. That's very kind,' Anna said.

He turned to Gracie. 'Don't worry. I'll see to everything. Go with Miss Grayson. She'll look after you.'

Anna took Gracie's arm. 'Come on, dear.' She led her over to where Beatrice was still waiting for the chauffeur to return with the Lanchester. 'I must look after her,' she said. 'I'll take her home on the train.'

'I wouldn't hear of it,' Beatrice replied. 'She must come in the car with us.'

'That's very kind of you. Are you sure there's room?' Anna said.

Gracie hung back. 'I don't want to go home. What will I say to Mum? And Dad? I can't ...' She choked on a sob.

'I'll come with you and explain,' Anna said.

'Ah, here's George at last,' said Beatrice. 'But where's Alfred? Oh, this is too much.' She marched up to the car as the chauffeur pulled into the kerb.

'Sorry I'm late, Your Ladyship. There was a policeman at the end of the road stopping everyone. There's been an accident,' he said.

'I know that. Where is my cousin? You were supposed to pick him up first.'

'Mr Alfred said he would make his own way home. He met up with some pals and then he was going to see if his car was fixed.'

'Gambling pals, I expect.' Beatrice sighed. 'Well, let's be on our way then.' She turned to Gracie. 'Come along, Miss Mitchell. We'll take you home.'

Reluctantly, Gracie climbed up into the Lanchester and sat behind the chauffeur between Anna and Lady Beatrice.

The journey back to Midchester was made almost in silence. At first, Lady Beatrice's friends tried to make conversation, but the disastrous ending to the day was uppermost in their minds and they soon ran out of things to say.

Anna sat holding her friend's hand, thinking about what had happened. Everyone was sure it had been an accident – a car driving too fast, the crowds. But as she'd turned towards the sound of the car, Anna was sure she'd glimpsed hands reaching out. But why? Was it an attempt to cause trouble for the suffragist supporters, to incur more bad publicity for the cause?

Anna shuddered. It could just as easily have been her or Gracie, or even Beatrice herself who'd been killed or injured. In fact, at first she'd thought it was Lady Beatrice lying there. From the back, in her jaunty little hat and dark blue dress Lily could easily have been mistaken for her. She shook her head. No, it must have been an accident. It was just someone eager to make contact with Beatrice.

Her thoughts were interrupted when Gracie spoke for the first time. 'Your Ladyship, please don't take me all the way home. The neighbours ...'

Beatrice touched her hand. 'Don't worry. We'll stop at the end of the road. Anna will walk with you from there, won't you?' she said, turning to her.

'Of course,' Anna replied. 'I'll come in with you – help you break the news.'

'Thank you,' Gracie whispered.

Anna gave the chauffeur directions and the car stopped at the corner of Chapel Lane. The two girls got out and Beatrice leaned down from the high seat, taking Anna's hand.

'I'm so sorry. Please let me know if there's anything I can do.'

Anna nodded, and she and Gracie began to walk with dragging steps towards the Mitchells' cottage. As Gracie pushed open the door, a voice called from the kitchen at the back of the house.

'Oh, good, you're home, girls. Just in time. I've taken a pie out of the oven and ...' Mrs Mitchell appeared in the doorway, the welcoming smile fading as she took in her daughter's tear-stained face and the presence of the factory-owner's daughter. 'What's happened? Where's Lily?'

Gracie burst into tears and rushed across to her mother. 'Oh, Mum,' she sobbed.

Mrs Mitchell patted her daughter's shoulder, looking across at Anna, a question in her eyes.

Anna hesitated. 'Is Mr Mitchell home? I think he should be here.'

'He's out but he'll be back soon. Tell me, please, what's happened to Lily?'

'There's been an accident ...' Anna said.

'Is she hurt? In hospital? Tell me ...'

Before Anna could explain, Gracie wailed, 'She's dead, Mum.'

Her mother paled and clutched the back of a chair. 'Dead? She can't be.'

'I'm afraid so, Mrs Mitchell.' Anna helped the older woman into a chair and said to Gracie, 'Could you make your mother a cup of tea while I explain?' She thought it best for her friend to be occupied.

Gracie nodded and went through to the scullery.

Sitting beside Mrs Mitchell, Anna told her how crowded the road along the seafront had been and how Lily had just been crossing the road when the car appeared, seemingly out of nowhere, and mowed her down. She didn't mention her suspicions or that she thought she'd recognized the car. And it wasn't the right time to mention the suffragist rally and the reason for the crowds either. She felt it would only add to Mrs Mitchell's distress if she knew why her daughters had been there.

She had just finished speaking when the door opened and Mr Mitchell came in. Catching sight of Anna he said, 'What's going on? Why's she here?' Seeing his wife's distress, he strode across and put his arm around her. 'The girls?' he asked.

Before she could reply, Gracie came in carrying a cup and saucer. Her father turned to her and said, 'Will somebody please tell me what's happened?'

Mrs Mitchell burst into tears. 'It's our Lily ...'

Anna explained once more. 'It was an accident. The car was travelling too fast and the promenade was so crowded,' she said.

'It was a good job Anna was there,' Gracie said.

Mrs Mitchell looked up sharply. 'Miss Grayson to you, girl,' she said.

Before Gracie could reply, Anna said, 'It doesn't matter. We're all a bit upset—'

'And how come she brought you home?' Mrs Mitchell interrupted.

'Miss Grayson was in Brighton with Lady Beatrice Winslow and some friends. They saw the accident. Lady Beatrice was kind enough to bring me back to Midchester and Anna – Miss Grayson, I mean – offered to come in with me.'

'Well, yes, it was kind. Thank you, Miss Grayson.' Mrs Mitchell seemed to have recovered a little, although she still twisted her sodden handkerchief between her fingers.

Mr Mitchell stood beside her, awkwardly rubbing her shoulder. 'Where did they take her?' he asked.

Gracie started to cry again. 'I don't know. They took her away in an ambulance.'

'Dr Peters was there too,' Anna said. 'He said he would see to everything. He'll call on you tomorrow and explain.' She stood up and hesitated. 'I really should go. It's getting late and my father will be worrying. If there's anything I can do ...'

None of them replied, too wrapped up in their grief to notice when she slipped out of the cottage, and walked through town to St Martin's Square. Dear, sweet Lily, she thought with a sob, remembering the girl's excitement at meeting Lady Beatrice. Preoccupied with thoughts of how badly the day had turned out, it was only as she reached her own front door that it occurred to her to wonder what Daniel had been doing in Brighton that day. How fortunate that he'd been there, though. He'd taken charge of the situation, calming Gracie's hysterics, while at the same time showing sympathy and compassion. What would she have done if he hadn't been there?

Millie opened the front door, peering round her for a glimpse of the big motor car.

'Have you had a good time, miss? I thought Lady Beatrice's chauffeur was bringing you home.'

As the maid took Anna's jacket and hat, she felt a burst of irritation at the maid's familiarity, although usually she didn't mind.

'I had to make a call on the way home,' she said shortly. 'Is my father home?'

'He's had his supper and is in the study. Do you want supper, miss?'

Anna shook her head. Food was the last thing on her mind, although she should have been hungry, having eaten nothing since their picnic lunch and that had been hours ago.

Millie was still chattering. 'I expect you had a nice meal while you were out. Did you have dinner at the Manor?'

'No, Millie, I didn't – and I'm not hungry. So please....' She put a hand to her forehead, suddenly feeling faint as the events of the day caught up with her.

'Miss, are you all right? Come on, sit down. I'm sorry – there's me chattering on and not realizing....' Millie guided Anna to a chair and rushed to the kitchen to fetch a glass of water.

Anna sat for a moment, taking deep breaths but when Millie returned, she only took a sip from the glass before standing up.

'I must speak to my father,' she said. 'Don't worry. I'm just tired.' She just didn't have the energy to face Millie's inevitable questions if she tried to tell her what had happened.

She went into her father's study, expecting to see him dozing in his chair or reading the evening paper. But he was seated at his desk, poring over some documents. He looked up with a vague smile.

'Oh, it's you, my dear. Did you have a good day out?'

'Not really, Father. There was an accident ...' Her voice caught on a sob.

'You weren't hurt?' He made to rise from his chair.

'No, someone in the crowd was killed – run down by a motor car. It was awful.' She was reluctant to tell him who the victim had been. It would have involved too many explanations and she was too upset to go into how she had become friends with the Mitchell sisters and why they had all been in Brighton on the same day. Of course, he was bound to hear that one of his employees had died but hopefully he wouldn't connect the incident with her.

'And you saw it? That must have been most distressing.' William looked concerned for a moment but his next words told her that it wasn't because she was upset. 'I do hope you won't be involved in any inquiry. I would hate for you to have to appear in court as a witness. Were you questioned at all?'

When she shook her head he looked relieved and, almost immediately, returned his attention to the papers on his desk.

In a way she was relieved that, once he'd made sure she hadn't been hurt, he took no further interest in what had happened. She hoped he wouldn't read about the accident in the newspapers, though. Still, she reflected, Brighton was out of the area covered by the *Midchester Gazette* and it was unlikely to be reported in the daily newspaper that her father usually read.

'I'm off to bed then. Goodnight, Father,' she said.

He looked up from his papers and smiled. 'Goodnight, my dear. Try not to dwell on that unpleasant incident.'

But as Millie helped her to get ready for bed, she could not help dwelling on it. The maid was eager to hear the details of her day out, but Anna pleaded tiredness and, promising to tell her about it in the morning, she said goodnight and got into bed.

Sleep would not come despite her exhaustion. Every time she closed her eyes, she could see the accident in her mind's eye, the hands stretching out, heard over and over the sound of the car, the thump as it hit Lily, and Gracie's heart-broken wails.

CHAPTER ELEVEN

THE NEXT DAY Anna pleaded a headache and stayed in her room. It was not like her to miss church and her father was concerned enough to come to her room before he left.

'Are you still upset after seeing that accident?' he asked. When she nodded he went on, 'Perhaps it is best for you to rest today.'

She didn't reply and, as he went out of the room she heard him muttering. 'I knew I shouldn't have let her go.'

She spent the rest of the day in her room, waving Millie away whenever she crept in to see if she could do anything.

The following morning she got up, determined to behave normally. She couldn't lie in bed brooding forever. That wouldn't bring Lily back, or help Gracie.

While she was dressing she satisfied Millie's curiosity, giving an edited version of the accident. She implied that the victim was a stranger, although Millie was bound to find out that the dead girl had been an employee in her father's factory. Midchester was a small town and gossip among the servants in neighbouring households was rife. She just hoped the story wouldn't find its way into the *Midchester Gazette*.

William Grayson had left for the factory and Anna had given Cook and Millie their orders for the day. Now, as she sat with her coffee in the morning room, she found herself once more going over and over what had happened. Perhaps she'd confide in Millie when she came in to take the coffee tray, she thought. Talking about it might help to clear her mind of the lurking suspicion that it had not been an accident at all. Poor Lily had just been in the way. Anna knew it wasn't the done thing to confide in one's servants but she had known Millie all her life – and who else was there for her to talk to? Her father had shown little interest and she had no real friends except for Bea. But would she wanted to be reminded of the tragic end of her triumphant day?

She was still brooding over the whole incident when there was a tap on the door and Millie entered.

'Dr Peters has called, Miss Anna. Are you at home?'

'Yes. Please show him in.' Anna's heart had begun to beat a little faster and she tried to compose herself, telling herself that he had probably only come to bring her up to date on Saturday's events.

She smoothed her skirt and folded her hands in her lap as Millie announced him.

'I hope I am not intruding,' the young doctor said.

'Not at all, Doctor. Do sit down. Would you like some coffee?' It was best to remain formal, Anna thought.

'Thank you.' He sat opposite her, drawing the chair a little closer and leaning towards her. 'I hope you are recovered from Saturday's dreadful scene.'

'Yes, thank you. Perfectly.' She rang for the maid and they remained silent until Millie had answered the bell, quickly returning with a fresh pot of coffee and another cup and saucer.

Anna felt the doctor's eyes on her as she poured the coffee and she tried to still the trembling of her hand. He reached out and took the pot from her. 'I believe you are still upset. It was a shocking thing to have happened, especially to someone whom I believe you were fond of.'

'I *was* fond of her.' Anna's voice caught on a sob and she checked herself. 'Oh, I expect you think that she and her sister weren't suitable friends, being my father's employees ...'

'It is not for me to judge,' he said. 'Besides, from what I have seen of them, they are nicely brought up girls. And you had your interest in the suffragist movement in common.'

To Anna's surprise, remembering their previous encounter when he had dismissed her attendance at the suffragist meeting as a misguided escapade, he sounded almost sympathetic.

'I hadn't known them very long but I was beginning to think of them as friends,' she said. 'I hadn't expected to see them in Brighton, though. I travelled to the rally with Lady Beatrice and her friends.' She picked up her cup and saucer, then put it down and said impetuously, 'Doctor – it *was* an accident, wasn't it?'

'Of course. What makes you think...?'

'I thought I saw ...' She hesitated.

'Go on.'

Haltingly she told him of her suspicions.

'I expect you think I am being foolish,' she said when she had finished and he did not reply.

'Not at all. There was a lot of confusion. I can see how you might ...' He paused. 'But, if it was deliberate, what reason would anyone have to hurt Lily?'

'Not Lily – Lady Beatrice.' Anna explained how, in those first moments of confusion she had thought it was her friend lying there. 'It was their similarity of height and dress – and when I saw the hat and the rosette – I thought it was Lady Beatrice's. Lily had copied the design of her hat.'

'But still, the question remains. Why?'

'I don't know. But many people are against the suffrage movement. Perhaps it wasn't meant for her to be killed – just to cause trouble. After all, Her Ladyship is one of their most prominent leaders and any bad publicity could hurt the cause.'

The doctor nodded thoughtfully and, after a few moments, said, 'Did anyone else see anything?'

'Gracie thought Lily was pushed as well, but she was so hysterical I don't think anyone took any notice of what she was saying.'

'I will give it some thought,' Daniel said. 'But there isn't really anything to go on. Maybe some other witness will come forward.'

Anna thanked him, pleased that he had not immediately dismissed her concerns.

He finished drinking his coffee and put the cup down and she thought he was about to leave, but he leaned towards her and said, 'Now, what I really came for, was to tell you that arrangements have been made for Lily's body to be brought back to Midchester later this week – after the inquest.'

'Oh. I had not realized. An inquest?'

'Of course. There is always an inquiry after such an accident. The question is, are you prepared to stand as a witness to what you thought you saw?'

Anna hesitated. Much as she desired justice for her friend, she dreaded the publicity and the effect it would have on her relationship with her father. He had looked so careworn recently that she was reluctant to give him any cause for worry.

'Do you think I should speak out?' she asked.

'I really don't think it would serve any purpose at the moment,' said Daniel. 'If we had some proof, if you were certain of what you saw – yes, perhaps. But ...'

Anna sighed. He had said 'we' which implied he was on her side. She would be guided by him, she decided.

'I think you're right,' she said. 'Besides, I'm thinking of my father and the effect all this would have on him. But Gracie is sure to say something if she is called.'

'I think the coroner is likely to dismiss anything Miss Mitchell says as the result of her shock and grief,' Daniel said.

'I agree but, as you say, there might be other witnesses.' Anna stood up. 'It is very kind of you to have come and told me all this.'

For the first time since entering the room, Daniel smiled. 'I was not being merely kind. I wanted to see you again. I think I offended you the last time I called and I wanted the chance to make amends. I spoke hastily and I am truly sorry.'

'I accept your apology, Doctor.'

'Daniel – I think we agreed that you would call me Daniel.'

He took her hand and she returned the pressure of his fingers. 'And you may call me Anna,' she said.

For just a few seconds the heaviness of her heart lifted a little and she smiled. But all too soon, Daniel brought her back to earth with his next words.

'I had to identify Lily at the mortuary. I said I was a friend of the family. Gracie had already gone back to Midchester with you and Lady Beatrice. Besides, I could not let her do it.'

'I must go and see her. I know she has friends and family but ...'

'I called there before coming here,' said Daniel. 'She is bearing up well, but I cannot say the same for her mother and father.'

'Those poor Mitchells. I wish I could do something to help but I fear they may blame me for getting the girls involved in the movement, even though I knew nothing about it until I spoke to the sisters at the factory that day.'

'I understood it was they who encouraged you. However, it is too late to think about blame. Besides, you didn't know that the girls were going to attend the rally.' He stood up. 'I'm afraid I must go. I'm due at the hospital.'

Anna accompanied him into the hall. Millie was nowhere to be seen so she handed him his hat and opened the front door. 'Thank you so much for coming.'

He took her hand. 'I will call again after the inquest if I may.'

'Please do.'

She watched until he had gone through the front gate and turned the corner before closing the door and returning to the morning room. Only then did she remember that she had not asked him why he had been in Brighton that day.

When Millie came in for the tray she was sitting by the window, deep in thought. Should she go and see the Mitchells? And if she did, what could she say to them? Perhaps she should leave them alone in their grief.

'I thought I heard the doctor leave,' the maid said. 'You should have rung for me to see him out.'

'You have enough to do, Millie. I am quite capable of opening the front door myself.' Seeing the hurt look on her face, Anna immediately regretted her sharpness. What was the matter with her these days? It wasn't like her to snap at the servants. 'I'm sorry, I am not myself,' she added.

'That's all right, miss. I expect you're still upset after seeing that girl killed.'

'Yes, that must be it. But I am feeling better today. I will take a walk after lunch.' She had decided that she would visit the Mitchells after all.

It was another warm, sunny day and Anna decided to stroll along the ramparts of the old city wall which partially surrounded Midchester. It was a pleasant walk with views over the parapet towards an expanse of parkland and the Downs beyond. She slowed as she neared the steps leading down to the archway which passed under the walls to Chapel Lane, and the huddle of cottages where the Mitchells lived.

Would she be welcome? That didn't matter. She must offer her condolences and then, if they seemed resentful of her intrusion, she would go. Even so, she hesitated before knocking on the door of the cottage. But when Gracie answered she smiled and greeted Anna warmly, despite the tear-stained face and swollen eyelids.

'Thank you for coming, Anna.' Gracie led her into the parlour and offered her a chair. 'Mum, it's Anna – Miss Grayson.'

Mrs Mitchell was sitting on the sofa, her hands in her lap clutching a wet handkerchief. She looked as if she had not moved since Anna was last there. She looked up and stared at Anna with dull eyes.

'What's she doing here?' she asked.

'I came to offer my condolences, Mrs Mitchell, and to see if there was anything I could do for you.'

'Do? What can anyone do? My baby's dead.' She put her head in her hands and began to weep.

'Perhaps I should go,' Anna whispered.

'No, please stay,' Gracie insisted. 'I'll make some tea.'

She left the room, leaving Anna looking helplessly at the grief-stricken woman. What could she say to comfort her? There were no words. She went and sat beside her on the sofa, put an arm around her shoulder, and made soothing noises. After a few moments, the sobs ceased and Mrs Mitchell looked up.

'Gracie says you saw what happened. Tell me everything.'

'It's as I told you the other evening – the road was crowded, people pushing and shoving. There was so much confusion. I'm really not sure exactly …' Anna couldn't tell the poor woman of her suspicions.

'But what were my girls doing there? Gracie said something about a rally. I thought they were just having a day at the seaside.' Her shoulders heaved with a suppressed sob.

'I expect they wanted to see what was going on,' Anna said, not sure how much Gracie had told her mother.

'It was that suffragette woman – filling their heads with all sorts of ideas. I knew no good would come of it.'

'They were just curious,' Anna said. As I was to start with, she thought. Before she could say any more, Gracie returned with the tea.

'It was kind of you to call, Miss Grayson,' she said, maintaining formality in deference to her mother.

'Does my father know about Lily?' Anna asked.

'Dad took a note on his way to work at the tannery. I suppose I should have gone to work too but I couldn't leave Mum. Dad had to go in – we can't afford to have two of us off.'

'I understand and I'm sure my father will too. Your mother needs you here at a time like this.'

'It's not Mr Grayson I'm worried about – it's that Johnson. Any excuse to dock your pay,' Gracie said, her fists clenched.

'But my father …'

'Begging your pardon, Anna, but your father doesn't know what goes on under his nose.'

'Gracie – this is not the time.' Mrs Mitchell had dried her tears and her voice was firm. 'Miss Grayson doesn't want to hear this.'

Oh, but I do, Anna thought. It seemed that the more she heard about Edward Johnson, the more reasons she found to mistrust him. The older woman was right, though. It wasn't the right time.

'It doesn't matter, Mrs Mitchell. Gracie is upset, naturally,' she said, standing up. 'I must go now, but you will let me know when the funeral is, won't you?'

'Of course.' Gracie saw her to the door and thanked her for coming.

Anna laid a hand on her friend's arm. 'I will see that you get paid for the time off. I don't want your mother to have any more worries.'

For a moment, she thought Gracie would make an angry response. She knew how proud and independent her friend was.

But her face softened and she said, 'Thank you. I know you mean well.'

Anna was preoccupied on the walk home, wondering what Gracie's comment about the factory manager had meant. It was true she did not like him, but she hadn't seriously thought he was up to no good. Had Gracie merely been voicing her own dislike of the man or was there something else? She resolved to speak to Father about it when he got home and this time she would not let him dismiss the subject.

CHAPTER TWELVE

ANNA WAS JUST turning the corner into St Martin's Square when she heard the sound of a motor car engine. It was still unusual to see cars in the city centre and, curious, she turned her head.

She recognized the maroon Hispano-Suiza straight away, although so much had happened recently that she had almost forgotten being driven home in the sporty little motor car after her visit to the Manor a couple of weeks ago. But was it the same car she thought she'd glimpsed in Brighton? Everything had happened so fast that she couldn't really be sure. Perhaps it was her dislike of Bea's cousin that was conjuring up these absurd suspicions.

However, she had no desire to see Alfred Ponsonby-Smythe again and she hurried round the corner, hoping that he hadn't seen her. But the vehicle turned the corner too and pulled up beside her.

'Miss Grayson. We meet again. What a pleasant surprise,' Alfred said, raising his hat. 'May I give you a lift anywhere?'

'No, thank you,' Anna replied. 'As you can see, I am almost home.'

He leaned down from the high seat and smiled his wolfish smile. 'Do you have to go home yet? How about a little spin in the motor? As you can see, I've got her back – good as new. My man in Brighton has done a splendid job. She's running sweet as a nut now. We could drive down to the harbour.'

'I don't think so, Mr Ponsonby-Smythe. It would not be appropriate, especially since I gather you already have an understanding with Lady Beatrice.' She started to walk towards St Martin's House, hoping he would take the hint and drive away.

'As I told you the other day, my dear cousin has turned me down, I'm afraid.' His mouth drooped at the corners, but a moment later he grinned and said airily, 'Oh, well. I suppose I'll have to find another rich heiress.' He laughed as if to show he was joking, but Anna wasn't deceived.

She managed to force a laugh too and replied, 'I'm afraid there's no use looking at me.'

'Touché, Miss Grayson,' he said, not a bit put out.

She didn't answer and turned to open her front gate, but before she could go in he spoke again. 'Miss Grayson, forgive me. I have been insensitive. I had quite forgotten that you were a witness to that dreadful accident the other day. My cousin tells me the young lady was a friend of yours. My condolences.'

Anna doubted his sincerity but she smiled and thanked him. He touched the brim of his hat again and started the motor.

'Goodbye, Miss Grayson – until we meet again.'

Inside the house, Anna leaned against the closed door, taking a deep breath. What was it about the man that raised her hackles? Despite his surface charm she just couldn't take to him. No wonder Bea had turned down his marriage proposal.

Her maid had no such reservations about the handsome man in his smart little car.

'Was that the gentleman who brought you home from Lady Beatrice's?' she asked, her eyes round with excitement. 'Did he drive you home this time?'

She had obviously been looking out of the window, awaiting her mistress's return.

This time Anna did not chide her for her familiarity. Millie had little enough excitement in her humdrum life. It was only natural for her to be curious about the possibility of a romance for her mistress.

'Mr Ponsonby-Smythe happened to be driving by and merely stopped to pass the time of day,' she said, handing her hat to the maid and going into the drawing room.

Millie followed and asked if she wanted tea.

'No, thank you. I had tea while I was out,' Anna replied, reflecting that the strong brew which Gracie had poured for her earlier had been almost undrinkable, although she had sipped at it for the sake of politeness. She would have enjoyed a cup of the delicately-scented brew she was used to. But it was nearly dinnertime and Millie needed to be in the kitchen helping Cook.

'Very well, miss.'

The maid did not comment but Anna could tell she was wondering where her mistress had taken tea if she had merely gone for a walk as she'd said. Perhaps she would confide in her later, in the privacy of her room. The urge to talk to someone about the accident and her involvement was strong – and who else was there?

As she dressed for dinner, Anna relived the encounter with Beatrice's cousin, wondering why he had waylaid her. It was obvious that he had deliberately turned into the square in order to speak to her. Was it just for a brief flirtation or did he have some other purpose? His mentioning the accident had seemed casual, almost an afterthought. Surely he couldn't have been involved? If he had driven to Brighton in his own motor car she might have been more suspicious, but he had joined Lady Beatrice's party because his own car was being repaired. Anna shook her head in denial. Just because she didn't like the man, there was no reason to suspect him of sinister motives. But still the thought persisted. How many maroon Hispano-Suizas were there in this part of Sussex?

She shook her head, telling herself she was being over-imaginative. What possible reason could Alfred have for wanting to harm Bea?

Just then, Millie entered the room to tell her that the master was home and dinner almost ready, and she dismissed her foolish thoughts. As Millie tidied the discarded clothes, she chattered on about the 'gentleman' and his motor car, scarcely seeming to notice Anna's monosyllabic answers. She had got it into her head that Anna had taken tea with Alfred and Anna didn't correct her. It was better that she didn't know about her involvement with the Mitchell sisters, she decided, stifling the impulse to confide in her in case she let something slip in front of her father.

At dinner, William ate sparingly, his forehead creased in a frown. Anna watched him apprehensively. He always seemed worried these days and she was reluctant to add to his concerns. She was about to ask what was wrong when he cleared his throat and looked up from his plate.

'I heard some disturbing news today,' he said. 'Johnson tells me the girl involved in that accident was one of my employees. Apparently she and her sister were having a day out and they got caught up in the crowd.' He looked at Anna keenly. 'Did you know she was from Midchester?'

Anna couldn't lie. She nodded. 'I recognized the sister,' she said. 'I saw the girls at the factory when I delivered that message to you.'

'I told Johnson the Mitchell girl could have a few days off – her father has had to go back to his work at the tannery and I thought she'd be needed at home.'

'That's kind of you, Father,' Anna said.

'Johnson wasn't happy about it – reminded me it's policy to give close relatives only one day off for the funeral – not a whole week.' William chewed thoughtfully. 'Usually I trust his judgment, but he even queried my decision to pay the Mitchell girl for her time off. I had to remind him that it was *my* decision.'

'I should think so, too, Father. After all, you *are* the boss. I think it's very good of you.' Anna thought it was the least he could do, but she was grateful to him. She knew that men like him seldom gave a thought to the problems of the workers. As long as they turned up on time and did their work, that was all that mattered.

'I'm sure I've made the right decision,' William said. 'I think we get more out of our workers if they are treated fairly. But I'm sure Johnson was thinking of the interests of the factory and the possible fall in production if we start letting people take days off when they think they need to.'

'You're probably right, Father,' Anna said.

'I'm going to my study,' he said, pushing his plate away.

'I'll ask Millie to bring your coffee in there,' Anna said.

As he opened the door she asked, 'Father, do you know when the funeral is? I thought I would order a wreath – on your behalf of course.'

'It's next Wednesday – at the Wesleyan chapel. By all means send a wreath, my dear. A kind thought.'

That night in bed, Anna's thoughts returned again to the horrifying picture of Lily's crumpled body and her own nausea at the sight of blood. In her mind, she saw again the hands reaching out, the flash of maroon as the car raced off before anyone took in what had happened, the driver seemingly unaware of the accident – if it was an accident.

Could it have been Alfred's car? Vehicles like his were a sufficiently rare sight in these early days of motoring that surely it could not be a coincidence. All her former suspicions rose to the surface, foolish as they might be. Had Alfred deliberately driven at Lily, mistaking her for his cousin? If so, what was his motive? And more importantly, if she had been pushed, whose hands had done the pushing? Did he have an accomplice?

Anna sighed and turned over in bed once more. She hadn't been able to get it out of her mind since it had happened. But now, she was forced to admit that her over-active imagination was playing tricks and conjuring up these wild stories. It was sheer foolishness to think that Lily's death had been anything other than a tragic accident.

A few days later, Anna dressed for Lily's funeral in the clothes she had not worn since the death of an elderly great aunt two years before. When she had asked Millie to get the black dress with its matching cape and bonnet from her wardrobe, the maid's eyebrows rose but she did not comment.

'It's for Lily's funeral,' she said, although she knew she need not explain.

'Does your father know you're going?' Millie asked.

'No – and he doesn't have to,' Anna said tartly, tempted to remind her maid that it was none of her business.

'I'm sure you can rely on me to say nothing,' Millie replied.

Anna could tell by her tone that she was offended and she hastened to make amends.

'I know that, Millie,' she said. 'But Father has such old-fashioned ideas about what is proper and I don't want to upset him. I feel it would show respect. After all, I was there when the accident happened and, besides, I knew the sisters already.'

Now, Anna walked through the quiet afternoon streets to the Wesleyan Chapel, hesitating when she reached the open door. The minister, who stood in the doorway, beckoned her in and someone moved to make room for her on a bench at the back. The building was full and she looked around for a familiar face. But, of course, it was unlikely she'd know anyone in this gathering of Lily's friends and relations.

Gracie and her parents were in the front row and Anna could hear Mrs Mitchell's crying. She bowed her head, stifling the sob which rose in her own throat.

It wasn't until the last hymn and prayer was over and people were filing out that she spotted Edward Johnson. She hung back as he passed, hoping he hadn't seen her. He was sure to report her presence to her father and, although she felt perfectly justified in attending, she could not face his certain disapproval.

She was the last to leave and, not wanting to intrude on the family's grief, she was about to hurry away when she felt a hand on her arm.

'Anna, thank you for coming,' Gracie said. 'Will you come back to the house?'

She shook her head, dreading an encounter with the factory overseer. Gracie sensed the reason for her reluctance and gave a grim smile.

'Don't worry. Johnson's gone back to work. Thinks the place will fall down without him.'

'It's not that. I don't want to intrude.'

'Please come. Mum wants to thank you for helping.'

'All right – but I can't stay long.'

The men of the family – father, uncles and cousins – had accompanied the coffin to the cemetery while the women returned to the cottage. The little front room was bursting at the seams with friends and neighbours who had prepared an array of sandwiches and pies.

Anna felt out of place as Gracie introduced her to her aunts and cousins. When she finally felt that her duty was done and she could escape, she went into the kitchen to say goodbye to Gracie, hesitating as she saw her friend in earnest conversation with Detective Hawker, the policeman who'd helped them after their first suffragist meeting.

Gracie smiled. 'You remember Sam, don't you?'

'Yes, of course. How do you do, Detective?'

'He's investigating the accident,' Gracie said.

'Unofficially – not that there's anything really to investigate,' the policeman said. 'My superiors are confident that it was just an accident, although the driver should have stopped. If we can track him down, he will be severely reprimanded.'

'I told Sam I thought Lily was pushed,' Gracie said with a sob.

'What about you, Miss Grayson? Did you see anything?'

Anna hesitated, not wanting to add to Gracie's distress if she discovered that her sister's death had been deliberate. Besides, she had almost convinced herself that she'd imagined those hands reaching out.

'Well, I'm not sure ...' she began.

'Anything you can remember will help. I promised Gracie I'd try to get to the bottom of it.'

'There was one thing – I thought at first it was Bea lying there in the road.'

'Bea?'

'Lady Beatrice Winslow,' Anna explained.

Sam Hawker nodded thoughtfully. 'If it was deliberate, it could

101

explain....' His voice tailed off and Gracie shook his arm.

'What – explain what?'

Sam hesitated. 'I couldn't think why anyone would want to hurt your sister – unless it was merely to disrupt the suffragist rally. But it was all over by the time the accident happened.'

'Do you think someone might have wanted to hurt Her Ladyship?' Anna asked.

'It's just a thought.' Sam patted Gracie's arm. 'I must get back to work now but I will make inquiries.'

'I must go too,' Anna said.

She hurried out of the cottage, glad to get away from the atmosphere of grief and – on Gracie's part – anger.

As she turned the corner, Sam Hawker called out to her. 'Miss Grayson, please wait a moment. I must talk to you.'

She waited for him to catch up with her and listened as he explained that he was only investigating Lily's death for Gracie's sake.

'I am not officially involved in the inquiry. In fact, if my superiors knew, I could be in trouble,' he said.

'Isn't there an official inquiry then?' Anna asked.

'There was, but it's been dropped. They say it was just an accident despite what several bystanders thought they saw.'

'But you're not so sure?'

'Not now. At first I was only trying to please Gracie. In fact, I had almost persuaded her that there was nothing more I could do.'

'What changed your mind?'

'Well, when you said you thought Lady Beatrice was the victim, it made me think. There was no motive for killing Lily, but Her Ladyship is a different matter.' He paused as if waiting for Anna to comment.

Should she mention Alfred and his little maroon car? But would he believe her? Alfred was a member of the upper classes and it would be his word against hers. She shook her head.

'I'm sorry, Detective Hawker. I would help if I could.'

'Well, if you remember anything, you will let me know, won't you?'

'Of course,' she said and walked quickly away.

Nearing her house, she wondered why she hadn't told Sam about her suspicions. Because I have no evidence, she told herself firmly. Alfred Ponsonby-Smythe has no motive for killing Bea. It's nonsense even to think such a thing.

CHAPTER THIRTEEN

ANNA HADN'T HEARD from Beatrice since their return from Brighton and she decided to send a note asking her to call. She had already written a few lines when it occurred to her that she could have telephoned the Manor. She gave a little laugh. When would she get used to the idea that she could actually talk to people at a distance? Well, I might as well finish the letter now, she thought. She was just signing her name when she heard the telephone ringing. She waited a moment, sealing her letter as she waited for Millie to answer it.

'I'll tell her right away,' she heard the maid say.

Curious, Anna went to the door without waiting for Millie to bring the message. Seeing the maid's white face, she took a step towards her.

'What's happened?'

'Oh, Miss Anna – it's the master. Johnson's bringing him home.'

Anna's hand went to her mouth and she rushed to the front door. A few minutes later, the Daimler pulled up with Johnson driving. William was slumped in the passenger seat and she hurried down the path.

'What is it? Has there been an accident?' she cried.

Johnson looked up at her. 'Don't be alarmed, miss. Mr Grayson was feeling a little unwell and I persuaded him to let me drive him home. I'm sure he just needs to rest.'

Anna called out for Millie and took her father's other arm. 'Millie, telephone Dr Brown and ask him to come at once,' Anna said.

'I don't need a doctor. Stop fussing,' William said, trying to shake off Anna's hand.

'Father, you don't look well. Let Dr Brown have a look at you – just to put my mind at rest.' She forced her lips into a smile. 'Please, Father?'

'All right. But there's nothing wrong with me, I'm just tired, that's all.'

Anna and Johnson helped him into the drawing room and persuaded him to lie down on the sofa. But when Anna tried to cover him with a shawl, he pushed her aside.

'I said don't fuss.' But his words lacked their usual forcefulness.

'Best leave him to rest, miss,' Johnson said.

Anna nodded and beckoned him aside.

'What happened?' she whispered. 'He seemed perfectly all right when he left for the factory this morning.'

It was true, although she had noted that he had not seemed his usual self lately. He was often lost in thought and would stay up working in his study long after she had retired for the night. But when she had attempted to question him he had snapped at her that there was nothing to worry about and she had given up asking.

Now, noting the shadows under his eyes, the pale clammy skin, her worries re-surfaced.

Johnson tried to reassure her. 'I think he's been overworking, miss. Perhaps he'll be better if you can persuade him to take a few days off. I'll make sure things keep running smoothly at the works.'

'Thank you, Johnson. I know Father depends on you.'

He gave a small smile of satisfaction.

'Thank you, miss,' he said. 'Would you like me to stay with you until the doctor gets here?'

'That won't be necessary, Johnson. I'm sure you'll be of far more use back at the factory.'

'Very well, miss.' He paused. 'Would you like me to put the car away before I go?'

'That's kind of you. We keep it in the old coach house.' She went down the path and pointed to the double gates at the side of the house.

He gave that little smile again, touched his cap and climbed up into the Daimler.

When he'd gone, Anna went back indoors. She leaned against the wall, taking a deep breath. She hadn't missed that smile on Johnson's face. He obviously liked driving the car. She guessed he also liked the thought of being in charge of the factory, but he didn't have to look so pleased about it, she thought. She remembered Gracie's dislike of the man but her father seemed to rely on him and she decided she would have to trust him for the time being.

She went back into the drawing room where she saw that her father had fallen asleep. Perhaps he *was* just tired, she thought hopefully, covering him with the shawl. She knelt beside him and took his hand. He was sure to be back at the factory in no time and running things his way, she told herself.

Millie came in and said, 'The doctor will be here in a few minutes, miss.' She looked a bit flustered and Anna couldn't help smiling. Like her, Millie had not got used to the telephone. It would probably have been quicker for her to run round to the doctor's, she thought.

The doorbell rang and Millie went to answer it, showing Dr Brown into the room. She felt a little prickle of disappointment that Daniel hadn't come instead, but then she remembered he was working at the hospital now. She stood and let Dr Brown take her place beside her father.

He did a thorough examination before turning to Anna and saying, 'I fear it is worse than you thought, Miss Grayson. Your father has suffered a seizure – just a slight one but....'

'But he seemed all right when he came in. I thought he was just tired. He's been overworking....' Anna couldn't go on, and tears started to fall.

'There, there, my dear. As I said, it is just a slight attack. With rest he should recover completely.'

'Are you sure?'

'Of course. Now, I suggest we get him up to his bed. He will be more comfortable there.'

Anna rang for Millie and asked her to fetch Joe, the gardener, thankful that it was his day to come in and cut the lawn.

He came in wiping his hands on a rag.

'What's to do, Miss Anna?' he asked.

'Father's not well. Can you help him upstairs, please?' she asked.

Joe nodded and bent to take William's arm. 'Come along, sir. Let's get you to bed.'

William started awake and began to protest violently, mumbling that he was perfectly capable of getting upstairs on his own. But his words were slurred and when he tried to stand, he slumped to one side.

'Now then, sir, you'll feel better when you've had a rest,' Joe said, supporting him on his weaker side. Anna and the doctor followed them up to William's room where Millie had run ahead and turned the coverlet down.

It was an effort to get the big man undressed and into bed but between them, Millie and Anna succeeded in making him comfortable. He slumped back on the pillows and closed his eyes.

Downstairs, Anna thanked the doctor and was about to show him out when he said, 'I think you should hire a nurse. It's going to be hard work looking after him.'

'But you said he'd get better. I'm sure I can mange for a little while.'

'Very well, my dear. But call me if there is any change in his condition.' He retrieved his hat from the hallstand and went out.

For the next few weeks, Anna scarcely had a moment to herself. She was constantly running up and down stairs, tending to her father. Millie tried to help but she had her own work to see to. By the end of the week, Anna was exhausted and was beginning to think Dr Brown had been right in suggesting they hire a nurse.

But Father seemed to be on the mend, so despite her exhaustion, she decided to continue caring for him herself for the time being. He was far happier when she was the one bringing his food and helping him to wash. Millie had repeatedly offered to take over but William became agitated and pushed her away. How much more would he resent a stranger looking after him?

She looked down at him now, realizing that he had lost weight; his face was drawn and his eyes sunken and shadowed.

She touched his shoulder gently. 'I've brought you some broth, Father,' she said. 'Try to eat a little.'

He opened his eyes and struggled to sit up.

'I don't want broth. I need a proper meal,' he said, his words sounding much clearer now.

Anna forced a smile. 'You must be feeling better then,' she said. 'I'll ask Cook to make your favourite steak and kidney pie for supper.' She helped him up, stacking the pillows behind him and put the tray in his lap. 'Are you sure you can manage?' she asked.

'Of course.' He took the spoon and raised it to his mouth. 'Always fussing,' he mumbled.

But Anna could see that his hand trembled and she moved to help him. Impatiently, he pushed her away, spilling some of the broth onto the satin coverlet.

'Now look what you've done,' he said sharply.

'I'll get Millie to clean that up later. Meanwhile, if you're sure you can manage I'll leave you to it.' Anna stood up and left the room quickly so that he would not see how upset she was.

She went to her own room and sank into the chair by the window, sighing as she wondered how much longer she could carry on like this.

Naturally, she was pleased that Father seemed to be on the road to recovery but he was becoming increasingly bad-tempered. She knew it was because he was fretting about the factory and longed to get back to work. Johnson had called the day before and reassured him that everything was going well. The new order was almost completed and there was more work on the books. But he continued to worry.

Anna understood that for someone who had always been in control, it must be irksome to have to rely on other people. He still couldn't get out of bed unaided and staggered if he tried to walk more than a few steps. It would be some time before he was fit enough to go back to running the business.

She sighed and went upstairs to fetch the used crockery. William had finished the broth and now lay back against the pillows with his eyes closed. Millie had removed the soiled bedcover and replaced it with an old candlewick bedspread, and Anna pulled it up over William's chest. He stirred and mumbled, opened his eyes and said, 'Oh, it's you. I wasn't asleep, you know. In fact, I want to get up now.'

'No, Father. You must stay in bed until Dr Brown says you may get up. We'll talk about it when he calls this afternoon.'

'I can't stay here forever,' he protested.

'You're getting better every day. Perhaps you can go downstairs tomorrow.'

'I need to get back to the factory though. I'm sure Johnson is doing his best but there are things only I can deal with.'

'Is there anything I can do, Father? Perhaps I could call at the factory, take a look at the books for you.'

'Certainly not. What could you do anyway? You know nothing about running a business.'

And whose fault is that, Anna asked silently. 'You could tell me what to look out for, though.'

'No. Out of the question. I will just have to rely on Johnson. He's a good man. I'm sure everything is satisfactory.'

William sank back on the pillows with a sigh and Anna knew it was no good arguing. Still, she resolved as she went slowly downstairs, perhaps she would go along to the factory without telling Father. She had no idea what she would do when she got there but she'd think of something.

If only there was someone she could talk things over with, Anna thought. She knew her father had been worried about something before he was taken ill – in fact, she was sure it was worry that had brought on his attack. What could it be, though? After all, shortly before he'd been taken ill he'd mentioned a big order so he couldn't be worrying about their financial situation.

Perhaps she was fretting over nothing, she thought, as she stacked the dirty crockery in the sink. Cook was busy at the range and Millie was upstairs cleaning the bathroom. She was about to start washing the dishes when Millie returned and insisted on taking over.

'Go and sit down, miss. I'll make you a nice cup of tea when I've finished here,' she said.

Anna went into the morning room and tried to relax. But she couldn't stop worrying – about her father's health, the factory, the Mitchells. She'd had so much on her mind lately that when Bea telephoned, asking if she'd be willing to hand out leaflets, she realized she had hardly given the suffragist cause a thought.

The following day, Anna was tidying her father's room. Millie had protested that it was her job but Anna insisted.

'You have far too much to do these days, what with running up and down stairs all day helping with Father,' she said.

Reluctantly, Millie had lent her an apron and showed her where the dusters and polish were. She had just finished re-arranging the brushes and combs on the dressing table, trying to move quietly so as not to disturb her father, when Millie came in, panting from her run up the stairs.

'It's Lady Beatrice. Shall I say you're not at home, miss?'

'On the telephone?' Anna hadn't heard the ring. 'Just take a message, Millie. Can't you see I'm busy?' she said.

'No, Miss Anna. She's come to call. I've put her in the drawing room.'

'Oh, dear. I'd better go down then. Tell her I'll be with her in a minute.'

Anna patted her hair and took off her apron. She glanced in the mirror and wiped a smudge of dust off her nose with her handkerchief. She really wasn't in a fit state to receive visitors. But it had been so long since she'd spoken to anyone other than the servants and the doctor. A cup of tea and a chat with her friend would take her mind off her worries for a while.

When she entered the drawing room, Bea stood up and came towards her, taking both her hands.

'My dear, I didn't realize Mr Grayson was ill and that you were nursing him yourself or I would have called before. Is there anything I can do?'

'That's very kind but I'm managing, Bea. Do sit down. Millie will bring us tea in a moment.'

'How are you, Anna? And how is your father now?' Bea asked.

'He's doing well. I'm hoping he'll be able to come downstairs in a day or two.'

'And what about you? You must be exhausted.'

'I am a little tired,' Anna confessed. 'But you don't want to hear my troubles. Tell me what you've been up to.'

'I've been to meetings and rallies all over the place,' Bea said. 'Up north, to London....'

'And are we any nearer to success?' Anna asked. 'I haven't had time to read the papers so I have no idea what's been happening.'

Bea's face grew sombre. 'I'm sorry to say we are no nearer achieving our goal. Although more and more women are rallying round, the powers that be have set their minds firmly against us.'

'I thought some of the men in Parliament were sympathetic,' Anna said.

'Not enough of them, I'm afraid.' Bea sighed. 'Ever since that dreadful incident with the King's horse the tide has turned against us. But that hasn't stopped Mrs Pankhurst's followers. They are becoming more and more militant which, in my view, does not help our cause at all. I still believe our way is best.'

Well, they haven't achieved much so far, Anna thought. But she did not say so aloud. She did not want to upset her new friend. Besides, since her father's illness, the 'cause' as Bea called it, did not seem so important.

Bea, however, had lost none of her passionate zeal and she chatted brightly about the meetings and rallies she'd attended since she and Anna had last met.

'And the next big one is in Hyde Park next month,' she said. 'You will come, won't you?'

When Anna didn't reply she hastened to apologize.

'I'm sorry, my dear. I wasn't thinking. I've been running on about my life when I should be asking about you. I know that with your father so ill, you've been far too busy to think about the cause.'

'I can't come to London,' Anna said abruptly. Then, seeing the look of disappointment on her friend's face, she spoke more gently. 'You do understand, don't you? I'm sorry but it's impossible as things are at the moment.'

Bea set down her cup and saucer and frowned.

'I do admire you for nursing your father yourself,' she said. 'But surely you could hire a nurse, my dear, even if it's just for one day.'

'Father prefers me to look after him,' Anna said, adding hastily. 'I don't mind, really I don't. Besides, he's getting better every day.'

'Perhaps he'll be well enough for you to attend the rally by then.'

'Maybe,' Anna said.

'You don't seem very enthusiastic about it,' Bea said.

'I am but....' She hesitated. 'I'm just remembering what happened at the last one.'

'Oh, yes, your friend – Lily, wasn't it?'

Anna was hurt that Bea seemed to dismiss so casually what had been such a traumatic experience for her. She still hadn't quite decided that Lily's death had really been accidental. But since she'd heard nothing more from either Daniel or Detective Hawker, she had tried to put it out of her mind. Everyone else seemed convinced that it had been an accident and without proof, she knew she would just be dismissed as a hysterical woman with an over-active imagination.

'I still can't get over it,' Anna said.

'I understand, really I do. But you must try to put it behind you.' Bea stood up.

'I do hope you'll change your mind about the rally. For one thing, it would do you good to get out of the house. Being cooped up here looking after your father has given you too much time to brood over that unfortunate incident.'

'But it seems that there's always trouble at these events. I daren't get mixed up in anything else for my father's sake. If he got to hear of it while he's not well, it could set him back. Give me time to think about it.'

'Very well. But I do hope you'll come. We need all the support we can get.'

Anna rang for Millie to see Bea out but as her friend left the room she said impulsively, 'You will take care, won't you? I'd hate for anything to happen to you.'

Bea laughed. 'Don't worry about me. Thanks to my self-defence lessons, I can hold my own with the hecklers – and I'll make sure I don't get arrested.'

After she'd gone, Anna sat down and poured herself some more tea but it had gone cold. She contemplated ringing for more but changed her mind. Bea was right. She spent far too much time on her own, brooding over what had happened to Lily. Besides, she had plenty to do. She should go upstairs right now and check on Father.

But she didn't move.

What had possessed her to warn Bea to take care? Did she really think someone had pushed Lily into the road, mistaking her for Lady Beatrice? Such nonsense, she told herself, but the thought would not go away. Yes, it was nonsense to suspect Alfred Ponsonby-Smythe of having anything to do with the accident. But there were plenty of other suspects – people who hated the 'votes for women' brigade and would do anything to discredit them.

Sighing, Anna picked up the tea tray and took it through to the kitchen. Cook was busy rolling out pastry.

'The Master's got his appetite back, I see,' she said. 'I hope he enjoys his steak and kidney pie.'

Anna smiled. 'Yes, I'm sure he will. I really believe he's getting better,' she said. 'I'll just pop up and see if he needs anything.'

William was sitting on the edge of the bed when Anna entered the room. She rushed towards him and took his arm.

'You shouldn't try to get up on your own, Father,' she protested. 'Let me help you.'

He brushed her aside. 'I'm perfectly all right. It's about time I got up instead of lying around here all day.'

His face was red and there were beads of sweat on his forehead. He was obviously still far from well but Anna knew that remonstrating with him would only make him more stubborn. She took a deep breath and said, 'I'm pleased you're feeling better, Father. Perhaps you'd like to sit in the chair by the window for a while.'

He seemed about to protest but with a sigh, he allowed Anna to help him over to the chair and arrange a cushion behind him. She covered his knees with an afghan and pulled a small table towards him.

'Cook has made a steak and kidney pie, Father – your favourite. I'll bring it up in a moment.'

'I'd rather come down to the dining room,' he said.

'I think you should wait and see what Dr Brown says,' Anna said firmly, while bracing herself for an angry outburst.

But William gave a tired smile. 'I expect you're right, my dear.'

She smiled in return and left the room, but as she made her way slowly downstairs she reflected sombrely on the change in her father. It was so sad to see the once powerful and dominant man reduced to this. Still, at least his health seemed to be improving and Anna hoped that before too long he would be back to his old self. Once he was fit again, perhaps she would be able to think about joining Beatrice for the rally in London. But even as the thought came to her, she chided herself for her selfishness. She straightened her shoulders with a sigh. The suffragist cause would have to wait until her father was completely recovered. She did not really begrudge giving up her own life to care for him but aside from that, she knew how guilty she would feel if she did anything to upset him and precipitated another seizure.

CHAPTER FOURTEEN

A FEW DAYS later, Johnson called with some invoices for William to sign. When Anna showed him into the bedroom, he expressed his pleasure at seeing his employer sitting up by the window, the newspaper open on his knee.

'Well, sir, Miss Anna said you were much better. Can we hope to see you back at the factory before long?'

Before William could reply, Anna said, 'I don't think he's ready to return to work yet. But it depends on Dr Brown. He is due to call tomorrow.'

Johnson gave a short laugh. 'We must abide by the good doctor's decision, then, eh, sir? It wouldn't do to do too much too soon.'

Anna flinched at his familiarity, but William did not seem to mind. He echoed the man's laugh. 'No fear of that, Johnson. Between Brown and young Anna, I've been forced to toe the line. But don't worry – I'll be back in harness soon enough.'

'I'm sure you will, sir.'

'But not just yet, Father. You haven't even been downstairs yet,' Anna protested.

'No time like the present,' said William, casting aside his newspaper and struggling out of the chair. 'Johnson can give me a hand.' He took a few unsteady steps. 'Come on, man. Lend me your arm.'

'No, Father, please wait....'

But William ignored her and gestured to Johnson, who obeyed to take his arm.

It was a slow descent as, with Anna hovering anxiously behind, they negotiated the steep stairs. William was breathing heavily, but he brushed aside Anna's concern and gestured to her to open the door to his study.

By the time Johnson had helped him into his leather armchair,

William was breathing heavily and his face had taken on an almost purple hue. Anna rushed towards him.

'Father, are you all right?'

'Don't fuss, girl.' He turned to Johnson. 'Pour me a brandy, there's a good fellow.'

'But Dr Brown said....' Anna intervened.

'Never mind that. Do as I say, Johnson.'

After a hesitant glance at Anna, Johnson went to the sideboard and picked up the decanter.

William took the glass and gulped it down, waving Anna's protests away.

'Go on about your household tasks, my dear. Johnson and I have business to discuss. I'll call you if I need you.'

She knew it was useless to protest and left the room, closing the door behind her. She lingered in the hallway for a few moments with her ear to the door. She wasn't sure why she was so anxious to hear what they had to talk about apart from feeling resentful of her father's abrupt dismissal of her. But she could only hear a faint murmur of voices and she went down the passage to the kitchen where Millie was laying up the tray for tea.

'Is the master all right, miss?' she asked. 'Should he have come downstairs?'

Cook turned from stirring a pot on the stove.

'None of your business, Millie,' she said sharply.

'It's all right, Cook,' Anna said. 'We're all concerned about the master.' She sat down at the kitchen table and put her head in her hands. 'I couldn't stop him. He was determined and, with Mr Johnson to help....'

'Maybe it's a good sign, miss – that he's feeling better,' Cook said.

'I still wish he'd waited till Dr Brown had been.' She turned to Millie. 'Don't bother taking tea in to them. They're talking business and don't want to be disturbed.'

She followed Millie into the drawing room and waited till the maid had put down the tray. When she was alone, she didn't pour the tea but paced to the window and stared out at the sodden garden. While she had been nursing her father, the leaves had all gone from the trees and autumn was well on its way. The day of the London rally was drawing near and a little flicker of excitement rose in her breast. She had been so wrapped up in nursing her father that she'd almost forgotten it.

She turned away from the window and sat down to pour her tea but after a few sips, she left the cup on the tray as her thoughts whirled this way and that. Despite the improvement in her father's health, she still wasn't sure if she should go, but she couldn't let Beatrice down.

Why shouldn't I go, though, she asked herself. Millie and Cook can keep an eye on Father. After all, he is so much better now. By the time of the rally he might even be back at the factory. Besides, after being cooped up at home all these weeks, surely I deserve an outing.

A frown creased her face. How selfish she was. Was it wishful thinking on her part that Father was getting better, or was he just being stubborn? She would have to wait and see what Dr Brown said when he called the next day. Thinking about the doctor inevitably brought Daniel to mind. If only he would call. She felt she could confide in him – not only her worries about Father, but the niggling doubt which still lingered in her mind concerning Lily's so-called accident. But he had not been in touch since Father had been taken ill.

Over the next few days, William seemed to get a little stronger and Dr Brown agreed that he would soon be ready to go back to work, although he would have to take things gently for a while.

'I think I'll go down to the factory tomorrow,' he said at dinner one evening. 'I know Johnson's been keeping things running while I've been laid up, but I need to see for myself.'

'I worry that you'll overdo it,' Anna said, passing him the dish of potatoes. 'I know you think I'm fussing,' she continued before he could reply. 'But I do wish you'd listen to Dr Brown. You were very ill, Father, and it takes time to recover completely.'

'I'm perfectly all right.' He thrust a piece of meat in his mouth and chewed vigorously, then continued with his meal, waving aside Anna's concerned looks.

She knew it was useless to press the point. Bea had asked her to call the following afternoon if she could be spared, so she changed the subject, telling Father that she would be going out and that Millie would see to his tea.

'I may not be here myself. I might still be at the factory,' he said. 'Only for a short while,' he added hastily when she made to protest.

He finished his meal and stood up. 'I'm very pleased you are keeping up your friendship with Lady Winslow. You shouldn't be cooped up here looking after me – although I appreciate all you've done in the last few weeks, my dear.'

'It was a pleasure, Father.' She touched his hand as he passed her chair. 'You're all I've got.'

'You should be thinking of marriage, my dear.'

Anna gave a little laugh. 'No chance of that,' she said.

'Well, there's one young man who's interested in you and you know I would approve.'

Anna knew he was talking about Edward Johnson, but he was the last person she would contemplate marrying. She had not given a thought to her father's hints in the past and she had dared to hope that, since he had not brought the subject up again, he had accepted that she was not interested.

She was about to say so, when William said, 'Although he is not quite a gentleman, Edward Johnson is a hard-working young man and would be an excellent match. I will not be around forever, and I can think of no one more fitted to take over the factory when I'm gone. And, as your husband ...'

'Father, don't speak of such a thing. You are almost well again.' Anna was horrified. 'Besides, I don't think ...'

William held up his hand, interrupting her protest. 'I have already told him I do not object.' He stood up and pushed his chair back, ending the discussion.

Anna remained at the table staring down at her empty plate. How could he make these plans without consulting her? William's illness had given Johnson an excuse to call frequently, and she had noticed his increasing familiarity both with her and her father. It had only furthered her dislike of him. How could Father think she would ever contemplate marriage to such a man?

The following day when William had left for the factory, Anna went up to her room to change for her engagement with Lady Beatrice. It was such a long time since she'd had any social engagements and she had taken to wearing her plainest day dresses, suitable for nursing her father.

Millie knocked on the door as she was taking down an afternoon dress with a lace collar and she called to the maid to enter.

'What do you think, Millie?' she asked, holding the garment up against her.

'I love that one, miss. It suits you. But it's more suitable for summer, don't you think?' She hesitated. 'Sorry, miss. It's not really for me to say.'

'Don't be silly. I asked for your opinion. I think you're right. I had hardly noticed summer was over. Oh dear, I think I shall need some new clothes for winter.'

Millie went to the wardrobe and pushed aside the hangers. 'Here you are, miss. Perfect for a day like today. It's a bit fresh out but sunny.' She held out a wool gown in a shade of russet. It had a matching jacket with a fitted waist and a flared peplum. 'Is Lady Beatrice sending the car for you?' she asked.

Anna shook her head. 'I decided to walk up to the Manor,' she said. 'I've been cooped up indoors for so long and, as you say, it's a lovely day.'

Millie helped her to change and she left the house, walking briskly through the town and up the hill towards the open country. She breathed deeply, enjoying the fresh autumnal tang in the air.

As she reached the gates to the Manor, she startled at the sound of a horn and turned to see Alfred Ponsonby-Smythe. He leaned over to open the passenger door and said, 'Hop in, Miss Grayson. You must be tired after that long walk from town.' He grinned his wolfish grin and Anna inwardly shuddered. But she felt she could hardly refuse. Besides, she would only have to endure his company for a short while.

The butler greeted them as the motor car halted in front of the house. Alfred got out and opened the door for Anna, then got back in and, giving a cheeky wave, drove off towards the mews behind the house.

'This way, miss,' the butler said, showing her into the drawing room, where she'd had tea on her previous visit. This time, to her relief, there was no sign of Lady Winslow. A few minutes later, Bea strode into the room and, with a welcoming smile, bade her sit down.

'Tea will be served in a few moments,' she said. 'Meanwhile, you must tell me all your news.'

Anna gave a little laugh. 'I'm afraid there's not much to tell. As you know, I've been looking after Father which has left me little time for anything else.'

'Of course – you haven't been able to attend any of our suffragist meetings which is a pity. But what I meant was, did your policeman friend find out any more about the accident? I know you were concerned about what really happened.'

'I still think it was deliberate. I'm sure I saw someone push poor Lily.'

'But why? I don't understand.' Bea seemed genuinely puzzled and Anna decided it was time to share her suspicions with her friend.

She hesitated, then took the plunge. 'Hasn't it occurred to you that Lily may not have been the intended victim?'

'But who...?' Bea looked puzzled for a moment. Then her face cleared. 'You mean – you think someone meant to harm me?'

Anna had had plenty of time to think over the past few weeks and Lily's accident had never been far from her mind.

'It was my first thought – once I realized it was no accident. Someone deliberately pushed Lily into the path of that car and it must have been a mistake – after all, who'd want to hurt poor Lily?' A sob caught in her throat and she paused. 'At first I thought it was you lying there – her dress was the same colour. And her hat – she told me she had copied the design of yours.'

'But why would anyone want to harm me? It doesn't make sense,' Bea said, shaking her head. 'No – it must have been an accident. I can't imagine it being anything else.'

'I wish I could agree with you,' Anna said. 'But Lily didn't deserve to die and I think we owe it to her and her family to find out the truth.'

Bea nodded. 'I suppose you're right. Have you any idea...?'

'I thought someone might have meant to harm the suffragist movement. They probably didn't mean for someone to die, but if you were injured, you wouldn't be able to organize these meetings and rallies.'

'No, Anna. I'm sure you're wrong. The movement doesn't need me. There are plenty of others ready to take up the banner.'

'I suppose so.' Anna wasn't really ready to drop the subject but at that moment, the maid came in with the tea trolley. 'Is Lady Winslow not joining us today?' she asked, sensing that Bea wished to change the subject.

'She is not feeling very well and is keeping to her room today.'

Anna was relieved. She had felt embarrassed by Lady Winslow's scrutiny on her previous visit. She had made it plain that she did not approve of her daughter's commitment to the cause and the unsuitable friends she was making.

When the maid had left the room, Bea indicated that Anna should help herself to the tempting array of dainty sandwiches and cakes on the tray. She poured the tea and said, 'Now let's talk of more pleasant things. You will come to London, I hope.'

'I'm not sure at the moment.'

'But you told me your father had recovered. Isn't he at the factory today?'

'I still worry about him. Dr Brown was very reluctant to allow him back to work but he can be very stubborn. Suppose he has a relapse?'

Bea put down her cup and saucer. 'Anna, my dear, you cannot spend your life worrying about him. Whether you are at home or in London will make no difference. Besides, you've hardly been out of the house lately. You need an outside interest. Please say you will come.'

Anna smiled. 'Very well.'

'Good. Now, let's make plans.' Bea launched into the programme for the rally which would take place in Hyde Park, together with groups from all over the country.

Anna found herself getting excited despite a twinge of conscience at the thought of deceiving her father yet again. She fell in with Bea's plans, telling herself that if he showed the slightest sign of a return to ill health, she would not go.

Despite Anna's protests, Mr Ponsonby-Smythe had insisted on driving her home and Bea had done nothing to discourage him. She sat in embarrassed silence on the short journey into town, sighing with relief when they pulled up outside the house. Her relief was short-lived when she saw her father looking out of the drawing room window. She had not expected him to be home so early.

Hastily thanking her companion and saying 'goodbye', she hurried up the path, planting a smile on her face as William came into the hall.

'Hello, Father. Did you have a good day?' she said brightly.

Ignoring her question he said, 'I did not realize you were so friendly with that young man. I thought you were having tea with Lady Beatrice.'

'We are not exactly friends,' Anna said. 'He is Bea's cousin – he very kindly offered to drive me home.'

'Well, I don't think you should be alone with him again. People will talk.'

Anna didn't care. She knew she'd done nothing wrong. Still, she tried to appease him by saying, 'He was just being kind. It is a long walk from the Manor and the wind has turned chilly. Besides, he confided in me that he wishes to marry Lady Beatrice.' She didn't add that her friend had turned him down.

William seemed to accept this and, waiting until Anna had hung up her jacket, he followed her into the drawing room and sat down in front of the fire. He looked tired and Anna was sure he had overdone things at the factory.

She rang the bell for Millie and asked the maid to bring tea for the master.

'I don't want tea,' he said. 'A whisky and soda's more like it.'

Anna opened her mouth to protest. She knew Dr Brown would not approve. But what harm could it do? She nodded and asked Millie to pour the drink.

'Would you like tea, miss?' Millie asked.

'No, thank you. I had tea at the Manor.'

When Millie had left the room, William settled back in his chair, cradling the glass in his hands.

'And what has Lady Beatrice been up to?' he asked. 'I hear she got herself mixed up with that Votes for Women crowd. I hope she hasn't tried to involve you in all that nonsense.'

Anna felt herself colouring and hoped he would think it was the heat from the fire. 'We talked about the Church Ladies' Guild and raising money for the orphans,' she said. It was true but that had not been the only topic of conversation. Now was not the time to mention a trip to London, she decided.

CHAPTER FIFTEEN

TO ANNA'S SURPRISE, there was quite a crowd waiting for the London train, despite the heavy rain which had greeted her on awakening that morning. The crisp autumn days had given way to the onset of winter with a driving wind which made holding an umbrella almost impossible.

But despite the dismal day, the ladies gathered at Midchester station chatted cheerfully, their spirits undaunted. As the train drew into the station with a hiss of steam, Lady Beatrice gathered her flock around her with last minute instructions.

'When we reach Victoria, be careful to stay together, ladies. Mrs Hughes and Miss Spencer will make their way to the station forecourt and unfurl the banner. You will range yourselves behind them in an orderly manner and wait for the word to march off. The ladies from the Surrey group will already be there and we will wait for the Kent contingent before we leave the station.' She paused and gave a satisfied smile. 'It will be a most impressive display.'

Anna had never been to London before and she found it hard to control her excitement as the train pulled out of the station. As the town was left behind and they progressed through the countryside, even the vista of sodden fields stretching on either side of the swollen river, couldn't dampen her enthusiasm.

She had felt a twinge of conscience as she'd lied to her father about why she was going to London. She knew he would forbid it if he knew the reason. It wasn't good for his health to get agitated – so she told herself.

When she had mentioned shopping, he had pressed a handful of coins on her, saying, 'Buy yourself something nice, my dear.'

Feeling guilty at her deception, she had tried to refuse but he had insisted.

'Even I have heard of Mr Selfridge's famous store,' he said. 'I know you are going on this shopping trip as chaperone to Lady Beatrice but you must get something out of it too. You deserve a treat after your care of me over the past few months.'

Anna had eventually accepted gracefully, deciding that if it was at all possible she would appease her conscience by buying a present for him. Although she had no idea where Selfridge's was, she'd think about it later, she thought as the train pulled into Victoria station.

Her companions began to gather up their bags and straighten their hats, chattering excitedly. The station concourse was crowded and Anna lost sight of Lady Beatrice as she was caught up in the surge of movement towards the entrance.

Outside the station, a cacophony of noise greeted her – taxicabs sounding their horns, horse-drawn buses clopping past, vendors shouting their wares. Fortunately, the rain had stopped although there was still a chill breeze. As Anna gazed about her, bewildered but entranced, a hand grasped her arm.

'This way, Miss Grayson. The ladies are gathering over there,' a man's voice said in her ear.

She turned round sharply, about to pull away, colouring as she recognized Daniel Peters.

'What are you doing here?' she asked.

'The same as you,' he replied. 'I am marching to Hyde Park for the rally.'

'I did not realize you were one of our supporters,' she said, trying to ignore the pressure of his hand on her arm.

He grinned. 'Perhaps a certain young lady has persuaded me to change my mind,' he said.

Anna didn't reply but she could not help smiling. Her heart was beating a little faster but it wasn't because of Daniel's presence – was it? It must be the excitement of being in the big city. She allowed Daniel to guide her across the road to where the procession was forming up behind the two ladies carrying the banner. Other groups were spilling out of the main entrance to the station and a policeman appeared, waving his arms and trying to herd them across the road.

Anna recognized one or two supporters from the Brighton rally and greeted them cordially, introducing them to Daniel. As the crowd sorted itself into an orderly procession, she felt a secret pleasure that he stayed beside her, although he had dropped her arm when introduced to her friends. She remembered their earlier encounters when he had seemed to dismiss her support for the suffrage movement as the whim of someone who had nothing better to do. Was it really she who had caused him to change his mind, she wondered. No, he must surely have been referring to Beatrice and her impassioned speech at the Brighton rally.

Led by Mrs Hughes and Miss Spencer holding their banner aloft, the Sussex group formed up behind the marchers from Surrey and Kent. Then they were off, up Buckingham Palace Road and into Grosvenor Place.

As they marched along, Anna gazed about her, thrilled to be part of such a momentous occasion. In the excitement, she almost forgot that Daniel was walking beside her until he said, 'Do you know what's behind there?' He indicated the high brick wall which extended along the other side of the road.

She shook her head. The height and the blackened bricks gave it a grim look and she had imagined that it concealed a prison.

Daniel smiled and said, 'That is Buckingham Palace.'

Anna forced a smile. On any other occasion she would have been quite thrilled, but there were important things on her mind today and, besides, she had just realized her feet were starting to hurt. She had not imagined they would have to march so far. If only she hadn't worn her new shoes, she thought. She glanced ahead and, over the heads of her fellow marchers, she saw that the high wall curved to the right and beyond was an impressive arch adorned with sculpted figures.

'The Wellington Arch,' Daniel murmured in her ear.

'How much further?' she asked, trying to ignore the pinching of her shoes.

'Hyde Park is just the other side of the arch,' Daniel said.

Thank goodness, Anna thought. But her relief was short-lived as they crossed the wide road into Park Lane. They still had to cross the park which was huge. Some of the other supporters were flagging too until Lady Beatrice appeared alongside, urging them on with encouraging exhortations 'for the cause'.

As they entered the park, a group of ragged youths began catcalling and one threw a clod of mud which just missed Anna. Daniel grasped her arm and she was grateful for his support.

Beatrice urged the marchers to step up the pace and some of them began to chant, 'Votes for Women', overriding the increasingly loud and abusive shouts.

On reaching the platform which had been erected in a corner of the park, the marchers ranged themselves in front of it. Beatrice mounted the steps to join the other suffragist leaders and began to speak, her voice strong and confident as she made the case for women having the vote.

As she had in Brighton, she emphasized their peaceful intentions. 'We do not condone the militant acts of the Women's Political and Social Union. We believe that reasoned argument will sway our members of Parliament. I'm confident that in time we shall prevail.'

As Beatrice's voice rose in an impassioned appeal, Anna managed to forget her aching feet and sore toes, the cold wind penetrating her thin jacket. A loud cheer went up as her friend concluded, 'We will not give up the fight' and Anna's heart swelled with pride at being part of this historical moment.

Other speakers followed and, as she listened, she could scarcely believe that only a few months ago, she'd hardly given a thought to whether or not women should have the vote. It had seemed a useless ambition to her then, one which wouldn't make much difference to her, or to the women employed by her father. Bea's reasoned arguments had changed her mind.

She turned to Daniel with a warm smile and it was only then that she realized he had been holding her hand the whole time. She did not pull away, although she hoped none of the others had noticed.

The last speeches were over and, despite the heckling from bystanders, the rally had passed off relatively peacefully. There had been no need of intervention from the line of policemen who had ranged themselves at the back of the crowd, truncheons at the ready, almost as if they were craving the outbreak of a disturbance.

As Beatrice stepped down from the platform, a man rushed at her, spitting in her face and shouting foul abuse. Anna gasped and stepped forwards to intervene but Daniel grabbed her arm, holding her back.

'I must help her,' Anna said, pulling away as the man pulled at Bea's sash, ripping it away from her bodice. But before she could get near, Bea stuck out her foot, hooking it under the man's leg. She grabbed his arm and twisted it, flipping him over onto his back. A cheer went up from the surrounding throng and Bea grinned, her hands on her hips as she gazed down at her fallen opponent.

'So that's what she's been learning,' Anna said. 'She made it look so easy.'

'It was foolish of her,' Daniel said. 'She could have been hurt.'

'More likely to have been hurt if she hadn't,' Anna said. 'I think I'll take lessons too.'

'I do hope not,' Daniel said.

'It's nothing to do with you.'

Daniel's face reddened. 'I'm not presuming to lecture you. I merely meant that I hoped it wouldn't be necessary. I wouldn't want you to be harmed.'

Anna wasn't mollified and was about to retort, when she heard an argument behind her. A policeman stood over Bea's victim while another wrote in his notebook.

'You say he attacked you first, Your Ladyship?' he asked.

'He did. And I was only defending myself,' Beatrice replied.

The policeman turned to the man. 'You're sure you don't want to press charges, sir?'

'Just get her away from me.' The man groaned and attempted to get up.

The crowds had begun to disperse, but a few of Bea's supporters who were still waiting nearby began to cheer.

'Now ladies, no more trouble, please,' the policeman said.

'You can be sure *we* won't cause trouble,' Bea said, adjusting her torn sash and beckoning to her friends. 'Time we were getting home, I think.'

Anna's exhilaration faded as she thought of the long walk back to Victoria.

She hoped they were not expected to march behind the banner once more. To her relief, Beatrice said, 'We won't go back to the station yet. Let's go and have tea at the Park Lane Hotel.'

'An excellent idea. We'll take a cab,' said Daniel, taking Anna's arm.

'It's not far,' Beatrice protested.

'Well, I for one have done quite enough walking for one day,' said Daniel firmly, raising his hand as a taxicab slowed down alongside them.

There was room for four inside and Anna climbed in beside Mrs

Hughes and Miss Spencer. Daniel held the door open for Beatrice but she declined.

'I have a few leaflets left. I'll hand them out along the way and join you later,' she said.

Anna had already forgiven Daniel for his earlier remarks. He was only concerned for her safety after all. When he got into the cab, squeezing next to her in the narrow space, she allowed herself to relish the sensation of being so close to him. But it was only moments before they drew up to the grand entrance of the hotel and she couldn't help wishing that the journey could have been longer.

As they entered the hotel foyer, Anna gazed in awe at the brilliant chandeliers with their crystal teardrops catching the light. She had been used to attending ladies' night dinners at the Masonic Hall in Midchester and had thought the grand dining hall one of the most splendid rooms she'd ever been in. But this was entirely different and she felt quite dazed by the opulence which surrounded her. Gracie would have loved it too. What a pity she had not been able to come with them today.

A black-clad waiter led them to a table by the window which overlooked the park, and Daniel helped the ladies to their chairs. He seemed quite at home in these surroundings and Anna realized how little she really knew of the doctor and his background.

Tea was being served by the time Beatrice joined them, her face aglow.

'I've got rid of all the leaflets,' she said. 'I really believe people are coming round to our way of thinking.'

'It's about time,' Mrs Hughes said. 'This campaign has been going on for years. When will people see common sense?'

'I do hope you are right, Lady Beatrice,' said Daniel. 'One would hardly think so, though, given the behaviour of that young man.'

'He was just one person. Many more are supporting us now.'

The conversation grew animated but Anna hardly listened. At any other time, she would have enjoyed the delicate sandwiches and selection of cakes and pastries served to them. But she was only conscious of Daniel's presence at her side and the warmth of his expression whenever he turned to her.

The meal was over and Lady Beatrice declared that it was time to make a move if they were to catch their train. Daniel insisted on paying the bill and asked the concierge to call a cab for them.

While they waited, Anna noticed a gift shop at the side of the foyer. 'Is there time for me to buy something?' she asked.

'If you hurry,' Beatrice said.

'I want a gift for Father.'

Anna took only a minute to select a pair of onyx cuff-links, which the assistant placed in a decorative box.

'Taxi's here,' Daniel called, and she hurried to join her friends, pleased that she had something to show her father for her 'shopping trip', despite a small twinge of conscience.

She put her purchase in her bag and climbed into the taxi beside Daniel. It was a tight squeeze for the five of them but Anna didn't mind, pressed closely as she was against his side. She flushed at the thought and told herself to stop behaving so foolishly. She still could not stop the strange feelings which flooded over her and, although she did not want to part from Daniel, it was almost a relief when the cab deposited them at the entrance to Victoria Station.

'Are you travelling with us, Dr Peters?' Lady Beatrice asked as they joined the crowd of passengers surging towards the ticket barrier.

'I'm afraid I only have a third class ticket,' he said. 'I will rejoin you when we get to Midchester.'

Before Beatrice could say a word, he strode off down the platform, leaving Anna feeling most embarrassed on his behalf. There was no opportunity to examine her feelings on the journey home as she joined in the conversation with her fellow travellers. Her companions were full of excitement, discussing the rally and what it would mean for the furtherance of the cause. Anna tried to show an interest but she found it hard to put the pleasant memory of her hand in Daniel's out of her mind.

She thought she had succeeded, but when the train drew in to Midchester station, she found herself looking eagerly for him. The surge of disappointment when there was so sign of him was almost overwhelming, although she told herself not to be so foolish. He might have waited and escorted her home, though, she thought.

Beatrice's chauffeur was waiting on the station forecourt and Anna was grateful for the offer of a lift. The ache in her feet matched the ache in her heart and she longed to escape to her own room where she could try to make sense of her chaotic feelings.

As the car turned the corner into St Martin's Square, her heart began to race and all thoughts of Daniel and the rally fled. Dr Brown's carriage stood outside the house and Millie was waiting on the doorstep, looking up and down the road and twisting her apron in her hands.

CHAPTER SIXTEEN

ANNA JUMPED OUT of the car and raced up the steps, clutching at Millie's arm.

'What is it, Millie?'

'Oh, miss, I'm that glad you're home. It's the master – he's had another bad turn,' she sobbed.

'How bad?'

'I don't know. Dr Brown's with him now.'

'What happened?'

'He'd just got back from the factory and I went in to ask if he wanted dinner served straight away or to wait till you got back. He was at his desk, slumped over like. We got him up and into bed but....' Millie choked on a sob. 'Oh, miss, he looked dreadful....'

As Anna made to rush inside, Beatrice got out of the car and looked at her anxiously.

'Is everything all right?' she asked.

'My father's been taken ill. The doctor's with him. I must go....'

'Of course. Do let me know if there's anything I can do.'

Without bothering to reply, Anna hurried into the house and ran up the stairs, her tired and aching feet forgotten. She paused at the door to her father's room and took a deep breath before entering.

Dr Brown looked up from his examination of the patient. 'Ah, there you are, Miss Anna. Your father has been asking for you.'

'How is he?'

'It could be worse. He just needs rest and freedom from any stress. I did warn him that he had returned to work too soon.' He turned back to his patient. 'Didn't I tell you, William? Perhaps you'll take more notice of your daughter.'

William was sitting up in bed, propped up with several pillows. His face was very pale but he managed to smile at Anna.

'Lot of fuss about nothing,' he said. 'I'll be all right after a good night's sleep.'

Anna kissed his forehead and stroked his hair. 'I'm so sorry I wasn't here.'

'Nonsense. You deserved an outing. I hope you enjoyed your shopping trip, my dear.'

Dr Brown was about to leave the room but he turned and said, 'Shopping? But young Daniel told me....'

William struggled upright in the bed. 'What? Anna, what've you been up to?'

'Nothing, Father,' Anna stammered. 'As I told you, I went up to London on the train with Lady Beatrice. Daniel – Dr Peters – was on the same train.'

A bewildered look crossed her father's face. 'But, Brown, old man. How did you know that Peters was joining the ladies?' His face grew red and he struggled for breath. 'Is there something I should know about?'

'Father, calm yourself. I can assure you there was no impropriety.' Anna shot a look at Dr Brown and shook her head.

'Yes, a coincidence,' the doctor blustered. 'I must have got the wrong impression.' He picked up his bag. 'Now, William, don't forget – rest and quiet. No sneaking down to the factory until I give you the all clear. Johnson can take care of things for the time being.'

Anna followed him out of the room, anxious to ask what was wrong with her father and if things were worse than they seemed. But before she could speak he looked at her sternly.

'I gather your father does not know of your involvement with the suffrage movement.'

She flushed and shook her head.

'And he would not approve, would he?'

'Please don't say anything to him,' she pleaded. 'It would only upset him. As you say, he shouldn't have any worries in his present state of health.'

'You must tell him yourself, Miss Grayson. It would be better than hearing it from someone else or reading about it in the newspapers. Besides, now that he knows that Dr Peters accompanied you, he'll be thinking far worse. It is not the done thing for unmarried young ladies to travel in the company of a gentleman. You have your reputation to consider.'

'But there was a group of us – two other ladies besides Lady Beatrice.'

'But your father does not know that. No, my dear, you must tell him.'

'I will – when he is feeling a little stronger,' Anna said.

'See that you do,' the doctor said, picking up his hat and leaving the house.

When he'd gone, Anna went down to the kitchen and found Cook and Millie in a state of agitation.

'Is the master going to be all right?' asked Cook.

'I hope so. He just needs rest,' said Anna.

'I thought he went back to the factory too soon. I said so to Millie, didn't I?' Cook wiped her hands on her apron and proceeded to bustle around the kitchen. 'Well, the dinner's all spoiled and I don't know what I'll give you to eat, miss.'

'Don't worry about it, Cook. I'm not hungry. Perhaps a little broth for Father?' She turned to Millie. 'Could you light the fire in his room? It has turned rather chilly.'

Having something to do seemed to calm them and they went about their duties, leaving Anna feeling guilty and exhausted. What an end to such a wonderful and inspiring day, she thought – wonderful because of being with Daniel, and inspiring for the example of Lady Beatrice and her followers. But for the time being she must put all that out of her head. Father was the one she must think of now.

He must get well, she prayed. And when he recovered from this latest attack, she would confess all and hope that he'd understand. Deep down she had little confidence that he would. He was far too deeply entrenched in his views. She shrugged. She would just have to brave his anger, but she would deal with that when the time came. Until then, she must play the dutiful daughter once more.

For the next couple of weeks Anna had little opportunity to pursue her own interests. Her father was a demanding patient and once more she found herself constantly running up and down stairs to tend to him.

There was little that Dr Brown could do beyond admonishing William to rest and leave running the factory to Johnson. He called frequently to play chess with his old friend, which gave Anna a little respite from his demands.

She was very concerned about him, despite Dr Brown's assurance that he would get better with rest and freedom from worry. She could see there was something on his mind and she hoped he wasn't fretting about her involvement with Daniel. He hadn't mentioned it since her return from London and she was beginning to hope that he'd accepted her explanation that it had been a chance meeting. She really didn't want to upset him by telling him why she'd really she'd gone to London.

It was now almost the end of November and winter had set in with a vengeance with cold, icy winds and teeming rain. William wanted to come downstairs but Dr Brown insisted he stay in his room where a fire burned day and night. One day, as he was leaving, the doctor waylaid her in the hall.

'Have you spoken to your father yet?' he asked.

'No, Doctor. There has been no opportunity to bring up the subject. As you said, he mustn't be worried.'

'Quite right, my dear. Well, there is little chance of his finding out anything while he is housebound, but once he is up and about again he's bound to hear rumours. In a town this small, word gets around.'

'Please – you won't say anything, will you?' Anna was more worried about Father's reaction to her involvement with the suffragists than any possible romantic involvement with the young doctor.

'If you promise me that you will not attend any more of these silly rallies or women's meetings, I will keep quiet,' Dr Brown promised.

Anna's temper rose. How dare he call the cause 'silly'? With difficulty she swallowed her anger and managed to say quite meekly, 'Thank you, Doctor. You know I wouldn't do anything to upset Father in his present state of health.'

The doctor patted her arm.

'Good girl,' he said.

After he'd gone, Anna gave vent to her feelings with a vicious kick at the hallstand, bringing Millie rushing from the dining room.

'Are you all right, miss?' she asked.

'I stumbled,' Anna said, embarrassed by her lack of control.

She went into the morning room and sank into a chair by the window. She could do with a breath of air, she thought. She had planned to go out while Dr Brown was keeping Father company, but it had still been raining hard with a keen wind blowing from the east. Now the sun was breaking through and, although it was still chilly, she decided to ask

Millie to listen out for him while she took a turn in the park.

She hadn't been out of the house for days and, despite the cold, she found herself enjoying the fresh air. Winter had crept up on her unawares and she realized that the leaves had all gone from the trees, while the flowerbeds in the park were bedraggled and unkempt.

She reached the far side of the park and the gate which led through to the warren of streets where the Mitchells lived. She hadn't seen Gracie for weeks and she wondered how she was coping with the loss of her sister. With so much else on her mind lately, she realized somewhat guiltily that she had not given her friend much thought. There had been no more news about Lily's accident and she had almost convinced herself that that was just what it must have been – an accident. There had been nothing sinister about it – it was only her over-active imagination. At least that's what she told herself.

Should she call on the Mitchells? Of course, Gracie would be at work and Mrs Mitchell would hardly welcome a reminder of that dreadful day when she had brought the news of Lily's death.

She did not feel like returning home just yet, though, and, telling herself that Father would be perfectly all right for a bit longer, she turned her steps towards the factory. It wouldn't hurt to let Johnson know that she was quite capable of keeping an eye on things in her father's absence. And perhaps she would catch a glimpse of Gracie while she was there.

Even before she entered the factory yard, she could hear the machines and smell that combination of hot metal and oil. The noise was almost deafening and she wondered how the young women who worked there put up with it day after day. There was no one in the yard this time and she walked through the open doors, glancing at the rows of machines before opening the office door.

Edward Johnson, poring over some invoices, didn't look up when she entered but shouted, 'I've told you to knock before coming in here.'

'Excuse *me*, Mr Johnson, but I don't think *I* need to ...' Anna began, a flush rising to her cheeks.

He stood up, almost knocking the chair over in his haste. 'Oh, Miss Anna, I do beg your pardon. I thought it was one of the factory girls. They're always barging in here with one complaint or another.'

He straightened the chair and came round the desk, offering his hand. 'Do sit down, miss. It's a pleasure to see you. And how is your father – progressing well, I hope?' He pulled a chair out for her and bade her sit.

Anna swallowed her repugnance at his manner and managed a smile. The more she saw of him the more her dislike increased. Perhaps it was that he tried too hard to be pleasant, only to succeed in seeming insincere. Still, Father trusted and relied on him and she'd always thought him a good judge of character.

'Father's improving daily,' she said, sitting on the edge of the chair.

'Good, good.' Johnson nodded but there was no enthusiasm in his manner. 'However, I hope he doesn't come back to work too soon – after what happened last time.'

He sounded solicitous but Anna sensed something else in his manner. Perhaps he was enjoying being in charge of the factory and did not like the idea of going back to his former position, she thought.

'I'm sure he'll be guided by Dr Brown,' she said.

There was a short silence before Johnson asked her what had brought her to the factory.

'A message from Mr Grayson?' he asked.

Anna thought quickly. It wouldn't do to let him know that Father had no knowledge of her being here.

'No specific message. He was just wondering how things were going. Are there any new orders?'

'Very few at present, I'm afraid.' Johnson shrugged regretfully.

'Does my father realize this?'

'I have not mentioned it – don't want him worried.' Johnson paused. 'In his present state of health, I thought....'

'I suppose you're right. But he'll have to be told if the business is in trouble.'

Johnson held up his hand. 'I did not say that,' he said hastily. 'We are ticking over at present. There is no cause for alarm.'

Anna stood up. 'Very well. But you will keep me informed, won't you?'

He also stood and came round the desk, opening the door for her.

'I had not realized you took an interest in the business, Miss Anna,' he said.

Someone has to, was Anna's immediate thought. But she said nothing, merely smiled and bid him good day.

As she started to walk away, Johnson said, 'I think it best not to say anything to Mr Grayson at present, don't you?'

She nodded agreement.

As she left the factory, she spotted Gracie at her machine but the girl was engrossed in her work and did not look up.

It wasn't her friend who occupied her thoughts as she made her way through the narrow streets. She was thinking about the noisy machines, all of them churning out the needles that Grayson's was famous for. And the factory workers looked busy enough. Why had Johnson hinted otherwise?

If only she could talk to Father about it. But, apart from being reluctant to say or do anything that would bring on another attack, she knew that he would refuse to discuss things with her. It was not her place to worry about it, he would say. Perhaps he was right. After all, what did she know about running a factory?

She opened the front gate, sighing at the prospect of dealing once more with her father's irritable moods and the strain of keeping things from him. If only there was someone she could confide in. Her thoughts flew to Daniel but she hadn't seen him since their trip to London. Bea hadn't called either, although she had telephoned to invite Anna to attend a suffragist meeting in Haslemere the following week.

Anna had regretfully declined, giving her father's health as an excuse. But if she was honest, she was beginning to feel that the movement wasn't getting anywhere. Despite more men, some in high places, rallying to the cause, little progress had been made. The militant activities of the Pankhursts and the Women's Social and Political Union had resulted in so much bad publicity, it was alienating their former supporters, despite the suffragists' claim theirs was a peaceful campaign. All too often, Lady Beatrice's supporters were banded together in the same breath as 'those women'.

Millie took her coat, effectively banishing her sombre thoughts with her chatter.

'Did you enjoy your walk, miss? You must be cold. That's a nasty wind.'

'I needed the fresh air,' Anna said.

'The master seems a lot brighter today, miss. He wants to come downstairs for dinner,' Millie said.

'I don't know about that. I think we should wait and see what Dr Brown says.' She smiled at the maid. 'Still, I'm pleased he seems to be better. I'll go up to him.'

William was out of bed, sitting beside the fire with a shawl over his knees. He turned as Anna came into the room.

'Where have you been?' he asked. 'For a walk, Millie said.' He gestured to the window, where dark clouds had begun to gather. 'You don't walk in this weather. What have you been up to?'

'As Millie said, I went for a walk in the park. It was fine when I left the house. I'm sorry I left you alone so long, but Millie was here in case you needed anything.'

William gave a little grunt, staring into the fire and Anna hesitated by the door.

'*Do* you need anything, Father?' she asked.

He shook his head. 'Just to get out of this damn room and back to normal,' he said, looking up at her and reaching for her hand. 'Come and sit by me for a minute. There's something I want to discuss with you.'

Anna's heart sank. He sounded very serious. Had he found out about her involvement with the suffragists? But he didn't seem angry. Another thought rushed into her head. Had Dr Brown given him bad news about his health? She made up the fire and adjusted the shawl over her father's knees to allow time to compose herself, then sat in the chair opposite.

'What is it, Father?' she asked anxiously.

'Don't look so worried, my dear. I hope you will like what I have to say. I've had a lot of time to think while I've been lying idle. I'm worried about your future – if anything should happen to me....'

'No, Father. Don't say that. You're getting better – Dr Brown said so. As long as you don't overdo things and get plenty of rest....' Anna choked on a sob.

'That may well be, Anna. But you know me. I am not one to sit and do nothing. I want to get back to work and if that means....' He paused. 'It is God's will.'

Your will, Anna thought. You won't take advice but must go your own way.

William leaned forwards and took her hand. 'Please don't get upset, Anna. Let me tell you what I have in mind. You will not want for anything – I've made sure of that. The factory brings in a good income and with Johnson at the helm, it should continue to do well.'

Anna looked up and was about to tell him about the lack of new orders. But, mindful that she mustn't upset him, she managed to stop herself. Besides, she hadn't believed Johnson, although she was puzzled as to why he would lie.

William was still speaking and it was a moment before she realized what he was saying. 'It is the best thing for you, my dear, especially now that I have promoted him to manager. He has asked if he may court you and I have consented.' He leaned forwards and took Anna's hand. 'He will make a good, steady husband.'

CHAPTER SEVENTEEN

ANNA COULD SCARCELY believe she had heard aright.

'Father – I've already told you I will not marry him. I don't even like him,' she protested, snatching her hand away.

'Anna, it's for the best. I could not rest easy if I left you to fend for yourself. A woman alone is vulnerable to the wrong sort of man. Unmarried, you would still have this house but you'd have to sell the factory.' He leaned forwards and tried to take her hand again. 'I don't want to worry you, my dear, but we are not making as much money as in previous years. I dread to think you might be left destitute. This way, Grayson's will stay in the family and with Johnson in charge, things will pick up and the factory will continue to provide a living for you and any children you may have.'

Anna gasped. How dare he make these arrangements without first discussing them with her? And what did he mean about the factory staying in the family?

'It's all in my will, Anna. I have provided for you in the best way I know. The factory is left to Johnson if and when you marry.'

'But Father, I can't possibly....'

'Nonsense, Anna. I have explained – who better than a man who can provide for you as Edward Johnson will be able to?' He looked at her with a puzzled frown. 'There is no one else, is there?'

An image of Daniel Peters flashed through her mind. Should she speak up? She swiftly quelled the thought. After all, he had given her no real indication that he was interested in her, despite her treasured memory of his holding her hand during the London march. If he felt as she did, he surely would have called before now. Was he still working at the cottage hospital or had he left Midchester altogether? When Dr Brown called on his frequent visits she had been too reticent to ask him for news.

Regretfully, she shook her head at her father's inquiry and he smiled.

'Well then. It's settled. It will be a relief to me, my dear, to see you settled in case....'

Anna's shoulders slumped. She knew it was useless to argue once he had made up his mind about something. Usually she gave in for the sake of peace and quiet. But this was different. She should speak up. But how could she upset him in his present frail state? She dreaded that an argument might bring on another attack.

She smiled as if in agreement and said that she would go and see about dinner. It took a great deal of self-control not to slam the door and she stood outside on the landing, breathing deeply. So that was Johnson's game. He wanted to get his hands on the business. Not if I can help it, she thought. There must be some way to make Father see him for what he was.

Millie looked up from the bottom of the stairs with a worried frown. 'Are you all right, miss? It's not the master, is it?'

'Everything's fine, Millie. Nothing for you to worry about anyway.' She started downstairs, forcing a smile. 'Could you take a tray up to Father, please?'

'Very well, miss.'

When Anna took her place alone at the dining table, she found she was unable to swallow more than a few bites, although Cook had, as usual, prepared an appetizing meal. Her thoughts kept returning to her father's shocking announcement. Even if she didn't have feelings for Daniel, she would never have contemplated marrying Edward Johnson. She had never liked him, but that alone would not alter her father's opinion. She must find a valid reason to refuse him.

Should she tell Father that she suspected him of lying about the orders? No. He wouldn't believe her without proof. She would go to the factory again, preferably when Johnson wasn't there.

When Dr Brown called a few days later, he declared William fit to come downstairs.

'But you must not overdo it,' he admonished. 'No dealing with papers in your study, no telephoning the factory.'

William began to protest, but Anna intervened. 'You must listen to the doctor, Father. You don't want to be ill again.'

'I suppose I must,' William said with a sigh. Then, struggling to the edge of the bed he added, 'Come on then, help me up.'

Anna helped him into his dressing gown, despite his protesting that he preferred to get dressed.

'We don't want to tire you out,' she said.

Anna hadn't been to church for several weeks and the following Sunday, she found it hard to get away afterwards as everyone wanted to ask about her father.

'Yes, thank you, Mrs Collins. He is doing very well,' she said.

'Perhaps we shall see him in church too before long then,' the vicar's wife said. 'And we shall need your help with decorating the church for Christmas.'

'I'm sure I'll be able to spare the time now that Father is so much better.'

'We couldn't manage without you. You have such an artistic way, even though there's not much in the way of flowers at this time of year.'

'We have plenty of holly in the garden and I believe I spotted some Christmas roses coming into flower. Even if I don't have time to help with the decorating, I will get Joe to cut some greenery for the church.'

'Thank you. Oh, and ...'

'I'm sorry, Mrs Collins. I must get home. Father....' Anna guiltily fingered the bunch of keys in her pocket. She had hoped to escape quickly and visit the factory.

'I understand, dear. You mustn't leave him alone too long,' said Mrs Collins.

As Anna said goodbye and walked quickly away, she heard the vicar's wife say to her companion, 'Such a devoted daughter.' She blushed. If only they knew what I am about to do, she thought.

It was strange to enter the factory when no machines were running. Dust motes hung in the air and the smell of oil and metal still lingered. But it was eerily quiet and Anna found herself tiptoeing towards the office door. Suppose Johnson was there? But surely he would have no reason to be at the factory on a Sunday.

She threw open the door, but of course, the room was empty. She sat down at her father's desk and looked around. Where to start?

The desktop was bare, except for a blotter, an inkstand and a matching pen tray. Anna tried the drawers but they were locked and none of the keys she had taken from home fitted. She looked at the shelves behind the desk which were neatly filled with cardboard box files. She stood up and studied the labels – 'invoices', 'receipts', 'orders' – and the dates, some going back several years.

She pulled out the most recent file marked 'orders' and took it to the desk, gasping as she opened it up and saw that, contrary to what Johnson had told her, there was plenty of work coming in. But why would he lie?

She closed the file and put it back, careful to make sure it lined up with the others. It wouldn't do for the factory manager to realize that someone had been in here. The other files told the same story. The factory was doing well.

Frustrated, Anna tried the desk drawers again. There must be something here to give her a clue as to what was going on. Had Johnson hidden a spare key somewhere? She tipped the pens out of the tray but there was no key. She picked up the inkstand, removed the bottle from the ornate holder and there it was, nestled underneath.

The key opened the top drawer which contained nothing of interest, just a notepad, a receipt book and few elastic bands and drawing pins. But right at the back was another key and this one opened all the other drawers.

Her heart started to thump as she withdrew a large ledger. And as she turned the pages, she realized that the figures in this book bore no relation to the receipts and invoices she had seen in the files. This was the book she had seen Johnson carrying when he visited her father, the one that told him orders were down and costs going up.

What was he up to, she wondered. Surely it couldn't be in his interests to pretend that things were bad. It would make more sense for him to exaggerate how well the works was doing under his managership and so justify her father's confidence in him.

She sighed. It was all a bit too much for her to take in. After all, she had no real head for business, especially as Father had discouraged her from taking an interest in what went on in the factory. She closed the ledger, but as she went to replace it, she noticed something right at the back of the drawer.

'So that's it, 'she murmured, pulling out the little notebook and turning the pages. This was the real ledger, she realized, the record of how much money the works was really making. Johnson had been steadily siphoning off a certain amount of every batch of orders that came in. And he had been doctoring the costs of materials too. He must have squirreled away a vast amount of money in the weeks that her father had been ill, she thought, carefully replacing the notebook.

She glanced at the clock on the wall, noticing how much time had passed. Better get home before Father starts getting agitated, she thought. Re-locking the desk drawers and putting the key back where she had found it, she stood up and looked around, making sure that nothing looked disturbed.

She hurried outside, locked the door and crossed the yard. As she was re-fastening the padlock on the gate, she glanced up and saw a man coming across the road towards her. It was Johnson. Her hands started to shake and she almost dropped the bunch of keys. She managed to thrust them into her pocket, hoping he hadn't spotted her action. With an effort, she planted a smile on her face and turned as he drew near.

'Why, Miss Anna, what are you doing here on a Sunday?' he asked, raising his hat in greeting.

'I needed some air after church and decided to walk this way,' she said, pleased that her voice seemed steady. 'I know how hard you've been working since Father's illness and thought I might find you here.' She hoped she sounded sincere.

'I do come into the office sometimes for an hour or two on a Sunday. It is quieter and I can concentrate on the paperwork without interruption,' he said, giving her a wide smile. 'Well, it's always a pleasure to see you, Miss Anna, but was there any particular reason you wanted to see me?'

'Well, as you know, Father doesn't like me to interfere in the business so I can't speak freely when you come to the house.' She returned his smile. 'I know you're a bit worried about the lack of orders but I'd rather you didn't make too much of it to him. Dr Brown says he'll soon be fit enough to return to work and any worries are sure to set him back again.'

'I quite understand, Miss Anna.' Johnson got out his keys and unlocked the gate. 'Perhaps you'd like to come in for a while. I could show you the ledger.'

'That won't be necessary, Johnson,' she said.

'I do wish you'd call me Edward,' he said, reaching for her hand. 'After all, now that Mr Grayson has given his blessing, we should dispense with formality.'

She pulled away, trying to hide her dismay.

'I must go. Father will be worrying,' she said.

'Please, Anna. I'd like the opportunity to talk to you, to discuss something other than business.'

His familiarity made her cringe.

'I really don't think this is the right moment....' she snapped.

'You won't be able to avoid me forever.' His voice was sharp, but he made a conscious effort to placate her. 'You must believe your father has your best interests at heart – and that of the business.'

'Father is going to get well – I know it. And any arrangements he has made will no longer be necessary.' There was a slight hint of desperation in her voice. 'In the meantime, I'm sure everything is in order and you are doing your best to keep things running smoothly until he's fit for work again.'

'It is my pleasure, Miss Anna. Grayson's is a good firm to work for and I am happy to do my bit. Let's hope this lack of orders is just a temporary thing.'

Anna, pleased at the return to formality, kept her smile firmly in place as she thanked him for being so conscientious. But as she said goodbye and walked away, she was seething. The hypocrite, she thought.

Once at home, she managed to quell her anger and present a calm face to her father, who was reading the *Sunday Times*.

'Oh, there you are,' he said. 'Perhaps we can have lunch now. I expected you home some time ago.'

'I'm sorry, Father. I went for a stroll after church and walked a lot further than I meant to.'

She helped him out of his chair and held his arm as they started into the dining room. He was still a little unsteady on his feet but he shook her off impatiently. She didn't react and left him to take his place while she rang for Millie to start serving.

The meal progressed mainly in silence apart from a few questions from William about the church service and who had been there. Anna did not mention Mrs Collins's request to help with the Christmas decorations. It was always a very quiet time for the Graysons, being the anniversary of Lydia Grayson's death and Anna knew that any mention of the season would upset him.

She answered his questions absentmindedly, her thoughts busy with what she had discovered at the factory. She was still unsure how to approach the subject without causing her father to fly into a rage at being deceived. Even worse, he might refuse to believe her and accuse her of maligning Johnson in order to justify her refusal to marry him.

Perhaps it would be better to keep quiet for the time being. When Father was a little stronger he would be better able to deal with the problem. And by then she might have managed to get more proof of Johnson's wrongdoing. Of course, if Father brought up the subject of her marrying again, she would be forced to speak up.

She pushed her food around on the plate, having no appetite after the confrontation with the factory manager and what she had discovered at the office. How could she convince Father that his trusted manager was embezzling from the firm? There was the notebook of course, but she didn't think there would be another opportunity to get hold of it. Now that Johnson had seen her at the factory, he would be doubly certain to cover his traces in case she suspected anything.

She looked up to see that William had finished eating and was staring at her.

'An excellent meal, my dear,' he said, gesturing towards her plate. 'But you're not eating. I would have thought a walk in the fresh air would have given you an appetite.' He paused. 'You're not worried about anything, are you?'

Anna smiled and speared a potato on her fork.

'Not at all,' she said, forcing herself to swallow a few mouthfuls. 'The only thing I've been worried about lately is your health. But I can see you are much better so—'

'And have you thought anymore about my plans for your future?'

'No, Father, and I don't want to think about it. I've said I don't intend to marry. I'm quite content to stay at home, looking after the house – and you.'

'Well, we won't discuss it now. I know I can't force you, but it would set my mind at rest if you would agree.' He put his hand on his chest and drew a deep breath. 'Brown says I could have another attack at any time, you know.'

Now he was trying to make her feel guilty, she thought. But she waved his remark away and said, 'Nonsense, Father.'

The meal over, she insisted on William going to his room to rest.

'You haven't been up for long and I don't want you to tire yourself,' she said.

As usual, he protested but his voice lacked conviction and he allowed her to help him upstairs. He lay on the bed and Anna covered him with the counterpane. Before she had time to draw the curtains, he was asleep. She tiptoed away, pleased that she would have a little time to herself to think about everything.

She decided that she would send a note to Bea asking her to call. Due to her father's illness, she had rather neglected her friend. As she sat at her writing desk and got out notepaper and pen, she smiled, recalling that her friend had called her old-fashioned because she still preferred to write letters rather than use the telephone. She still hadn't got used to the noisy ring when someone called, and jumped whenever the sound echoed through the hall. She had to admit, though, that it had been a boon when Father was taken ill and she had to send for the doctor.

She wrote, apologizing for not keeping in touch and saying that she had something important to discuss. As she sealed the envelope, she realized that Bea would probably think it was something to do with the suffragists. It seemed an age since she had gone to the London rally with her and she felt a little guilty that she had given so little thought to the movement since then. There was so much else on her mind.

Perhaps she should have hinted that her problem had to do with Johnson and the factory, but she felt she couldn't put it in writing. Suppose she was wrong? Was she letting her dislike of the factory manager influence her? But after what she'd discovered that morning, she was convinced that something was amiss.

She found a stamp and stuck it on the envelope, deciding she would walk to the post box on the corner of the Square. But when she looked out of the window, she saw that it had started to rain so she placed the letter on the brass tray on the hallstand. Tomorrow would do, she thought. As she turned to go back into the drawing room, she saw the shadow of a man outlined against the glass panel in the front door.

Who would call unannounced on a rainy Sunday afternoon, she wondered. She really didn't feel up to being polite to visitors today and she turned away. She would tell Millie to inform whoever it was that she was not at home. But suppose it was Daniel? Her heart began to beat a little faster and she hurried to open the front door.

CHAPTER EIGHTEEN

'DO COME IN out of the rain,' Anna said, opening the door wider. But her face fell as the visitor lowered his umbrella to reveal Edward Johnson standing there.

'Thank you, miss,' he said, shaking the drops off the umbrella and stepping inside.

'I did not expect to see you again today,' Anna said, wondering why he had come. Surely she had made it plain this morning that she had no interest in furthering a relationship with him. Or could it be something else? Did he suspect she'd been in the office? But he was smiling widely as if he had quite forgotten their earlier confrontation.

As she took his coat and ushered him into the drawing room, she said, 'If you've called to see Father, I'm afraid he is resting at the moment. I do not want to disturb him.'

'No, Miss Anna, it is you I have come to see. I'm glad Mr Grayson isn't here. I wish to talk to you alone.'

Anna swallowed. Was he going to propose to her? She couldn't really believe that her father had led him to believe that she would welcome his advances. She almost wished he was about to probe into her reasons for being outside the works that morning. She would find that so much easier to deal with. To give herself time to think, she offered him tea and rang for Millie.

While they waited for the maid to bring in the tray, she chatted brightly about the weather, Mr Collins's sermon that morning and her relief that her father seemed to be getting better.

Johnson said that he hoped Mr Grayson would be able to return to work soon, but Anna didn't believe that for one moment, especially after what she had discovered earlier that day. So long as William was confined to the house, he was free to carry on his fraudulent activities.

Millie brought the tea in and Anna busied herself with the tray, filling their cups and handing a plate of dainty cucumber sandwiches to Johnson. He took one and crammed it into his mouth and she watched with distaste as he followed it with large gulp of tea.

She was about to speak when he said, 'I believe you are acquainted with the Mitchell girl. She told me you were very kind to her when her sister died.'

Anna nodded. 'How is she?'

'She is a very good worker. I have promoted her to overseer. It will mean an increase in her wage.'

'That will be a big help to her family,' Anna said. 'Her father doesn't earn much and they must be missing Lily's wages.'

She did not reveal that she knew Mr Mitchell had been dismissed from Grayson's.

'You have a kind heart, Miss Anna. It is not everyone who would take an interest in the welfare of their family's employees.'

'I was brought up to think of others,' Anna said and, uncomfortable with his personal remark, she busied herself with the tray. 'More tea, Mr Johnson?'

He shook his head. 'I did not come for tea, Miss Anna. Nor did I wish to inquire after your father. I have a very special reason for calling on you.'

Anna's stomach churned and she braced herself for his next words, but she looked up in surprise when he said, 'I believe you have become friendly with Lady Beatrice Winslow.'

'I don't see what it has to do with you, but yes – we both belong to the Church Ladies' Guild.'

'And you are acquainted with her cousin, Mr Ponsonby-Smythe?'

Anna glared at him. 'You are being very familiar, Mr Johnson. What is the purpose of these questions?'

'You have been seen in that man's car, gadding around the town. I wondered whether your father was aware of his interest in you.'

'Mr Ponsonby-Smythe is not interested in me as you put it. He merely gave me a lift home – at his cousin's request. Anyway, I am most certainly not interested in him.' Anna was angry. How dare he question her like this? And why?

She soon found out when Johnson sat back and, with a satisfied smirk on his face, said, 'I am very pleased to hear it. Ponsonby-Smythe is not good enough for you. He is a gambler – and worse. It is only your money he would be interested in.'

And he's not the only one, Anna thought, shaking her head. 'I have told you, there is nothing between us. We are merely acquaintances.'

Johnson leaned forwards and took her hand, lowering his voice. 'You see, Anna, my dear, I merely wished to find out if there was another man in your life.'

She tried to snatch her hand away, but he gripped it fast. 'I believe your father has spoken to you about the future – *our* future.' He gazed at her earnestly. 'You must know that I admire you immensely....'

With a great wrench, she managed free her hand. 'Mr Johnson, you must not say such things.'

'Why so formal, Anna? I thought you were going to call me Edward.' He reached for her hand again. 'I understood from your father that he would be agreeable to a match. I wish to marry you, Anna.'

Taking a deep breath, she said, 'My father may be agreeable but I am not.'

'Do not be so hasty, my dear. I admit you do not know me very well – yet. But I would be a good husband. You would not want for anything. I would continue to run the factory and make it prosper as your father has.'

'Is it me – or the factory that you want?' she asked, her eyes flashing.

He lowered his eyes and grimaced. 'I suppose it is natural you should think that, and it's true that your father offered it as an incentive ... but I *am* fond of you, Anna. I would be proud to call you my wife.'

Perhaps he was sincere, she thought. He certainly sounded it. But she remembered the evidence of his cunning that she'd found in his desk and she hardened her heart.

'Mr Johnson, I have no intention of getting married – to you or anyone else. I am content with my lot. Caring for Father is my life at present.'

'But what if he dies?'

Anna was shocked at his bluntness and she responded sharply. 'He is not going to die. Dr Brown says he is getting stronger every day.'

'I hope that is true, Anna, my dear,' Johnson said, softening his tone. 'But Mr Grayson is obviously worried about your future if anything should happen to him.' He attempted to take her hand again. 'It is what he wishes – what I wish too.'

Anna sighed. 'I'm sorry, but it is not what *I* wish.' She stood up and stepped towards the door. 'When Father wakes, I will tell him that you called, but I will say nothing of this conversation. Now, I think you had better leave. We have nothing more to say to each other.'

Johnson stood up too. 'Very well. I'll go. But this is not the end of the matter.' He grasped her arm and pulled her towards him, his face twisted in an ugly grimace. 'I think I can make you change your mind.'

'Nothing will make me change my mind,' Anna said defiantly, pulling away from him.

'Oh, you will when you hear what I have to say.' He grasped her arms and thrust his face towards hers. 'What do you think your father will say when he hears what you've been up to?'

Despite the churning in her stomach, Anna stood her ground. 'I have no idea what you're talking about.'

'I think you do, miss.' He grinned and let go of her. Then, in what appeared to be a change of subject, he said, 'Did you know that the factory is so noisy that the girls can't hear each other speak – and yet they gossip all the time? They read each other's lips, you know.' He nodded. 'Oh, yes. What they don't realize is that I, too, have learned to lip-read. It is a very useful accomplishment.'

'I cannot imagine what that has to do with me.'

'You have been the subject of their tittle-tattle, my dear. For instance, I know why you were in Brighton that day. Your father thinks you went to the races but you were a long way from the racecourse. Is it just a coincidence that Lady Beatrice was holding one of her rallies on the seafront?'

'It is none of your business how I spend my time,' Anna retorted.

'But it is. I do not want my future wife consorting with those trouble-makers. Those suffragettes are not worthy of the name of women.'

As she started to protest, he made a grab for her again, his fingers tightening painfully on her wrist. 'I mean to have you, Anna – and the factory. So think carefully. I know how your father feels about the Votes for Women movement, so if you don't want him to find out about your involvement with them, you will re-consider my offer.' He pushed past her into the hall and, ignoring a startled Millie, he grabbed his coat off the hallstand.

Anna waved the maid away and said as calmly as she could. 'It's all right, Millie. I will see Mr Johnson out.'

She handed him his hat and, realizing that Millie was still hovering, she said politely, 'Thank you for calling, Mr Johnson. I'll tell Father you've been.'

'Goodbye, Miss Anna, and don't forget what I said.'

To the maid it must have looked like a polite exchange between acquaintances and Anna did her best to keep her tone neutral. 'I won't, Mr Johnson.'

She opened the front door for him and, as he stepped out on to the porch, he turned and whispered. 'Your secret is safe with me – as long as—'

Her temper flared and without stopping to think she said, 'I am not the only one with secrets, Mr Johnson.'

She slammed the door behind him and leaned against it, breathing heavily. What had possessed her to say that? He had seen her at the factory that morning but would he realize that she'd opened the desk drawer and seen his private ledger? If so, he was bound to destroy it, or hide it elsewhere. What proof would she have then that he had been defrauding the company?

Millie came out of the drawing room with the tea tray and, seeing Anna still leaning against the front door, asked, 'Is something wrong, miss?'

'No, Millie. I'm a little tired, that's all. Would you make some more tea, please? I'll go and sit down for a while.'

She sank into a chair beside the fire, and closed her eyes. What should she do? Who could she turn to? Of course, if Father was well enough, she would have told him straightaway what she suspected of Johnson. But then, it wouldn't have happened at all if he had still been running things.

One thing was certain though – she had more of a hold over the factory manager than he had over her. He could not coerce her into marriage now.

When Millie returned, she sat up straight and took a deep breath. 'If that man calls again, you must say I am not at home.'

'But he usually asks to see the master.'

'Tell him Father is not well enough for visitors.'

'But, miss—'

'Don't argue, Millie. I don't want him in the house.'

'Very well, miss.' She poured the tea and handed Anna a cup. 'I never did like him anyway.' She bit her lip. 'Sorry, Miss Anna – it's not my place to say....'

'Never mind. I don't like him either.' She gave a shaky laugh. 'Would you believe – my father wants me to marry him.'

'Oh, miss, surely not. He's not good enough for you.'

'My thoughts exactly, Millie. But don't worry, I turned him down.'

'Good. Now, miss – is there anything else?'

'Could you go up and see if Father's awake? Don't tell him Johnson was here. I don't want him to know for the moment.'

'Of course, miss.'

When the maid had left the room, Anna leaned back in the chair and sighed. Thank goodness for Millie, who had been with the family so long that a certain familiarity had grown up between them and it was good to be able to show her true feelings when they were alone. Anna still didn't feel ready to confide her discoveries about the factory manager, though. After all, what could Millie do about it?

Dr Brown called the next afternoon and Anna greeted him with some surprise. 'I was not expecting you, Doctor. I thought Father was much better. He's coming downstairs every day now. But I'm making sure he rests as well.'

'I have called as a friend, Miss Anna. I have some unexpected free time so I wondered if William would enjoy a game of chess.'

'I'm sure he would, Doctor. But what about your patients? This is such a busy time of year for you normally.'

'I'm pleased to tell you I have some help now. I have taken on an assistant. And if things work out I shall be offering him a partnership.'

Anna's heart began to thump. Could he be talking about Daniel? But surely he had said that he could not afford to buy into the practice. That was why he'd been working at the cottage hospital. She tried to calm herself and said, 'I hope this does not mean that you are thinking of retiring.'

'Not just yet. But when the time comes, I am sure Dr Peters will prove to be an excellent replacement.' Dr Brown smiled and said, 'Well, what about that chess game?'

It was hard to answer calmly, due to the racing of her heart, but she opened the door and showed him in.

'Father, look who's here. Shall I get the chess board out?' she asked brightly.

William was sitting in his chair by the fire but he struggled to rise and shake his old friend's hand. While the two men exchanged greetings, Anna pulled a small table out and set up the chess board. But her hands were shaking as she tried to take in what the old doctor had said. Would Daniel call on her now that he would be living nearby? And if he did, could she confide in him?

She had debated speaking to her father about Johnson's visit but she had refrained, sure that he would not believe her accusations. Father was sure to see her suspicions as an excuse to refuse Johnson's proposal. He had always trusted the man and, besides, he had made up his mind that marriage to the factory manager was the only possible future for his daughter.

Leaving the two men to their chess game, Anna left the room, her mind still reeling from Dr Brown's announcement. And, as she made her way to the kitchen to check on Cook's preparations for dinner, she made up her mind. If Daniel didn't call on her soon, she would brave the telephone and ask him to come. She could always say she was worried about Father. But she must confide in somebody or she would go mad.

CHAPTER NINETEEN

BREAKFAST SEEMED TO be later and later these days as it took some time to help William downstairs and into the dining room. He now refused to use his walking stick and Anna hovered behind him, anxious in case he should fall. As usual, he became irritable when she tried to help but in a way, she was glad he was getting back to his old forceful self.

This morning, instead of hiding behind his newspaper, he seemed disposed to conversation, pleased with himself for having beaten Dr Brown in two games last night.

'I haven't lost my touch,' he said.

'Well done, Father. It's good of the doctor to spend time with you. He's a busy man.'

'He told me he is thinking of retiring – partly anyway. When young Peters joins the practice, he'll have more time for his hobbies. You know he loves fishing too and, when I'm a bit fitter, we plan to go on a fishing trip – lovely trout streams they have over there in Hampshire.'

Anna could hardly believe it. William had been wrapped up in the business all his life with no time for hobbies. But uppermost in her thoughts was the mention of Daniel. She spread marmalade on her toast, looking down at her plate and hoping her father would not notice the telltale flush which crept up her cheeks.

'Dr Brown mentioned that he had taken on an assistant, but I understood that Dr Peters could not afford to buy into the practice,' she said.

'Well, it seems his circumstances have changed. A distant relative has died and left him some money. Not much, but enough to get him started with Brown.'

'That's wonderful. I know that's what he wanted.'

'I did not realize you were so well acquainted with young Peters,' William said, looking up from his plate and frowning.

'Hardly. But he called after tending to Cook's burns to see how she did and we spoke a little.' That was true enough but she didn't want to remind Father of the trip to London, or to enlighten him about Daniel's presence at Lily's accident.

To forestall any further discussion of the young doctor, she stood up and began to clear the table.

'Let Millie do that,' William said. 'Sit down. I want to talk to you.'

Stifling a sigh, Anna sat down again. 'Yes, Father. What about?'

'Since I've been ill, I've hardly realized how much time has flown by. Christmas will be upon us soon and I thought it might be nice to invite Edward for dinner. He lives alone and—'

'Edward? Oh, you mean Johnson.' Anna still refused to call the man by his Christian name.

Since being practically thrown out of the house the last time he'd called, he had telephoned several times. But Millie had obeyed orders and said that Anna was not at home and the master sleeping. Anna had not told her father but she knew he would soon be asking why the factory manager hadn't called lately.

But asking him to Christmas dinner was going a bit far, she thought.

'I don't think that would be appropriate, Father,' she said.

'Why ever not? You know the man admires you, has asked permission to court you. What better way for you to get to know each better than for him to spend Christmas with us?'

Because I don't want to get to know him. I know enough about him already. Anna could not voice the thought aloud. Instead she reminded William that ever since her mother's death seven years ago, they had passed the Christmas holiday very quietly, going to church in the morning and exchanging small gifts with each other and the servants in the afternoon.

'I understand, Anna, my dear. It was a very painful time for us. But isn't it time we moved on? I thought having a guest here for dinner might help.'

'Perhaps you're right, Father,' she said, thinking quickly. 'Why don't we make a party of it – invite a few others. Dr Brown lives alone too, doesn't he?'

William didn't look pleased but he nodded and said, 'Of course, my dear. Invite who you like. But not too many people, please.' He put a hand on his chest. 'My health, you know....'

'Don't worry. Just a few acquaintances. I'm sure Cook will be pleased. She loves having an opportunity to try out her special recipes.' Anna jumped up from her chair and kissed her father's cheek. 'I'll go and talk to her right away.'

She rushed out of the room before William could remark on her change of heart. It wasn't just the thought of not having to entertain Johnson alone on Christmas Day. Now that Daniel was staying at Dr Brown's, she could invite him too.

The next couple of weeks were busy ones for Anna. Now that her father did not need her so much, she had time to help decorate the church, as well as organizing a party for the patients in the cottage hospital which would take place on Boxing Day.

St Martin's House was enveloped in the spicy smells of baking cakes and pastries as Cook prepared an array of delicacies both for the hospital party and Anna's expected guests.

Those patients who were well enough were sent home before the holiday, but there were always a few too weak or unable to care for themselves who had to stay in hospital. Matron and the staff did their best to make their stay a happy one and the ladies of the Church Guild contributed by supplying extra delicacies and small gifts.

Anna had always enjoyed being involved, finding it a pleasant antidote to the more sombre atmosphere of Christmas in her own home. This year, however, she was really looking forward to a much more pleasurable day. Daniel had accepted her invitation and that was enough to chase all other worries from her head.

She was determined not to let Edward Johnson throw a shadow over it, having decided to ignore his threat to expose her suffragist involvement to her father. She was confident that she knew enough of his activities to make him keep quiet.

On Christmas morning, Anna was up before it was light but Cook had beaten her to it.

She and Millie were in the kitchen, their sleeves rolled up as they bustled around preparing the mountain of food.

'Have I done enough potatoes, Miss Anna?' Millie asked as she appeared in the doorway.

'Enough for an army, I'd say,' she said with a laugh.

'Well, these men have hearty appetites, you know,' Cook said, opening the over door and letting out a cloud of steam, redolent with the aroma of goose fat.

'Can I help?' Anna asked.

'No, thank you. You've enough to do getting the master downstairs. Breakfast is laid so just ring the bell when you're ready.'

Anna withdrew and went slowly back upstairs, opening her father's door quietly. He was just stirring but he refused her offers to help him dress. As usual, he became irritable with what he called her fussing.

'Well, don't try to come down on your own. Call me when you're ready,' she said.

In her own room she tidied her hair, which was already falling loose from its pins due to the steaminess of the kitchen. She smoothed her skirt and straightened her collar, wanting to look her best for their guests – one guest in particular, she acknowledged with a smile. She could not remember feeling so excited about Christmas since the year before her mother had died and no one, especially not Edward Johnson, was going to spoil it.

But first there was church. Father was determined to go with her and they would have to leave early in order to get there on time. Dr Brown had promised to call for them in his carriage but William moved so slowly these days, and getting him up the step and into the carriage would take time.

Anna couldn't help hoping that Daniel would be joining them but it was so long since they'd last met that she was a little apprehensive too. Had she imagined the warmth that had grown between them on that autumn day in London? And if she hadn't, why had he not made some attempt to see her?

'Anna, where are you?'

Her father's voice roused her from her chaotic thoughts and she hurried into his room.

'I'm here, Father. Are you ready to come downstairs?'

'I've been ready these past ten minutes. Didn't you hear me call?'

'Sorry, Father.'

'Well, if you're too busy, I'm quite capable of going downstairs alone. But I was obeying orders.' The ghost of a smile touched his lips and Anna smiled back. He must really be feeling better if he was in a teasing mood. It seemed that Christmas Day was going to turn out well, despite her misgivings concerning Johnson.

When Dr Brown's carriage pulled up outside, Anna's heart began to flutter. She had included Daniel in the invitation and she hoped he would join them for church too. She tried to remain calm as she helped her father on with his coat, wrapping a muffler round his neck.

Millie answered the door and Anna heard the old doctor's gruff tones.

'Merry Christmas, Millie.' He came into the hall, stamping his feet and rubbing his hands. 'Nippy out there. Good morning, William. I see you're wrapped up well.'

Swallowing her disappointment that there was no sign of Daniel, Anna wished the doctor good morning and, with a last instruction to Millie, she followed the two men down the front path.

'Young Peters not with you then?' William asked when they were settled in the carriage for the short drive to the church.

'He had to go and see a patient at the hospital. He's still working there at the moment, you know. He's joining me in the new year.'

'More time for fishing then – when you have an assistant,' William laughed.

Dr Brown joined in. 'Yes. Anyway he sends his apologies and hopes to be able to join us for dinner later on.'

During the service, Anna was pleased to see that her father was joining in the carol singing with some of his former gusto. But she couldn't concentrate, her glance constantly straying to the back of the church in case Daniel had managed to get there. She had hoped to be able to speak to him before Johnson turned up at the house. Perhaps she could hint at what she had discovered about the factory manager and seek his advice.

When they got back to St Martin's House, Daniel had still not arrived but to Anna's dismay, as Millie was taking their coats, she announced that Mr Johnson had arrived.

'I've put him in the drawing room, miss, and given him a sherry.'

'Thank you, Millie. I think we could all do with a drink to warm us up.'

William greeted Johnson cordially and introduced him to the doctor, before pouring sherry for everyone. Johnson stood up hastily and took Anna's hand.

'It's good to see you again, Miss Anna. And you, sir, looking so well.'

'I'm getting stronger every day, thanks to the good doctor here,' William said.

'I had very little to do with it,' Dr Brown said. 'Grayson is a very stubborn man – he was determined to get well.'

'Perhaps you'll be back at the factory again before too long, sir,' Johnson said.

'Not too soon, though,' Dr Brown said. 'We don't want another relapse, do we?'

'Of course not,' Johnson said. 'Anyway, sir, you know you can rely on me to keep things running for you.'

Anna stood up. 'I must see how the dinner's progressing,' she said, rushing out of the room. She could not bear to listen to the manager's oily tones a minute longer. Why could her father not see through him?

She breathed deeply, controlling her annoyance and went into the kitchen.

Before she could speak, Cook said, 'It's all ready, miss. Millie will serve in ten minutes if you'd like to get your guests seated.'

'Dr Peters hasn't arrived yet, but I think we should start anyway. Dr Brown said he's been delayed with a patient. He'll join us when he can get away.'

'Very well, miss.'

They had finished their soup and Anna rang for Millie to bring in the goose. Almost staggering under the weight of the dish, the little woman placed it in front of William and went to fetch the vegetables.

Anna glanced anxiously at her father, hoping that his heightened colour was due to the sherry and the company, rather than the exertions of the morning. But he seemed to be enjoying himself as he picked up the carving knife and fork.

Just as he was about to start carving, Johnson leaned forwards and said, 'Would you like me to do that, sir?'

Anna almost leapt from her seat. The cheek of him. Did he think he was already one of the family? Before she could speak, William said, 'I can manage, thank you, Johnson,' and, turning to Anna, he asked, 'Would you like leg or breast, my dear?'

'Breast, please, Father.'

Anna bit her lip, trying to hide her smile at the look of discomfiture on Johnson's face. Oh, yes, you know you've overstepped the mark, she thought. That was good, though. If he continued to behave like that, perhaps her father would begin to see his true nature.

Anna wasn't enjoying her food, her ears tuned for the sound of the doorbell. The conversation buzzed around her, but she did not join in, although she was pleased to note that Johnson seemed a little uncomfortable, especially when the two older men began discussing their work on the hospital committee and other charitable organizations.

'It's good of you to keep me up to date with these things, Brown. I wish I could do more but—' William waved his fork.

'You'll soon be back with us,' Dr Brown assured him. 'You have made amazing progress over the past few weeks.'

'Mainly thanks to my daughter's nursing,' William said, laying a hand over Anna's. 'What would I have done without you, my dear?'

Johnson, who had been silent throughout most of the meal, leaned forwards and said, 'You are fortunate, sir, to have such a devoted daughter.'

'I appreciate it, Johnson. But sadly, I know I shall lose her one day.'

Anna almost choked on her pudding. Please don't start that again, Father, she pleaded silently. At that moment the doorbell rang and Anna stood up.

'That will be Dr Peters,' she said, stammering a little. 'I'll let him in as Millie is so busy in the kitchen.'

Daniel was profuse in his apologies, explaining that the case he'd been dealing with had proved more serious than he'd first thought. 'I had to stay and make sure he was being looked after.'

'I understand, but you're here now. Have you eaten? We saved some goose for you.' Anna strove to keep her voice even, despite the fluttering in her chest.

'That's very kind but they fed me at the hospital. Besides, I don't want to put you to any trouble.'

'Well, at least have some of Cook's excellent plum pudding. We are just having ours.'

Anna led him into the dining room where a place was still laid for him. He greeted the menfolk, wishing them a happy Christmas and sat down. Dr Brown straightaway asked him about his patient and a discussion of the man's symptoms ensued. Johnson looked bored and William interrupted, saying how pleased he was to be well enough to entertain.

Anna, fighting to keep her emotions under control, could scarcely manage to finish her dessert, but she was glad of the buzz of conversation which served to cover her agitation. Pleased as she was that Daniel had finally arrived, she found herself tongue-tied and unable to join in the conversation.

When the meal was over, she rang for Millie and said they would take coffee in the drawing room. As they made their way across the hall, Daniel took Anna's arm and said quietly, 'Is there any chance we can be alone? I need to talk to you.'

Although Anna's heart leapt, she told herself firmly that he was unlikely to want to talk about the subject she most desired. It must be something to do with Lily, she thought.

'It's unlikely while we have other guests,' she said. 'Is it important?'

'Very.' Raising his voice, his said, 'I do hope you will be at the hospital for the party tomorrow. The doctors and nurses have laid on some special entertainment for the patients.'

'Yes, I'll be there,' Anna replied.

When they were all seated, she announced that she had gifts to distribute. 'But we'll wait for Millie to bring the coffee,' she said.

There was much laughter as she pulled the packages from under the Christmas tree and handed them round and Anna felt happier than she had for a long time, although she glanced anxiously at her father from time to time. However, William seemed to be more like his old self, and he got up from his chair unaided to kiss her cheek after unwrapping his present of a pair of onyx cuff links – the ones she had bought in London.

Then it was Johnson's turn to unwrap his gift. Much as she'd hated the idea, she had felt duty-bound to provide something for him and had given him a box of handkerchiefs. She cringed at his effusive thanks, which were out of all proportion to the present itself, and hastily handed Dr Brown's package to him.

She had left Daniel to the last and she watched anxiously as he opened the parcel, breathing a sigh of relief as his eyes lit up.

'You made this?' he asked, holding up the hand-knitted scarf.

When she nodded, he smiled warmly. 'Just what I need when I get called out on these cold nights,' he said.

The conversation turned to general topics as they sat and drank their coffee, nibbling on nuts and sweetmeats, despite the huge meal they had just consumed. The heat of the fire had made William sleepy and his eyes were closing but he started awake as Daniel spoke about Lady Beatrice and her work for the suffragist cause.

Anna shook her head in warning but Daniel didn't seem to notice and she held her breath as Dr Brown replied, 'I deplore their methods but I daresay votes for women will come in time. After all, look at all the social changes there have been in the past few years.'

She was almost moved to protest that Lady Beatrice's methods were not those of the militant suffragettes but she was anxious not to upset her father. Any controversy seemed to raise his blood pressure and left him gasping for breath and clutching his chest.

Daniel, however, had no such qualms. Since the London rally, he had become convinced that Lady Beatrice and her supporters had the right idea and he was not afraid to contradict the older doctor.

Anna noticed that Johnson had not joined in the discussion but was leaning back in his chair with a faint smirk on his face.

William was wide awake now and he said, 'Well, I'm sure I wouldn't want my daughter to get mixed up with them. Politics is no subject for a woman.'

Johnson leaned forwards. 'Quite right, sir.'

Anna opened her mouth to protest but Dr Brown put a hand on her arm and shook his head.

'Perhaps we should talk of pleasanter things,' he said.

'I think Mr Grayson has a point, though,' Johnson said, with a sly glance at Anna. 'Imagine if the girls in the factory started wanting the vote and agitating for change.'

'Perhaps change is needed,' said Daniel.

'Now then, Daniel, let's not get too heated. It's Christmas Day after all.' Dr Brown turned to Anna. 'My dear, shall we have some music?'

But as she nodded and stood to go over to the piano, she heard Daniel ask, 'Are you all right, sir?'

She rushed to her father's side. 'I'm so sorry, Father. We shouldn't have upset you.'

'I'm just tired, that's all.'

'Perhaps you should rest. It has been a long day for you,' said Dr Brown.

He and Daniel helped William from his chair and up the stairs, leaving Anna to tend to him.

161

By the time she came down, the men were getting ready to leave, apologizing for their hasty departure.

'Best to let your father rest, my dear. Too much excitement for him,' Dr Brown said.

As Millie helped them with their coats and hats, Daniel took Anna's hand. 'I'm sorry we haven't had a chance to talk,' he said quietly. 'Perhaps tomorrow?'

Before she could reply, Johnson's voice interrupted. 'Thank you for the dinner, Miss Anna. I do hope your father will be all right. But do tell him I will continue to see that everything goes well at the factory.'

Why did he have to take every opportunity to reinforce his so-called reliability? Did he really think he was indispensable?

She smiled and thanked him as politeness dictated but underneath her blood was boiling. Daniel and Dr Brown made their farewells and left, Johnson lingering behind just long enough so that Anna had no chance to speak to Daniel further.

She took a deep breath, the tightness of her smile relaxing as she closed the front door. She almost danced into the dining room, ignoring Millie's protests as she helped to stack the used dishes. She would see Daniel again tomorrow.

CHAPTER TWENTY

As the time for the party drew near, Anna could hardly contain her excitement at the prospect of seeing Daniel again. Why did he need to speak to her alone? Despite trying to convince herself that he had news about the investigation into Lily's death, she couldn't help hoping that he had something more personal on his mind.

'Stand still, Miss Anna,' Millie said. 'I'll never get your hair done at this rate.'

'Oh, Millie – a party. It seems so long since I had any fun.'

'I don't see what's so special about it. You always help out on these occasions.'

'Yes, but I've been shut up indoors with Father all these weeks. It'll be good to get back to my usual activities.' Anna hoped Millie would think this was the real reason for her flushed cheeks and sparkling eyes.

Yesterday she had been a little annoyed with Daniel for speaking out about his beliefs. But she admired him all the same. He obviously hadn't realized how her father felt about women's suffrage. Her real anger had been reserved for Johnson and his sly remarks. It had completely spoilt what had been up until then a pleasant social occasion.

Millie fastened the last pin in Anna's hair and stood back. 'There, Miss Anna, it looks a treat. And that blue dress really suits you.'

Anna looked at herself in the mirror and had to agree. She determined to put all thoughts of the disastrous end to yesterday's dinner from her mind.

After a good night's sleep, William seemed much better. Heated discussions always got him agitated, especially if anyone disagreed with him. She would have to be very careful in future but, oh, how tired she was of always being on her guard, anxious to keep the peace.

She patted the smooth bun and stood up. 'Dr Brown will be here soon. Better make sure Father's all right and say goodbye to him.'

'Don't you worry about the master. Me and Cook will take care of him. You just go and enjoy yourself.'

The drive in Dr Brown's carriage to the hospital on the outskirts of Midchester seemed to take forever, although it was only a short distance.

As they dismounted from the carriage, Matron and the chief surgeon greeted them on the steps.

'So pleased you could come, Miss Grayson,' Matron said. 'Mr Grayson not with you?'

'He's much better but he did not feel up to coming out today.'

The surgeon rubbed his hands. 'Don't blame him. It's bitter out here. Let's go inside.'

They followed him along an echoing corridor to the door of the children's ward, from which came the sound of music and laughter.

A Christmas tree had been erected in the corner behind the nurses' desk and coloured paper chains were looped across the ceiling. A piano had been wheeled in too and was wedged in a corner of the now crowded ward.

Some of the children had been sent home for the holiday, but those not well enough to leave were propped up in their beds. Several patients from the other wards had been wheeled in so that they could join in as well. Anna took in the scene, her heart sinking when she could not see Daniel among the doctors and nurses gathered round the beds. Perhaps he was tending to someone too sick to join the party, she thought.

But he *would* be here – he had promised.

Matron held up a hand for silence and announced that they would start by singing carols.

'*Away in a Manger*,' she said, gesturing to a nurse who sat at the piano.

The music started up and the nurses began to sing, the children joining in with wavering voices.

Anna went and sat on the edge of a bed, glancing at Matron as she did so. But it seemed the strict rules were relaxed on this special day. She took the hand of a small boy who was trying his best to sing, the words punctuated with coughs.

'What's your name?' she whispered.

'Freddie, miss. I've got whooping cough.'

164

'Well, don't try to sing too much, Freddie.' She squeezed his hand and he smiled up at her.

The medley of carols came to an end with a smattering of applause and Matron stepped forwards. 'And now, we have a very important guest,' she said. 'Please welcome Father Christmas.'

The children cheered as the door burst open, and a very fat man with a snowy beard and dressed in a red robe entered. He waved and smiled, depositing his heavy sack under the tree.

At first, Anna thought it was one of the hospital porters but when he shouted, 'Merry Christmas, children,' her heart leapt. It was Daniel. So that was why he had not been here when she arrived.

He began to distribute presents from his sack, pausing at each bedside for a cheerful or comforting word with the young patients. There was something for everyone, even the staff and helpers, and soon the room was filled with the sound of tearing paper and excited exclamations.

Daniel reached the bed where Anna sat and handed Freddie a parcel.

'Hello, Daniel,' she whispered as the boy began to unwrap his present.

'Miss Anna, I'm pleased you could come.' He delved into his sack and brought out a small parcel.

She took it from him but hesitated to unwrap it, wondering why he was being so formal. Everyone was too busy opening their gifts to notice them and she had hoped for some warmth, a smile at least.

'Thank you,' she said, swallowing the lump in her throat.

He picked up his sack, pausing before moving on to the next bed. But he did not speak and she wondered why he had changed towards her when only yesterday he had seemed so anxious to talk to her alone.

Disappointed, Anna was unable to enjoy the rest of the party, although she tried her best to amuse little Freddie who had taken a fancy to her, and refused to let her leave his side.

'Play with me,' he pleaded, holding up the little wooden engine that had been his gift from Santa Claus.

Somehow she managed to get through the rest of the afternoon, persuading Freddie to eat some of the jelly and ice cream. But all the while her thoughts were with Daniel, who was at the other end of the ward, helping with the older patients.

A burst of laughter reached her and she glanced up from the game she was playing with Freddie to see Daniel's head thrown back as he joined in. Well, at least he's having a good time, she thought. If he was so keen to talk to me, surely he would have come over and sat with me.

At last the party wound down and Matron decreed it was time everyone was back in their proper places. The hospital porters wheeled the grown-ups back to their respective wards and the nurses started their round of giving out medicine and settling the children for the night.

The volunteers began clearing away the remains of the food and torn wrapping paper. As Anna was carrying a tray through to the ward kitchen, she bumped into Daniel. A blush suffused her cheeks and she tried to pass without speaking. It was obvious he really did not want to speak to her, despite telling her the previous day that he had something important to say.

He followed her into the kitchen and grabbed her arm. 'Put that down, Anna.'

At his harsh tone, she turned on him. 'Can't you see I'm busy?' she said.

'I'm sure you're not too busy to hear what I have to say,' he said. 'It's about Lily. I called on the Mitchells the other day and Detective Constable Hawker was there – he's spoken to several witnesses and is now sure that it was no accident. The trouble is, he has been investigating unofficially and he might be in trouble when he speaks to his superiors.'

'But he must—'

'Of course – and he will. He told me he doesn't care what they say. He wants justice for the Mitchell family.'

'I'm pleased they have someone on her side.'

Daniel nodded. 'You know he and Gracie are courting now?'

'Sam's a good man. I'm sure he and Gracie will be very happy.'

'And you? Will you be happy?'

'What do you mean?' Anna was flustered by the change of subject.

'Dr Brown tells me you and Edward Johnson are to be married.'

Anna almost dropped the tray she was still holding. 'Married? Who told him that?'

'Your father. It's all settled, he said.'

'But Daniel – Dr Peters – I have not accepted ...'

But Daniel did not stop to listen to her protests, striding out of the room and banging the door behind him.

She banged the tray down on the draining board. How dare Dr Brown repeat what her father had told him – and to Daniel, of all people? And how dare her father talk about her to his friend, especially as she had told him in no uncertain terms that she would never marry the factory manager.

She ran hot water into the sink and began washing the dishes, crashing the crockery onto the draining board. She would have to have stern words with her father, even at the risk of upsetting him and bringing on another attack. As for Daniel, at least he could have had the courtesy of listening to her. But as she re-played the scene in her mind, she began to calm down. Surely his angry reaction must mean that he had some feelings for her? But how could she let him know that she returned those feelings without being too forward?

By the time a nurse put her head round the door to tell her that Dr Brown was ready to leave, Anna was comforting herself with the thought that Daniel would soon be living in Dr Brown's house just round the corner, where she was sure to encounter him more often. A chance to correct his misapprehension was sure to present itself before long.

It was only as she was on her way home that she realized Daniel had not told her of Sam's progress in his investigation.

Daniel went back into the children's ward, wishing he had not slammed the door on Anna's words. He had not intended to bring up the subject of her impending engagement to the factory manager but he had wanted to hear it from her own lips. When she opened her mouth to speak, however, he found he could not bear to continue the conversation.

He made a round of the ward, settling the children in bed and admiring the presents that Santa Claus had brought them. With a warm smile and cheerful words, he managed to disguise his real feelings. But inside his thoughts churned. Should he go back and apologize for his hasty exit? But what could he say? No. He would just have to face up to the fact that Anna was lost to him.

Since their trip to London and the warmth that had developed between them, then he had dared to hope, especially when his financial circumstances had changed so dramatically.

Instead of continuing as a lowly registrar at the hospital or acting as locum to family doctors as and when necessary, he would eventually have his own practice.

God bless Dr Brown, who was nearing retirement and keen for Daniel to take over from him. It would be some time before his uncle's will was proved and his affairs were settled, but then he would be in a position to buy into the practice as well as buy a modest house for himself and – as he had fondly hoped – his future wife.

A small boy, his head swathed in bandages, tugged at Daniel's white coat, rousing him from his gloomy thoughts.

'Look what Father Christmas brought me,' the lad said, holding up a toy car.

'You must have been a good boy then,' Daniel said, ruffling his hair. 'Goodnight, sleep tight.'

'Good night, Doctor.'

A nurse stopped by the bed. 'You're very good with the children, doctor,' she said, smiling. 'Have you thought of specializing in paediatrics?'

'I prefer general practice. That's where my future lies,' he replied. But the thought crossed his mind that perhaps he would be better to go and train in a big London hospital, leave Midchester altogether. The thought of running into Anna once she was married was too much to bear. But then, how could he let Dr Brown down now that his plans were made?

The nurse was still smiling at him and he forced himself to smile back. She asked him if he would be attending the party and dance that the hospital held every year on New Year's Eve.

He had a feeling she was waiting for him to ask if she would be his partner and, although he was almost tempted, he let her down gently. 'I'm sorry, I won't be there,' he said. 'I'm on call.'

As the nurse walked away, he glanced up and saw Anna in the doorway but before he could speak, she turned away.

CHAPTER TWENTY-ONE

AFTER HIS ALMOST relapse at Christmas, William had made a good recovery, although it seemed that any disturbance was enough to set him back. Dr Brown had told Anna most emphatically that he should not be upset and she found herself thinking twice before she spoke, anxious not to introduce any topic of conversation that would start him off on one of his rants.

The doctor had also vetoed any return to work until he was fully recovered, which meant that Johnson was calling at the house more frequently.

Anna was sure that, now he was living close by, Daniel must be aware of these visits which would only reinforce his mistaken belief that she and the factory manager were engaged to be married, although no official announcement had been made.

There had been a violent outbreak of influenza in the early weeks of the year and both doctors had been extremely busy. Even Dr Brown, despite being semi-retired, had had to forego his games of chess with Anna's father. So, despite her hope that she could put things right with Daniel, there had been no opportunity to speak to him.

Meanwhile, Johnson was becoming more familiar as the days passed and she began to dread him turning up at the close of the day's business, ostensibly to consult with William. Anna contrived to be out when he was due, dreading his familiar remarks and leering looks.

As William did not need so much looking after these days, she had taken up her old activities, using the Church Ladies Guild as an excuse. She had also started attending suffrage meetings around the county with Lady Beatrice. Keeping busy served to take her mind off Daniel and their disastrous conversation at Christmas. How could she make him believe that she detested Johnson? Nothing would make her marry him – not even to please her father.

Although her enthusiasm for the cause had waned a little after Lily's accident and the attack on Beatrice in London, she had now renewed her support, writing letters and distributing leaflets. However, mindful of Johnson's threats to tell her father of her involvement, she tried to be discreet, not wishing to be the cause of a setback to his health.

Now, as spring approached, William seemed to be getting better every day, and was becoming increasingly impatient to be back at the factory. Anna tried to dissuade him, saying that he should be guided by Dr Brown and wait for the better weather before venturing outside. It had been a very cold, wet winter and only now, at the end of March were signs of spring appearing. The lilac outside the kitchen window had tiny buds and purple crocuses were massed at the base of the tree. But the daffodils, which usually brightened the garden at this time of year, were still struggling to make their appearance.

'Dr Brown says that the damp air is bad for you,' she said, as once more William declared his intention of visiting the factory. 'You are coming along so well, Father. You don't want another relapse now.'

She sighed with relief as he looked out of the window at the teeming rain and reluctantly agreed that he would stay home for today at least.

'But I must see for myself how things are,' he said. 'The last time Johnson came he hinted that the orders aren't coming in. Of course, I trust him implicitly, but I need to find out why.'

'Yes, Father,' Anna said, thinking it best not to upset him. He would find out soon enough that Johnson had not been telling the truth. She feared what effect the shock of discovering how the factory manager had deceived him would have on his precarious health. If only she had said something sooner. Or even taken the false ledger from the desk. It was a good thing she had left it there, though, as Johnson would have seen her with it when she encountered him at the factory gates.

The next day dawned bright and sunny, the first spring-like day of the year, although it was still very cold.

As Anna helped her father downstairs she knew what was coming. Hard as she tried to persuade him to stay home, he insisted on getting ready after breakfast.

'I'll take the car,' he said. 'I shall be perfectly all right – and I promise I won't stay too long, my dear.'

It would be the first time he had driven for months and Anna was worried.

'Let me come with you, Father,' she said, wrapping a scarf securely round his neck and tucking it into the collar of his coat.

'That's really not necessary, Anna.'

'I shall only worry while you're gone. Please Father.'

He shrugged. 'Oh, very well, then. But I don't want you interfering with things in the office. Leave everything to me.'

'Of course, Father.'

Anna gave in for the moment but she knew she would have to brave his annoyance before too long. She resolved to try and prepare him on the short journey to the factory.

She got into the passenger seat, glancing across at her father, relieved to see that, although he was breathing heavily, the exertion of opening the garage and getting the car started had not affected him too much. Perhaps she was worrying over nothing, she thought.

As they drove through the park, William took a deep breath. 'It's so good to be out in the fresh air – spring is on the way at last.'

Anna smiled and nodded distractedly. Then, after a brief hesitation, she made up her mind. 'Father, there's something I must tell you. It's about Johnson....'

'Has he made a formal proposal then? You know he has my blessing....'

'No, Father. I've already told you I don't want to marry him.' She hesitated but she knew she must speak up before they reached the factory. 'No, it's something else.'

But William wouldn't listen as she haltingly tried to warn him that he should not trust the man.

'Nonsense – you are just looking for an excuse to refuse him.' His face had reddened and his hands tightened on the wheel and Anna was afraid she had gone too far. How would she feel if he had another attack now? She didn't answer and sat staring ahead for the rest of the short drive.

As the car turned into the factory gates, William turned to her and said, 'I want no more of this nonsense, Anna. He is a good man and you must believe that I have made these plans for your own good.'

'Yes, Father,' she said. Her voice was meek, but inside she was incandescent with rage.

Johnson came to the works door as they got down from the car and shook William's hand effusively.

'It's so good to see you back, sir,' he said. 'You're looking very well.' He turned to Anna. 'And you, too, Miss Anna. Come into the office.'

As William entered and sat in his chair behind the desk, Anna thought a trace of annoyance showed on Johnson's face. It was obvious to her that he had come to think of the office and its furnishings as his own domain over the past weeks. Well, Father's back now and there will soon be some changes around here, she thought with satisfaction.

Johnson reached for one of the ledgers down from the shelf and laid it on the desk.

'I think you'll find all is in order, sir,' he said. A knock came at the office door and he looked up in annoyance. 'Come in,' he shouted.

One of the machine operators put her head round the door and said timidly, 'Mr Johnson – there's something wrong with my machine. I think it's jammed.'

The manager gave a grimace of annoyance and snapped, 'What have you done, girl?'

'Nothing, sir. It just jammed.'

'Well, can't one of the others unjam it then?'

Before she could speak, William looked up from the ledger and said, 'Better go and see to it, Johnson, while I go through these figures.'

Johnson sighed and strode onto the factory floor and Anna seized her chance. She came round the desk and tried to open the drawer where the ledger was hidden, but of course it was locked.

'What on earth are you doing, Anna?' William asked.

'I'll show you if you just give me your key. Quickly, before he comes back,' Anna whispered.

'I don't understand. What...?'

'Please – give me the key, Father.'

William fumbled in his pocket and she snatched the key-ring from him, hurriedly fitting the key into the lock. Pulling open the drawer, she thrust her hand under the pile of papers.

After a moment's rummaging she sighed. 'It's gone. He must have hidden it....'

'Hidden? Anna, please tell me....'

'Later, Father. He's coming back.' She re-locked the drawer and gave the keys to William.

When Johnson entered, he was followed by one of the factory girls bearing a tray. The girl put it on the desk and Anna smiled at her and said, 'Shall I pour?'

'Yes, yes,' Johnson said impatiently. 'You, girl – get back to your machine.'

Anna poured the coffee and handed cups to Johnson and her father. She sat on the opposite side of the desk, trying to look calm and silently willing her father not to question her in front of the manager.

'Is it fixed?' William asked.

'Just a minor problem, sir,' the manager replied.

'Does this sort of thing happen often?'

'Oh, no, sir. Everything is in order.'

The men became engrossed in business talk, discussing figures and the maintenance of the machines, so after a few sips of her coffee, Anna excused herself. She had plenty to say about the figures but this was not the right time, she decided. Without the secret ledger, she had no way of backing up her claim that Johnson was skimming off the factory's profits.

She put her cup down and walked out into the factory. The machines were going at full pelt and out here, the noise was deafening. She walked between the rows, watching the women working. Gracie was at the far end and she made her way towards her, smiling a greeting.

It had been weeks since they'd last met and she was anxious to know how the family were coping – not just with the grief of Lily's death but the loss of her wages.

'How are you, Gracie?' she asked.

The other girl shook her head and took one hand off the machine to point to her ears.

'Later,' she mouthed, gesturing towards the clock on the wall.

It was ten minutes to twelve. Anna nodded and pointed to the main door. She knew that on fine days, the factory employees went into the yard to eat their dinner-time sandwiches. She hoped her father would remain closeted with Johnson so that she would have time for a chat with her friend.

She wandered outside and looked around. It seemed busy enough, despite Johnson's pessimism. A cart was being loaded up while the horse stood, flicking his tail and blinking in the sunshine. She went over and stroked his nose, smiling at the two men who were manhandling the heavy wooden boxes onto the back of the cart.

They touched their caps and greeted her politely but did not pause in their work until the factory fell silent as the machines were switched off. A stream of young women flowed out of the building, laughing and chattering. They chose a sheltered corner of the yard out of the cold wind and sat down to unwrap their sandwiches.

Gracie came over to where Anna stood and said, 'What brings you down here? Haven't seen you for months. Thought you'd forgotten all about me.'

'Of course not.'

'Thought you'd been hobnobbing with your posh friends – no time for the likes of me.'

Why did she have to be so prickly, seeing slights where none were intended, Anna asked herself. She hastened to placate her friend.

'I've had no time for anybody. As you know, my father's been ill. I've hardly been out of the house lately.'

'I'm sorry. It's just – well, you helped when Lily died and I thought we were becoming friends. But you didn't call and....'

'I'm sorry too. I should have sent a note – at least asked how you were coping. But time flies so fast and I was so busy with Father.'

Grace put a hand on her arm. 'It's all right. I do understand. Come and sit down. I must eat my sandwiches – it'll be time to go back in soon.' She led Anna away from the other girls and they sat on a box.

'So, what's been going on? Seen any more of that handsome young doctor?' Gracie asked.

Anna felt a blush creeping over her cheeks. 'Not really. He came to dinner at Christmas.'

Gracie smiled knowingly.

'He wasn't the only guest,' Anna protested. 'Besides, he's not interested in me.'

'Do you really think so? That's not the impression I got when we saw him in Brighton. And he was very helpful afterwards.'

'But I hardly know him.'

'Didn't you tell me he joined you on the London rally then? I don't think it was entirely due to his interest in the cause.'

'Oh, but he is interested – in the cause, I mean,' Anna protested.

'And what about you?' Gracie asked. 'I've been to a few suffrage meetings – wondered why you weren't there. Thought you'd lost interest.'

'Not at all. I just haven't had the time,' Anna said, relieved that they seemed to have moved on from the subject of Daniel. 'Looking after Father is a full-time job.'

'I would have thought you'd hire a nurse,' Gracie said.

Anna gave a short laugh. 'He wouldn't hear of it. Didn't want a strange woman in the house.' She shrugged. 'Anyway, he's better now, and I'm hoping to start getting involved again now.'

'That's good. I'm going to the next meeting. Perhaps I'll see you there. Not that we seem to be getting anywhere at the moment.'

'I'll try.' The women's suffrage movement was the last thing on Anna's mind at the moment. All she could think of was the factory problems and she decided to confide in Gracie. Perhaps the girl had noticed something amiss. After all, she was here every day. She put her hand on her friend's arm.

'There's something I want to ask you,' she said.

At that moment a bell rang and Gracie stood up, screwing up the paper bag that her food had been wrapped in.

'Quickly then. I have to go,' she said.

'It's too complicated to go into at the moment. Can we meet after you finish work?'

'Sunday afternoon would be better. We'd have more time to talk. Why don't you come round for tea?'

'I'd like that, but will your parents mind?'

'Mum would like to see you, I'm sure.' She glanced around, noticing that the other workers had already disappeared. 'I must get back, otherwise I'll have old Johnson after me,' she said, hurrying inside the factory, but turning to give a little wave at the door.

Anna followed slowly. Already the machines had started up again and the women were bent to their work. She did not envy Gracie having to spend another five hours in that noisy, dusty environment.

When she re-entered the office, William was still examining the ledger. He looked up with a satisfied smile. 'Well, Anna, my dear, it looks as if Johnson has been keeping the wheels turning for us in my absence. The orders have fallen off a little, it's true, but that is normal in business – everyone has their ups and downs.'

'They seem very busy out there,' Anna said, gesturing towards the factory floor.

Johnson nodded.

'Things are beginning to pick up nicely,' he said.

'Are you ready to come home now, Father?' Anna asked. 'You don't want to overdo it on your first day back.'

'I'm perfectly all right,' William snapped.

But Johnson stepped in. 'I think Miss Anna is right, sir. We've gone over the books and I'm sure I've satisfied you that things are running smoothly. You can leave everything to me.'

William leaned back in his chair with a sigh. 'Perhaps you're right. Thank goodness I have someone I can rely on.' He stood up and Anna fetched his coat and scarf.

As they turned to leave, Johnson said, 'May I call on you and Miss Anna, sir, after work?'

'Of course. You are always welcome – isn't he, Anna?'

She smiled and nodded but the familiar anger crept up on her. How dare Johnson assume he could call at any time, just because they'd invited him to Christmas dinner? Besides, she had made it quite clear she was not interested in him. Did he still think she was open to persuasion?

She was seething all the way home and she sat upright and silent in the car beside her father, wondering how she could convince him that he was wrong to trust the factory manager. If only she could get hold of that ledger. Perhaps Gracie could help. It should be easy enough to enlist her support, given the girl's obvious dislike of Edward Johnson.

By the time they reached home, William looked very tired and Anna persuaded him to have a rest after lunch. She was dreading the coming evening when Edward Johnson had said he would call. What could she say to him, short of accusing him outright? But if she did that, a confrontation could well upset her father enough to bring on another attack.

She could not settle to anything and it was almost a relief when Millie came in and told her that she was wanted on the telephone.

'Who is it, Millie?'

'Mrs Collins, miss – about the Easter flowers.'

Normally, she would have asked the maid to take a message but she got up and went into the hall. Overcoming her dislike of the telephone, she greeted the vicar's wife.

'What can I do for you, Mrs Collins?'

'Miss Bertram is indisposed and unable to do the flowers. I know you

have been occupied with looking after Mr Grayson but I wondered ...'
Mrs Collins hesitated.

'Of course, I'll do them,' Anna said. 'Father is so much better. I
think I can leave him for an hour or two.'

'Thank you, my dear. Such a relief. You always make such a good job
of it and, as it's Easter, we want the church looking especially beautiful.'

Anna agreed and was about to ring off when she had a thought.

'Could I call round and discuss the arrangements with you, Mrs
Collins?' she asked.

'Of course.'

'Would this evening be convenient? As you know, I don't like to
leave Father on his own but he has a friend coming later on.'

She sighed with relief when Mrs Collins agreed. She would make
sure she had left the house before Johnson arrived. But how long could
she carry on avoiding him?

William declared himself well enough to attend church on Good Friday
morning and Anna made sure he was well wrapped-up against the chill
wind. Despite the bright sunshine, it was still very cold and his breathing
was laboured after the short walk from St Martin's Square.

Anna settled him in his pew, ignoring his usual admonitions not to
fuss. The service wasn't due to start for a few minutes and several of
their friends came up to greet them.

'It's good to see you out and about again, Mr Grayson,' said Mrs
Collins. 'Anna has made a beautiful job of the flowers, hasn't she?'

'Very nice,' said William.

'Well done, my dear,' the vicar's wife said, turning to Anna.

'Well, I did have some help,' Anna protested. Still, she was proud
of the display, although to reflect the meaning of the day, it was rather
sombre.

She had brought evergreens and ferns from the garden and wound
wreaths of holly round the base of each vase to represent the crown
of thorns. Tomorrow she would come and take it all away. Buckets
of spring flowers were already stored in the vestry and she would cut
sprays of blossom from the flowering cherry in the garden and bring
lilies from the greenhouse. Sunday's display would be a joyful celebration of the resurrection.

She bowed her head for the last prayer, adding a plea that she would be shown the right way to approach her father about the problems at the factory. Perhaps when she spoke to Gracie on Sunday, a solution would come to her, she thought.

Easter Sunday dawned bright and sunny and the wind had dropped. Accompanying Anna to church that morning William said, 'It's good to get out of the house again.'

During the service, Anna's thoughts started to wander, and she stole an occasional glance at her father. He seemed to be intent on the vicar's words and, when they stood up for the final hymn, he joined in the singing as he always had. Today he seemed truly well again, and she hoped and prayed it was so. But was he strong enough to cope with the knowledge that his trusted manager was an embezzler?

The walk home was slow, but it did not seem to have tired him as much as it had on Friday. He ate his roast lamb with obvious enjoyment and complimented Cook on the meal. When Anna suggested he have a rest afterwards, she expected him to protest. It was a relief when he admitted to feeling tired and went up to his room.

While he was lying down, she could walk round to Gracie's cottage and spend an hour with her friend.

Mrs Mitchell seemed pleased to see her and inquired after her father. 'We was so sorry to hear he was ill,' she said. 'But Gracie tells me he's on the mend.'

'Thank you, Mrs Mitchell, he's much better now.'

'And back at the factory, I hear.'

'It'll be a while before he can come back permanently. He only popped in the other day to see how things were,' Anna said.

'And glad we were to see him,' Gracie said, bustling around and getting out cups and saucers. 'I don't think I can put up with that Johnson much longer – throwing his weight around and acting like he owns the place.'

'Well, he is in charge while Mr Grayson's not there,' Mrs Mitchell said.

'S'pose so – but I don't have to like it,' Gracie said, thumping the teapot down on the table.

'I take it Mr Johnson is not popular among the factory workers,' Anna said.

'You can say that again. The girls can't stand him – creeping around, finding fault all the time. And docking their wages for the slightest thing.'

Anna remembered Gracie mentioning something about this when Lily had been injured after the suffrage meeting.

'I wonder if my father knows about that,' she said, taking a deep breath. Perhaps this would be a good moment to voice her suspicions.

Before she could speak, a knock came at the front door and Gracie flew to open it, her face wreathed in smiles.

'That'll be Sam,' she said.

Anna hardly recognized Detective Constable Hawker out of uniform, but then she had not seen him since Lily's funeral.

'You remember Miss Grayson, don't you, Sam?' Gracie said.

Sam Hawker doffed his cap and said, 'Of course. How are you, miss?'

'I'm well, thank you, Detective.'

'I didn't get the chance to tell you the other day,' Gracie said. 'Sam and me are walking out.'

'So I heard. Dr Peters told me. Congratulations. How long has this been going on?' Anna realized with a guilty start just how long she'd been out of touch with her friend.

'Come and sit down, Sam – we're just about to start tea,' Gracie said as her mother brought in a plate of sandwiches and a fruit cake.

'Go and call your father, Gracie,' said Mrs Mitchell. 'He's out in that garden all day, forgets the time,' she added, turning to Anna. 'Takes his mind off Lily, he says. Still, better than brooding indoors.'

Anna nodded but could not find the right words. Fortunately, Gracie and her father came in at that moment.

'Look Dad, Sam's here,' Gracie said brightly.

The older man nodded a greeting and went to wash his hands in the scullery before taking his place at the table.

'So – how did you two become friends?' Anna asked Gracie.

'We've kept in touch since that first day – you remember the meeting where we met?' She giggled at the memory of their escape from arrest, but the smile left her face as she continued, 'That was when poor Lily got hurt – and then....' She choked on a sob. 'Why did it happen? Why?'

Mr Mitchell put down his cup, slopping the tea into the saucer, and stood up abruptly. As he stumbled out of the room, Mrs Mitchell said,

'He still can't bear to talk about her,' and hurried after him.

Sam put his arm round her and stroked her hair. 'Don't cry, Gracie, love. I can't bear to see you cry.'

'Why? Why?' Gracie repeated.

Anna sat in embarrassed silence. In the first few weeks after Lily's death, she had often asked herself the same question but the police had seemed satisfied that it had been a tragic accident. And despite her suspicion that it was deliberate and that Beatrice had been the intended victim, she had no real evidence to support it. And when she'd mentioned it, her friend had brushed aside her concerns with a laugh.

'Who would want to kill me?' she had asked. 'No, the idea is ridiculous.'

Anna had appeared to accept it and, as the weeks passed and no further harm came to Beatrice, she had dismissed the matter from her mind. After all, with her father's illness and the problems at the factory, she had had enough to think about.

But then Daniel had told her that the detective too was convinced Lily had been run down deliberately. Her mind had been so full of Johnson's activities that she hadn't really given it as much thought as she might have. Now, at Sam Hawker's next words, she was forced to think again.

'I haven't given up, you know,' he said. 'Since I've been promoted to detective, I thought I'd get the chance to investigate further, but my inspector has told me to drop it. Still, I'm sure there was something fishy about it. We never found the car that was responsible and, given that make of motor car is rare in these parts, we should have tracked it down. Even if it was a genuine accident, the man deserves prosecuting for not stopping.'

Anna couldn't help thinking of Alfred Ponsonby-Smythe's sporty little vehicle, but his car had been with the mechanic, which was why he had travelled to Brighton with Lady Beatrice's party. Besides, he had no reason to kill Bea. It was ridiculous even to suspect him.

Gracie was still crying,

'What good would it do to prosecute the driver anyway?' she snapped. 'It won't bring Lily back, will it?'

'No – but at least someone would pay,' Mrs Mitchell said, coming back into the room.

'Is Dad all right?' Gracie asked.

'Best leave him out there for a bit. He's digging like mad, getting it out of his system.' Mrs Mitchell sat down and began pouring the tea and handing cups round. 'Anyway, we shouldn't be bothering Miss Grayson with all this. Let's try and enjoy our meal.'

'You're right, Ma. Sorry, Anna.' Gracie offered Anna a sandwich and said, 'You wanted to talk to me about something. Was it to do with the suffrage meeting?'

Anna glanced at Sam and Gracie hastened to reassure her that it was all right to talk in front of him.

'He's one of our supporters,' she said, 'although his boss wouldn't be too happy if he found out.'

She hesitated. 'It wasn't about that but ...'

'Well, go on,' Gracie urged.

Why not, Anna thought. Perhaps Sam could advise her on the best course of action.

'It's to do with the factory. I'm worried about Johnson. I think he's been cheating my father.'

Ignoring Gracie's shocked gasp, she told her friend of the suspicions which had culminated in finding the false ledger.

'But when I looked in the desk a few days later, it was gone,' she said. 'I think he suspected I'd been rummaging around and he's hidden it somewhere else.'

'We'd need proof, Miss,' Sam said. 'Besides, we can't go in and investigate without your father's say-so. You must try to convince him of what you saw and get him to report it.'

'It will be difficult. He trusts Johnson completely. Besides, in his state of health....' Her voice trailed off.

Gracie spoke up eagerly. 'Perhaps I could find out something. It should be easy enough for me to keep an eye on him.'

That was what Anna had been hoping for, but before she could agree, Sam said, 'No, Gracie, love. I don't want you putting yourself in danger. Who knows what he'd do if he caught you snooping. He'd get you sacked at the very least.'

'Sam's right, Gracie,' Anna said. 'Anyway, when Father gets back to work he'll soon realize something's wrong. Johnson is bound to trip himself up some time.'

Anna finished her tea and, apologizing to Mrs Mitchell, stood up.

'I really must go. I don't like to leave Father alone too long.'

As Gracie saw her to the door she said, 'I'm sorry I upset your father, bringing it all up again. Perhaps I shouldn't come again.'

'Don't say that. It was nice to see you. Perhaps when Mr Grayson is a bit better you'll start coming to the meetings again. I've even managed to get some of the girls from work interested.'

'That's good,' Anna said. 'I'll try to come to the next one.'

She turned to leave but Gracie put a hand on her arm and whispered, 'Don't take any notice of Sam. I'm not scared of old Johnson. I'll keep my eyes open – and don't worry, I'll be careful.'

'Thank you, Gracie, but do take care.'

As she walked away, Anna's mind was a jumble of thoughts. Although she was grateful for Gracie's offer of help, Sam's remarks about Lily's death had almost eclipsed her worries about her father's manager. Until now, when the events of that dreadful day had been brought back to her, she had been almost ready to dismiss her doubts about the so-called accident, putting it down to an over-active imagination. But if Sam was still investigating, he must have doubts too.

As she lay in bed that night, she went over it all again before finally managing to fall asleep, only to wake with a start with that image of those reaching hands etched on her brain. It's only a dream, she told herself, settling down to try and get to sleep again. But deep down, she knew it was not.

CHAPTER TWENTY-TWO

THE FOLLOWING WEEK, William declared his intention of going to the factory again.

'It's time I got back to work regularly,' he said, finishing his breakfast and pushing the plate away. 'I can't bear this idleness. Besides, although Johnson has been doing a grand job, the workers need to see the boss in action.'

'Are you sure, Father? Has Dr Brown agreed that you're fit enough?'

'Never mind what Brown says,' William snapped.

'But, Father ...'

'You worry too much, my dear.' He smiled and patted Anna's arm. 'I'll just go in for a couple of hours each day. But I need to inspect the goods – make sure they're up to standard. If there's been a drop in quality that could be why we're not getting as many orders.'

'Did Johnson say he was worried about anything?' Anna asked.

'No. He was very reassuring and I have complete confidence in him. But I must see for myself.'

'I understand, Father.'

Although Anna was still concerned about his health, she was pleased in a way that he felt up to taking charge once more. Surely he would soon realize what was going on at the factory. Perhaps she need not concern herself with it after all. Besides, she had other things on her mind since her visit to the Mitchells last Sunday.

As she busied herself with household tasks, she could not get the frequently recurring dream out of her head – the image of those hands shoving Lily into the road.

She shuddered at the memory, trying to tell herself it was only a dream, but something persisted in niggling at the back of her mind. Well, at least Sam Hawker was trying to do something about it. But so much time had passed it was unlikely he would find a witness now.

She was helping Millie to hang the washing out on the line when a thought struck her and she paused with the pegs in her hand, a pillow case hanging by a single peg.

Millie, struggling with a sheet, looked at her in concern.

'What's the matter, miss? Still worried about the master?'

Anna shook her head. 'No, it's all right, Millie. I just had a thought, that's all. Something I must do.'

She finished pegging the pillow case and turned to help Millie with the sheet, then leaving Millie to carry on hanging out the laundry, she went indoors.

Much as she hated using the telephone, she had decided to speak to Bea about her suspicions.

Fortunately, Beatrice was at home and seemed delighted to hear from her.

'Why don't you call this afternoon?' she said. 'I'll send the car for you.'

William returned home from the factory in time to join her for lunch and she was pleased to see that he didn't seem to have suffered any ill effects from his hours at work. In fact, he was very cheerful, praising Johnson for his management as well as the workers for keeping up production in his absence.

'The machines are all running smoothly and the goods are of excellent quality,' he said, tucking into his roast beef with great enthusiasm.

Anna didn't reply, biting her lip to prevent herself from voicing her doubts. She couldn't believe that her father could so easily be duped.

William paused with his fork halfway to his mouth.

'You're very quiet, Anna. You're not still concerned about my health, I hope? I must assure you I feel very well.'

'I'm pleased, Father. Perhaps you needed something to occupy you. You certainly look better today.'

'By the way, Johnson sends his regards. He was sorry to miss you when he called the other evening but I explained that you take your duties to the church very seriously. He admires you for that.'

Anna swallowed nervously and kept her eyes on her plate. She knew what was coming.

'Have you given any more thought to his proposal, my dear? He deserves an answer.'

'I've already told you, Father. I don't wish to marry him – or anyone else for that matter.' She pushed her chair back and rushed out of the room.

Upstairs, she sat at her dressing table and stared into the mirror at her flushed cheeks, the suspicion of tears trembling on her lashes. It was not true that she did not wish to marry. If Daniel had asked her she'd have said yes with no hesitation, despite the fact that she hardly knew him. Right from their very first meeting, she'd known that he was the one she had been waiting for. But she hadn't seen him for weeks and she had no idea how he really felt about her.

She brushed her hand across her eyes, mentally berating herself for her foolishness. There were more important things to think about than her romantic dreams, she told herself.

The little clock on the mantel chimed and she realized that Bea's chauffeur would be here soon. As she started to tidy herself in readiness, a knock came at the bedroom door and Millie came in.

'Sorry to disturb you, miss. The master would like a word with you.'

'I can't talk to him now, Millie. I'm due to call on Lady Beatrice and the car will be here any minute. Tell him we can discuss whatever it is at dinner tonight.'

Millie hesitated. 'Are you sure, miss? He seemed a bit put out.'

'We had a disagreement at lunch. I'm sure he'll have calmed down by the time I get back.'

'Very well, miss.'

She turned to leave but Anna could see that she was nervous about delivering the message and she called her back. 'Don't worry, Millie. It was nothing really. I just don't feel I can deal with it at the moment.'

The maid withdrew and she finished getting ready to go out, descending the stairs just as a knock came at the front door. Her father was still in the dining room and she called out a hurried goodbye. She would have to brave his displeasure when she got home, but for now she would put all thoughts of Johnson and the factory to the back of her mind.

As the Lanchester drew up at the front of the Manor, Beatrice came down the steps to greet her.

'It's a lovely day. Let's walk in the garden for a bit. It's too early for tea and besides, I want the chance to talk to you without Mother chiming in every two seconds.' She laughed and took Anna's arm. 'Now, I know your father's been ill and you've been playing the dutiful daughter but you could have telephoned before. I've missed you.'

'I'm sorry, Bea. You must forgive me for neglecting you – and the movement. I just haven't been in the right frame of mind lately.'

'I understand and I forgive you.'

Bea led her to bench in a small arbour facing the lake. An early rambling rose trailed over a nearby wall, filling the air with its delicious scent. Bees foraged among the blooms and brilliant blue dragonflies darted across the surface of the pond. Summer had arrived almost without her noticing it. Turning her face up to the sun, Anna felt herself relaxing for the first time in weeks until her friend's next words brought her back to reality and the reason for her visit.

'I enjoy seeing you at any time, Anna. But on the telephone you said you had something important you wished to speak about. Was it to do with the movement? I'm afraid things haven't been forging ahead as quickly as I'd hoped.'

'Yes. Gracie said the same thing when I saw her last week.'

'I fear our friends in the WSPU are harming our cause with their antics. You must have read in the newspapers about them breaking windows and causing all sorts of mayhem.'

'I'm afraid I haven't had much time for reading the papers lately,' Anna said. She took a deep breath. 'I wanted to talk about something more personal really. I'm not sure if I ought to....' She paused. How could she voice her suspicions and possibly spoil a friendship?

'Well, go on. You can't leave me in suspense.'

'It's about your cousin.'

'Alfred?' Bea laughed aloud. 'What's he been up to? Don't say he's been making improper advances? I know he has an eye for the ladies but ...'

'No, really. It's nothing like that,' Anna protested, blushing a little as she recalled Alfred's flirtatious remarks at their previous meetings. 'I just wondered – you told me once that he wanted to marry you and—'

'As I told you, I turned him down. He's only after my money, you know.' Bea looked keenly at her. 'Why do you ask? Is he pursuing you now? Please say that he isn't.' She took Anna's hand. 'My dear, he's a bad lot and if he is showing interest in you, it will be because he thinks you have money.'

'I thought he had means of his own,' Anna said.

'He had – past tense. He's gone though his inheritance in record time, gambling mostly. I've helped him out once or twice but the last time he came to me for a so-called loan, I refused him.'

Anna hastened to reassure her friend. 'I have no feelings for your cousin at all – in fact, I must confess I dislike him intensely.'

'So what did you want to tell me about him then?'

Still Anna hesitated. Could her suspicions be correct? When Beatrice had turned Alfred down, had he thought his only way to get his hands on her money was to have her killed? Of course, that would depend on whether he would inherit if she died, but how could she ask such an impertinent question of her friend?

'Oh, it was nothing really,' she said hastily as a maid came across the grass to say that tea was served and would they join Lady Winslow in the drawing room.

Bea raised her eyebrows. 'You can't say it's nothing when you telephoned especially. Come on, tell me.'

'Not now, in front of your mother,' she whispered. 'Perhaps later.'

Lady Winslow was seated in the same chair that she had occupied on Anna's previous visit, looking as if she had not moved since then. She raised a languid hand in greeting.

'I suppose you're going to discuss votes for women all through tea,' she said, fixing Anna with a steely glare. 'Don't encourage her, Miss Grayson. It is a lost cause anyway.'

Beatrice poured the tea and handed a cup to Anna.

'Take no notice of Mother,' she said. 'If she was young and fit, she would be up with us carrying a banner. She was quite a rebel in her day.'

Anna smiled tentatively. It was hard to believe of the old lady sitting there so upright and regal-looking. Lady Winslow nodded and the ghost of a smile appeared.

'It's true, Miss Grayson,' she said. Then, turning to her daughter, she leaned forwards and tapped her on the knee. 'But at least I had the good sense to put my youthful indiscretions behind me, to marry and settle down before it was too late.'

'Marriage,' Beatrice scoffed. 'Is that all there is to look forward to? And who would I marry anyway?'

'Your fault, my dear. Unlike me, you have left it too late – all the eligible young men are spoken for.'

'And those that are not, are only after my money,' Beatrice said.

Anna sipped her tea, embarrassed by this exchange, but she looked up when Lady Winslow said, 'And who will get your money if you die without a husband or children? There is only your cousin left now. It will all go to him – and I know you don't want him to have it.'

'Mother, please don't talk about dying. I am still young and healthy. There is plenty of time to think about the future. Now, let us change the subject. We should not be talking of this in front of our guest.' She turned to Anna. 'Please forgive us. It is an old argument.'

Anna smiled, although, given her suspicions about the accident, she thought Beatrice should not talk so lightly. But instead of saying so, she bowed to her friend's desire to change the subject and said, 'Perhaps we can speak of the progress of your campaign – if Lady Winslow doesn't mind.'

The old lady waved a hand. 'Please continue.'

'Thank you, Lady Winslow. As I expect you know, I have been nursing my father recently and I have been rather out of touch with developments.'

'The papers are biased,' Bea snapped. 'They only report the more sensational activities such as those of Mrs Pankhurst and her followers. As I said earlier, I think they do more damage to the cause than anything. I do appreciate their zeal, though.'

'I heard some have been arrested,' Anna said.

'Oh, yes – and they are treated abominably in jail.' Bea sighed. 'I can't help admiring their fortitude, but will it make the powers that be listen to us?'

'Do you really think our way is best then? Our efforts don't seem to have brought success either,' Anna said. 'I sometimes wonder if we'll ever get anywhere.'

'It will come eventually, I'm sure of it. After all, women in New Zealand and Finland have had the vote for some years now. Even some of the states of America are allowing votes for women. We must keep up the fight,' Bea said emphatically. 'But no chaining ourselves to railings. I still think our way is best – reasoned argument and an appeal to the good sense of some of our more liberal politicians.'

'You're right, of course, if we could only get them to listen,' Anna agreed.

'I have been getting up a petition—' She was interrupted by a contemptuous snort from Lady Winslow but, ignoring her mother, Bea continued, 'Yes, another one. This one we will deliver in person to the door of Number Ten. We have several hundred signatures already.'

'Well done,' said Anna.

'Perhaps you could persuade your friend Gracie Mitchell to sign. And you could ask her to get some of her fellow workers interested too.'

Anna hesitated. 'I thought Gracie might have lost interest in the cause since the death of her sister. But she seems as keen as ever. And she's already spoken to some of the factory girls. She still blames herself for encouraging Lily to come on the rally, though.'

'But it was an accident. It could have happened anywhere – nothing to do with the rally.'

Now was her chance to voice her doubts, Anna thought. 'I'm not so sure it was an accident and neither does Gracie's friend, Detective Constable Hawker.'

'What do you mean? I know you hinted at something before but surely it must have been an accident.'

'Bea, I hesitate to say this but – well, when I saw Lily lying in the road I thought it was you. It was the hat, you see. Lily had copied the design of yours.' A sob caught in her throat. 'She admired you so much. And she was so proud of that hat.'

Bea laid a hand on Anna's arm and said in a low voice, 'I'm sure you're wrong. Why would anyone want to harm me?' She nodded towards her mother who was nodding in her chair. 'Let's not upset Mother with this. We'll talk later.' She picked up the silver bell on the table and rang for the maid, then in a louder voice, said, 'I'm sorry you have to go so soon.' She gave Lady Winslow a gentle shake. 'Mother, Miss Grayson is leaving now.'

Lady Winslow sat up with a start. 'Oh, do forgive me, Miss Grayson. How rude of me. You must come again when I'm feeling more wide awake.'

'That's quite all right, Lady Winslow. Thank you for having me.'

The two young women walked through the hall and out on to the terrace. While they waited for George to bring the car round, Bea said, 'Quickly, tell me why you think someone was trying to harm me.'

Anna explained that she had seen someone push Lily into the road, just as the car sped round the corner.

'But surely it wasn't intentional – just someone wanting to speak to me – if indeed they did think it was me,' Bea protested.

'Or it could have been someone trying to disrupt the rally – but it was over by then.'

That seemed a more logical explanation than a deliberate attempt on Beatrice's life but Anna still wasn't convinced.

'We can't afford any negative publicity, though, so perhaps you're right,' Bea said. 'Well, there's nothing we can do about it now. Finding out who was responsible won't bring Lily back.'

'That's what Mrs Mitchell said. But suppose it happens again?'

'Why should it? Surely it was just a spur of the moment thing?'

'I'm not so sure,' Anna said. She didn't know how Bea would take it but she couldn't keep silent any longer. 'It occurred to me that it may have had nothing to do with the rally or the suffragists at all.' She paused and took a deep breath. 'Bea, I think whoever was responsible meant to harm you – personally.'

'What nonsense,' Bea cried. 'What makes you think that? And who on earth...?' She stopped abruptly, a hand to her mouth. 'Alfred – you mean Alfred, don't you?'

Anna nodded miserably, wishing she hadn't spoken.

To her astonishment, Bea burst out laughing. 'Oh, Anna, what an imagination you have. Alfred – a murderer!' She could hardly speak for laughing. 'Oh, I admit he's after my money and he was furious when I rejected him. But he's a spineless fool. He wouldn't have the nerve.'

'I'm sorry, Bea. Maybe I'm being foolish. But this whole thing has been playing on my mind. I've been having dreams about you being pushed into the road. And then there's the car ...'

'But Alfred didn't have his car that day. It was being repaired. That's why he came with us, remember?'

Anna still wasn't convinced but she thought it best to drop the subject – for now. 'Please forgive me, Bea. As you say, I probably imagined it. I won't mention it again.'

'I accept your apology, my dear – but only because I know you have my interests at heart.'

'Thank you.' Anna touched her friend's arm. 'You won't mention this to Alfred, will you?'

'Of course not, although I think it would amuse him.' Bea began to laugh again.

'Please, Bea,' Anna pleaded.

'Very well, I won't say a word,' Bea said with a smile.

Just then the Lanchester appeared round the corner and pulled up in front of the terrace steps, and Anna said goodbye to her friend. On the short journey home, she silently berated herself. She had handled it all wrong, she thought. She should have waited until Sam Hawker had some positive proof that Lily's death had been no accident. Perhaps then, Bea would have taken her seriously. Knowing that Alfred had been trying to borrow money from Bea and been refused, Anna was now more concerned than ever for her friend's safety. If he knew for certain that he would inherit her wealth if she died, what was to stop him trying to manufacture another 'accident'?

CHAPTER TWENTY-THREE

As SPRING TURNED to summer, William began to go to the factory every day although, on Dr Brown's advice, he only spent a couple of hours there.

'Best not to overdo it at first,' the doctor had said. 'Work up to it gradually and you'll soon be back to normal.' His hearty manner had barely disguised the worried glance he threw at Anna, who was hovering behind her father's chair.

As she saw him to the door he said in a low voice, 'I am relying on you to make sure he obeys orders. I know how stubborn he can be.'

'Are you sure he should be doing this?' Anna asked, an anxious frown creasing her forehead.

'It will do him more good than sitting at home worrying about what's happening in his absence. That sort of stress can't be good for him.'

Anna had to agree. She had seen how frustrated her father had become as he gradually got his strength back.

Two weeks later, he certainly seemed to be almost back to his old self, although she wished he wasn't so short-tempered. He had always been inclined to get tetchy if he disagreed with the vicar's sermon or something he'd read in the newspaper. But these days he seemed more irascible than ever. She tried to understand. His illness had often left him frustrated at not being able to do the things he usually did.

This morning he had rustled the pages of his paper and cleared his throat before speaking. Anna tensed, wondering what had upset him now. She hoped that Bea's rival, Mrs Pankhurst, had not been causing more disruption in her campaign for the right of women to vote.

'It's these Serbs. Always up in arms and causing trouble,' said William. 'These Balkan countries are a hotbed of discontent.'

'How does that affect us, Father? These countries are nothing to do with England, are they?' She didn't really want to discuss it but she was so relieved that he wasn't ranting about the suffrage campaign that she tried to show an interest. But as usual, he dismissed her remark.

'You wouldn't understand, my dear. These things have a way of spiralling out of control and who knows what will happen next.'

'Perhaps you could explain then, Father. I would like to understand.' She managed to hide her frustration at his attitude and keep her voice even.

He threw down the paper and stood up.

'I haven't got time to go into it now, Anna. I'm due at the factory.'

Tight-lipped, she rang the bell for Millie. 'Perhaps I'd better get on with my household duties then,' she said.

He did not react to her sarcastic tone but said, 'I'm sure you have plenty to keep you busy, my dear. You don't need to be worrying about things you can't control.'

She didn't reply but followed him into the hall and silently handed him his hat and cane.

When the front door had closed, she let out a breath and marched into the kitchen. Forcing a smile, she gave Cook her orders for the day and went into the morning room where she paced up and down in fury. As her annoyance with her father gradually subsided, she told herself she should be grateful he had recovered to the point where he could take an interest in affairs outside the home. The weeks when he had lain in bed or sat listlessly in his chair, gazing out of the window, had been quite frightening. Despite their frequent disagreements and her wish that he would be a bit more flexible in his ideas, she loved him dearly.

Her reverie was interrupted when Millie entered the room and asked if she could get her anything.

'No, thank you,' Anna said shortly.

'Are you going out today then, miss?'

'I hadn't planned to,' Anna said. 'I have some letters to write.' Truthfully, she did not know what to do with herself. After seeing Gracie the other day, she would like to have asked her if she'd had any luck in finding out what Johnson was up to. But she dared not visit the factory while her father was there and she was reluctant to call at the girl's home when she had finished work for the day.

She lapsed into thought, only realizing that Millie was still there when the maid said, 'Are you all right, miss? You don't seem your usual self, if you don't mind me saying so.'

'I'm quite well,' she said sharply.

As Millie went to leave the room, she relented and said, 'I'm sorry. I didn't mean to snap. Yes, I am well, but I do have something on my mind.' She had to confide in someone and the older woman had been with the family so long that Anna knew she could trust her. It would be a relief to unburden herself. She gestured to a chair and said, 'Please sit down.'

'What is it, miss? Have I done something wrong?'

'Of course not.' Anna hastened to reassure her. 'I would like your advice, that's all.'

'Mine? Really?'

'Yes, Millie. You have been a friend as well as a servant all these years and you have been very good at keeping my secrets. I knew I could rely on you when you kept quiet about the blood on my coat.' She gave a little laugh. 'I was terrified he'd find out I had been at that meeting.'

'I did not think it was any of my business, miss. You are a grown woman – not the little girl whose scrapes I used to deal with.'

'Still, Millie, I don't know what I would have done without you to cover up my little escapades.'

'You never did anything really wrong. The master has strong views about what is right and proper – he does not realize that young women today need more in their lives than looking after a house and doing good works. You have told me yourself about the girls you went to school with who are working in offices, becoming school teachers and suchlike.'

It was one of the longest speeches Anna had heard from her maid and she was grateful for her support.

'I wanted to be a teacher too,' she said.

'I know, and if your poor mother had lived, she would have persuaded the master to let you train as such.' She paused and took a deep breath. 'But, miss, getting involved with the suffragists! Are you sure you're doing the right thing?'

'I was never more sure of anything,' Anna declared. 'But that wasn't what I wanted to discuss.'

'What is it then? Are you worried about the master?'

'No – well, a little, perhaps.' She paused. Should she confide her suspicions about Edward Johnson? But she had to tell someone. With a sigh, she made a decision. 'You know Mr Johnson, Father's manager, don't you?'

Millie pursed her lips. 'What about him?'

'He wants to marry me.'

'Marry you? The cheek of the man. You're worth ten of him. So that's why he's always calling.'

Her face reddened and Anna smiled at her vehemence. Millie's reaction entirely matched her own thoughts.

'I gather you don't approve,' she said with a wry smile.

'It's not really my place to approve or disapprove, but I think you could do better,' Millie declared.

'Then you'll be relieved to know that I refused him. My father is very angry with me – he wants me to accept Mr Johnson's proposal, thinks it will secure my future if anything happens to him. He is going to change his will, leave the factory to Johnson.'

'He can't do that.' Millie clapped a hand over her mouth. 'I'm sorry, Miss Anna. I shouldn't have said that. I'm just thinking of you, that's all.'

'Don't apologize, Millie. It was my first reaction as well, but, you know how Father is, once he's made up his mind....' her voice trailed off.

'He can't force you, though, can he?'

'I suppose not.' Anna put her head in her hands. 'Oh, Millie, what am I going to do? I hate that man.'

She was about to tell Millie why when a smile crossed the maid's face. 'You must tell your father there is someone else.'

'I can't do that. He would want to know who ...' she paused, blushing. 'Besides, there isn't anybody.'

'What about the handsome young doctor?'

'Daniel? Dr Peters, you mean?' Anna shook her head. 'You're wrong, Millie.'

Her heart had started to beat a little faster at Millie's words. If only she was right. However, that did not solve the problem of what to do about Johnson..

After a short silence, Millie stood up. 'I'd better get on. Cook will be needing a hand in the kitchen.'

'Very well. Thank you for listening anyway. I'll sort it out somehow.'

When she'd gone, Anna realized that she had not mentioned the reason for her dislike of Edward Johnson. Millie couldn't do anything about it anyway, but she must seek advice from someone. Perhaps she could telephone Daniel, ask him to call. She could use the excuse that she was worried about Father. But as she picked up the telephone receiver, she hesitated. Perhaps it would be better to send him a note. She sat at her writing desk and got out pen and paper. Daniel might not be romantically interested in her, but she hoped she could count on him as a friend. Surely he'd be able to advise her. She would also send a note to Gracie, asking if Sam had any more news about Lily's accident. Despite being so worried about Father and the future of the factory, she had not forgotten the tragedy that had befallen the Mitchell family, or her fears for Lady Beatrice.

She wrote to Gracie first, giving herself time to think about how she would word her letter to Daniel. She sealed the envelope and pulled a fresh sheet of paper towards her. After a few moments of biting the end of her pen, she dipped it into the inkwell and began to write but when she read it through, she screwed the paper up and threw it into the waste paper basket. How could she ask him for help after what had happened between them at the hospital party? Besides, he probably still thought she was engaged to marry Edward Johnson. And if he believed her story that the factory manager was stealing from the firm, what he could do about it anyway? Like Sam, he would say she needed proof.

She pushed her chair back with an angry jerk. Why did her life have to be so complicated, she asked herself.

'I need some fresh air,' she muttered.

A good brisk walk would help clear her head and maybe she could sort out her muddled feelings. She picked up the note for Gracie, deciding to take it to the post office rather than hand-deliver it.

She went into the kitchen and said to Cook, 'Father will be home for lunch and I'll be back by then.'

'Very good, miss,' Cook replied.

Anna hurried outside, glancing up into the clear blue sky. It was good to be outdoors on such a day, she thought, as she crossed the Square and walked through the narrow streets into the High Street. The town was crowded and she realized it was market day, but she didn't loiter to look at the stalls as she usually did. After she had posted her letter, she decided it was too hot to fight her way through the crowds and she turned down a side street which led to the park.

As she crossed the road to the park gates a voice hailed her.

'Good morning, Miss Anna. How are you – and how is your father?'

Her heart started to beat faster as she turned her head to see Daniel hurrying towards her, carrying his doctor's bag.

She steadied herself with her hand on the park railing.

'Good morning, Dr Peters. I'm well, thank you. So is Father.'

'I'm pleased to hear it.'

Daniel smiled at her and she tried to control the fluttering in her breast. He was behaving as if their meeting all those months ago had not ended in him flying out of the room and banging the door. She had replayed that scene in her mind so often and had almost convinced herself that his angry reaction had been because he couldn't bear the thought of her marrying another man. But if that were so, why had he not tried to see her, to seek an explanation?

She pushed open the park gate and started to walk away, unwilling to expose herself to yet another disagreement. But she stopped when Daniel said, 'Anna, please, will you walk with me a little?'

She glanced around. The park was deserted except for a gardener tending one of the flower beds and he was far enough away not to be aware of them. She nodded and walked on, leaving him to follow.

Daniel hurried after her and took her arm. He led her to a nearby bench and put his bag on the ground, saying, 'I'll understand if you don't want to listen but please ...'

Anna sat on the bench and folded her hands in her lap. She looked out across the park without speaking.

Daniel coughed. 'I feel really bad for not contacting you before. I know I behaved badly at Christmas. I want to apologize for being so hasty.'

'You've had plenty of time to call,' Anna said.

'I know – and I won't insult you by telling you how busy I've been – although I have.'

'So why...?'

'I was embarrassed. I was upset at the thought of you marrying that – that – boor. He is not good enough for you. And besides ...' His voice trailed off and Anna turned to look at him, surprised to see how miserable he looked.

So he did care for her after all. 'I told you – I'm not getting married.'

'I know that now. Every week I've looked in the *Gazette* at the marriage announcements, convinced I would see your name linked with that man's.' His voice hardened at the mention of Johnson.

'You could have asked Dr Brown – he knows what goes on in my family.'

'Mr Grayson told him it was all arranged, that you were waiting till his health improved.'

'My father is the one who wants it. I have no intention of marrying ...'

'I see.'

Daniel had interrupted before Anna could add the name of the factory manager. Now he would be under the impression that she did not want to get married at all. How could she let him know that it would depend on who was proposing without embarrassing herself – or him? When he did not speak for a few minutes, she decided to change the subject.

'Have you heard any more from Detective Hawker?' she asked.

'I'm afraid not. The last time I spoke to him, he said he felt too much time had passed. It is almost a year since it happened. People forget or get confused about what they saw.'

'I saw him the other day at Gracie's. He said he hadn't given up but I think you're right – what more can he do?'

'What about you, Anna? Do you still think it was deliberate?'

Anna hesitated.

'Come on – tell me. You seemed quite convinced at the time.'

'I was,' Anna admitted. 'But then I told myself I had imagined it. There was such confusion and now, as you say, so much time has gone by, I can't be sure ...'

Daniel nodded. 'I hoped Hawker could get to the bottom of it – it would help Gracie and her family. But I think we must accept now, there's nothing more we can do.'

'I don't know. I'm still worried,' Anna said.

'Worried? What about?'

'Bea – Lady Beatrice.'

'You really think she was the intended victim then?'

'I'm sure of it.'

Daniel looked sceptical and Anna took the plunge, telling him about her cousin who would inherit Bea's wealth if she died without marrying.

'He has gambling debts and is desperate for money,' she concluded.

'But he was at the races – nowhere near the rally,' Daniel said.

'But the car – the one that hit Lily – it was maroon, the same colour as Alfred's. I didn't think anything of it at the time as he had told us his car was being repaired. That's why he came in Bea's Lanchester with us.'

'Well, then....'

'But it's such an uncommon colour and make of car.'

Daniel thought for a moment.

'You have a point,' he said. 'Was Ponsonby-Smythe's car at a garage in Brighton then?'

'Yes, and he didn't come back to Midchester with us. Perhaps it had been fixed and he drove it down to the seafront.'

'If you're right, he must have had an accomplice, someone willing to push a defenceless woman into the road just as he came along.' Daniel shook his head. 'No, it doesn't make sense. Who would do such a thing? And besides, how could he be sure Lady Beatrice – or Lily as it turned out – would be killed, not just injured?'

'You're right, of course. It was just an idea. And what difference does it make now?' Anna sighed. 'I just keep worrying that if Alfred did intend to harm Bea, he might try again.'

Daniel covered Anna's hand with his own.

'You have a kind heart, Anna. Always worrying about other people – Gracie and her family, your father, and now Lady Beatrice.' He smiled. 'And you throw yourself into your charitable work – the church, the hospital, not to mention the suffrage cause. But what about you – your own life?'

'I am quite content,' Anna said, although the pressure of his hand on hers was causing her heart to beat faster and she could feel the blush stealing over her face.

'I hope that's true,' Daniel said, removing his hand and preparing to stand. 'I'm pleased we met but I'm afraid I must go. I was on my way to visit a patient.'

'I'm pleased too,' Anna said.

'So – we're friends again?'

'Of course.'

'And you won't keep worrying about Lady Beatrice?'

'I'll try not to.' Anna attempted a smile.

'But there's still something on your mind, isn't there?'

Could she tell him what was going on at the factory? It wasn't as if he could do anything about it anyway. She shook her head.

'No. Everything's fine.'

'You know you can always talk to me. Just telephone or send a note. I'll call any time.'

'Thank you. I will.'

He raised his hat, picked up his bag and strode away.

Anna stood looking after him for a few minutes before walking on. She went over their conversation, looking for some clue as to his feelings for her. He had said they were friends, but dare she hope for more? She sighed. It would have to do for now. At any rate, she felt better for having told him her concerns about Bea. And he hadn't laughed or dismissed her worries as the product of a hysterical female's over-active imagination as some men would have.

Perhaps she *would* telephone and ask him to call, if she could word the invitation without seeming too forward.

CHAPTER TWENTY-FOUR

ANNA GLANCED OUT of the window as the Daimler pulled up outside and her father got out of the car. As usual, she looked for signs of stress, and today she was pleased to see that he looked better than he had for a long time. Perhaps getting back to work had been good for him after all.

She smiled as she hurried to open the front door.

'Have you had a good day, Father?' she asked, but he did not return her smile. 'Is something the matter?'

'Just a little tired, my dear. I'll be fine once I've had a drink.'

William pushed past her, shrugged off his coat and went into the drawing room, sinking into a chair and running his hand through his hair. Anna followed him, going to the sideboard, pouring him a glass of whisky.

'There is something wrong. What is it, Father?'

'Nothing to concern yourself with. One of the machines broke down and we lost a batch of needles. The metal jammed in the machine.'

'Was anyone hurt?' Anna knew that sometimes when a jam occurred, pieces of metal could fly off, causing injury to the machine-minders.

'Not this time, fortunately.' William took a sip from his glass. 'I'm afraid I had words with Johnson. It's his job to see that the machines are maintained properly.'

Good, Anna thought. Perhaps now Father would see that Johnson wasn't the paragon he was thought to be. But at his next words, the familiar anger rose and she bit her lip to stop herself saying what she really thought.

'He pointed out to me that as he had been doing more of the administration work, he had delegated the maintenance to one of the men. I had to eat my words.'

So he had managed to wriggle out of it. When would Father realize the man's deviousness? Anna pretended to agree, knowing that if she argued, William would only get upset.

'So, is it all fixed now then?' she asked.

'I think so. Although we could ill afford to lose that batch. It was a special order. I've had the girls working extra hours to make up for it.'

Anna was about to speak when her father said, 'I know what you're going to say.' He raised his hand. 'And, yes, of course they will be paid for the extra time.' He gave a dry laugh. 'I had words with Johnson about that as well.'

At that moment, Millie announced that dinner was served and they went into the dining room. The meal progressed mainly in silence as usual, but Anna was pleased that her father had told her a little about the problems at the factory. It was so unusual for him to confide in her. She dared to hope that perhaps he was beginning to change his attitude.

When Millie came in to clear away the dishes, William announced that Dr Brown would be calling round for his usual game of chess.

'I hope you won't be bored with the company of two old men,' he said.

'Not at all. I have a meeting at the church hall,' she said, hoping he wouldn't ask what it was in aid of.

Bea had telephoned earlier that day to ask if she would be attending the suffrage meeting that evening. She had not intended to go but now she felt the need to get out of the house. Her heart wasn't really in it tonight, though. She was more concerned with the incident at the factory earlier that day.

On entering the hall, she was pleased to see that Gracie was there and she went to sit with her, hoping there would be an opportunity to ask her about it.

'I'm glad you could come,' Gracie whispered over the burst of applause that greeted Lady Beatrice as she mounted the platform and began to speak.

Anna tried to forget her worries about the factory, and gave all her attention to her friend's impassioned plea to support their sisters in the rival suffragette movement.

'They are being treated abominably in jail,' Bea said. 'We may not agree with their methods but we must applaud their bravery in sticking to their principles.'

Several of the women present began to applaud but Bea held up a hand for silence. 'We must all do what we can. I don't ask you to get involved in violent and unlawful acts, but we can help by writing letters – to the newspapers, your member of Parliament, anyone you know who has influence. And there's the Bank Holiday Rally....'

Bea began to outline her plans for supporting those who had been arrested, saying she was having pamphlets printed to let people know what was really happening to their jailed sisters.

'The newspapers are biased against us. We are not always told the truth,' she said.

Anna knew how true that was, having listened to her father's diatribes as he read his morning paper. His attitude was that they deserved everything they got. Anna didn't dare to disagree, although she would have loved to tell him that Bea had visited a friend in prison and been shocked at what she'd seen.

Despite her best intentions, her thoughts began to drift to the problem that had assumed far more importance in her mind than the cause. There must be some way to expose Edward Johnson for the criminal he was. She had hoped that now Father was visiting the factory daily, he would realize that all was not well. But since his illness, he had come to depend on his manager and would not hear a word against him.

Another burst of applause roused her and she joined in with the clapping enthusiastically, although she had scarcely taken in a word that had been said. Lady Beatrice thanked everyone for coming and lively chatter broke out, accompanying the scraping of chairs as the meeting drew to a close.

Bea made her way towards Anna through the crowd, her face aglow.

'That went well,' she said. 'It's been a bit slow lately but I think I've fired them up. We can't let things stand still – we must keep fighting.'

'Don't you ever get discouraged?' Anna asked.

'Of course I do. This campaign has been going on for years, but we mustn't lose our enthusiasm.'

'You're doing a really good job, Your ladyship,' Gracie said.

'Well, I hope I can count on your support for the Bank Holiday Rally. We'll be touring the surrounding villages, stopping in each one to speak and hand out pamphlets.'

'I don't think I can be there that day, Your Ladyship. I'm sorry but it's the works outing and I've promised to help with the refreshments.'

'You then, Anna? You must come.'

'I'm sorry, Bea. My father expects me to attend the outing too – it's a firm's tradition.'

Bea looked disappointed but she said, 'Perhaps next time then.'

'Of course.' Anna linked her arm in Gracie's and the two of them left the hall.

Dusk was falling as they walked slowly through the deserted town and Anna was enjoying the freedom of being out in the warm summer evening, enjoying the company of her friend too.

Gracie had already told her more about the accident with the machine earlier that day and had been loud in her condemnation of Johnson's laxness. 'Poor Bert could have been badly hurt,' she said.

'Was it really Johnson's fault?' Anna asked.

'Well, he's in charge of the maintenance.'

'I had hoped that once Father was back at work, he'd realize that all is not well at the factory.' Anna stopped walking and faced Gracie. 'Have you managed to find out anything?'

'I'm keeping my eye on him. But he stays behind when everyone's gone – that's when he does his so-called book-keeping.'

'I wish I could catch him in the act.'

Gracie was silent and Anna had to be content with that, and for the rest of the short walk to St Martin's Square, they talked about the factory outing which was to be on the August Bank Holiday Monday in two weeks' time. It was a tradition that had been started by Anna's grandfather, and one she looked forward to as eagerly as the factory workers and their wives and children. The factory girls were also allowed to invite their sweethearts – so long as they were officially engaged to be married.

Anna's mother had always provided the picnic food and she had continued to do so. A few days beforehand, she would join Cook and Millie in the kitchen and the whole house would be redolent with the smell of baking – pork pies with rich golden crust, sausage rolls and vol au vents, as well as scones and cakes.

'Sam's managed to get the day off,' Gracie said. 'We're all looking forward to it.'

'I just hope we don't have to cancel it,' Anna said.

'What do you mean?'

'My father says there's going to be a war.'

'I did hear one of the men talking about trouble in one of those countries but that's nothing to do with us, is it?'

'I just hope you're right,' Anna said.

Gracie linked her arm in Anna's.

'Don't worry about it. It won't affect us, will it?'

Anna wasn't so sure. Her father seemed convinced that since the assassination of the Archduke a few weeks earlier, Britain was sure to be drawn into any conflict that arose. She didn't understand it herself, so how could she explain it to her friend?

She touched Gracie's arm and smiled.

'Whatever happens, we'll have our outing. You all deserve a treat after the year you've had – what with my father's illness and having to put up with being pushed around by Johnson. It's down to you all that the factory has kept going.'

Despite William's gloomy predictions as he read aloud from the paper that Monday morning, Anna was determined to enjoy the day out. He had not felt well enough to attend this year, although he had been disappointed at not being able to give out the prizes for the races as he usually did.

'You can stand in for me, my dear, and with Johnson there to see that things run smoothly, I'm sure I won't be missed,' he said.

Anna swallowed the retort that rose to her lips and smiled.

'I'll tell you all about it when I get home, Father. You just enjoy a quiet, peaceful day,' she said.

He had given permission for Joe, their gardener, to drive Anna up to the Downs in the Daimler and she went outside to supervise the loading of the food. She glanced up at the cloudless sky, pleased that the day would not be spoiled by rain. And she would not let her father's anxiety about the political situation spoil it either.

The Daimler stopped at the top of the hill, pulling in behind the charabanc that William had hired to bring the factory workers and their families. The open downland overlooking the nearby racecourse and the village in the valley was a favourite picnic spot. The charabanc spilled its load of excited picnickers on to the roadside and the driver opened the gate into the field. The men began to unload the boxes of food and crates of beer and when it was done, Joe came up to Anna and said, 'All done, miss. I'll be back to pick you up this evening.' He touched his cap before driving away.

Gracie was already there and Anna asked, 'Where's Sam? I thought you said he'd got the day off.'

'He's going to ride over on his bicycle.'

'Don't envy him coming up the hill in this heat,' Anna said, fanning her face with her hand. 'Let's get these tables moved into the shade otherwise the food will spoil.' She beckoned to two of the men, who set up the tables in the shade of a small copse backing onto the field.

Soon the picnic was under way. Children ran about, laughing and screaming at the unexpected freedom. While some of the women tried to organize them into games, the others helped to lay out the picnic fare.

She watched Johnson ordering the men around, the familiar dislike rising up again. Why can't he leave them to enjoy themselves, she thought. They're not at work now. Perhaps she should intervene.

Gracie, who was laying out plates of sandwiches, muttered. 'Just look at him – thinks he's the boss, doesn't he?'

Her friend's words made up her mind for her and she walked across to the factory manager, who was speaking to a group of men standing beside the beer table. Several of them had already opened bottles and were drinking and laughing while Johnson tried to remonstrate with them.

She wasn't very happy herself that they'd started drinking so early in the day but they worked hard all year and this was their day for enjoyment after all. She smiled as she approached and, ignoring Johnson, said with a smile, 'I'm pleased to see you're all having a good time.'

'Thank you, miss,' one of them replied.

'Thanks to Mr Grayson,' another added, holding up his glass in a toast. 'Here's to the boss, lads.'

They all drank a toast to the absent factory owner and Anna seized her chance to suggest that they helped to organize races for the children.

'My father always said this day out was for the families as well as the workers,' she said. 'It's good to see the little ones enjoying the sunshine and fresh air.'

Sam had just arrived, leaning his bicycle against the field gate. Gracie ran up to him, laughing, her face flushed. Anna watched them enviously. She hadn't seen Daniel for some time and now wished she'd invited him along. She shook her head. It wouldn't do, she realized. It was up to him to make a move – that's if he wanted to.

Daniel was at that moment handing out pamphlets in the nearby village. He was hot and tired and wishing he hadn't come. It was only the hope of seeing Anna that had induced him to give up his day off. When he had heard about the rally he had been so sure she'd be there. It had been hard to hide his disappointment when Lady Beatrice informed him that Anna was otherwise engaged.

'It's Grayson's annual works outing,' she said. 'They always provide a charabanc and a picnic on August bank Holiday.'

Daniel frowned. That Johnson fellow would there – she would be spending a whole day in his company. Despite her protests that she had no intention of marrying the factory manager, he still wasn't sure what the situation was. Dr Brown had seemed so certain that an engagement announcement was imminent.

Given his suspicions of the man, he would have tried to prevent it, even if he hadn't been in love with her himself. He handed out the pamphlets automatically, without his usual pleas to read them and take note of the aims of the movement. His mind was busy with more important things. Although it had been over a year since Lily's death, he knew Sam Hawker still wasn't satisfied. He must speak to the detective again. And he must try to see Anna too.

Lady Beatrice's imperious voice interrupted his thoughts as she gathered her followers around her in the village square.

'I think we've done all we can today,' she said. 'Thank you for your support. Now, fall in for the last march.' She pointed up the hill to the racecourse. 'Your transport home will be waiting for you.'

She led the way, sitting upright on her chestnut hunter, while the others straggled behind her. She began to chant the familiar cry, 'Votes for Women', although the only ones to hear as they left the village were a few sheep and a distant farm worker, who raised his head briefly then bent to his work again.

The chanting gave the weary group new heart and they took up the cry.

CHAPTER TWENTY-FIVE

THE HEAT HAD gone out of the day, the food was eaten, and the beer drunk and Anna thought they ought to start packing up to go home. The children still seemed to have plenty of energy. They were chasing each other across the grass, and in and out of the little copse on the edge of the field while the adults sat or lay in the shade, the men smoking, the women idly chatting. It seemed that no one wanted the day to end.

Anna looked down the hill to the village in the valley, taking in the view of the cottages surrounding the ancient church. It had been good to get out of the town and into the countryside, but now, it really was time to make a move. She stood up, her heart sinking as Johnson approached across the grass.

'Miss Anna, it has been a grand day, hasn't it?' he said. 'You must thank your father when you get home. He is a generous employer.'

Anna inclined her head but did not reply.

'And you, too, miss. I know you've worked hard today and behind the scenes as well.'

'It was my pleasure, Johnson.'

'Come now. I thought we had agreed you would call me Edward, especially now that—'

He turned at an interruption, his glance cold as Gracie approached.

'Miss Anna, may I speak with you a moment?' she asked.

'And what have you to say that is so important?' Johnson demanded.

'It's quite all right, Johnson.' Anna turned to Gracie. 'What is it?' She took the other girl's arm and led her away, leaving the manager staring after them.

'Nothing really. I just thought ...'

Anna gave a little laugh. 'Thank you for rescuing me,' she said.

'Maybe you should have joined Her Ladyship today instead of coming on the picnic,' Gracie said.

'Well, I do feel a little guilty for letting her down,' Anna confessed. 'But I've enjoyed it today, despite having to put up with Johnson for a whole day.'

'I've been keeping my eyes open as I promised but so far I haven't seen him doing anything suspicious.'

'I've tried to warn Father but he won't listen. And he won't give up on this idea of me marrying the man. He can't make me, though.' Anna glanced over her shoulder to see Johnson standing where they had left him, staring at her.

She shivered. 'He's threatened me, you know. Says he'll tell Father about me joining the suffragists.'

'Maybe you should tell Mr Grayson yourself. Then he won't have anything to hold over you,' Gracie suggested.

'Dr Brown knows – he said the same thing. He feels it would be less of a shock hearing it from me rather than an outsider.'

'He's right. I know you don't want your father upset but he's bound to find out sooner or later.'

Anna nodded, then said, 'Come on, we'd better get packed up.'

Inevitably, some of the glasses had got broken and she looked for a box to put the pieces in. She called to Johnson. 'Make sure there's no broken glass left in the field, won't you?' she said.

She turned away and started to pack the used crockery, pausing to look towards the village as she heard the sound of distant chanting. She laughed, clutching Gracie's arm and pointing down the hill.

'It's Bea and her suffragists,' she said, laughing.

'They're coming this way. Looks like we won't miss the rally after all,' Gracie said.

The rest of the party were now standing up and looking for the source of the noise. Some of the women dropped what they were doing and ran towards the field gate while the men looked on in disapproval.

The procession of about twenty suffragist supporters, carrying banners and chanting 'Votes for Women', reached the top of the hill. They were led by Lady Beatrice seated on Hector, her chestnut hunter, holding her banner proudly aloft. Seeing the women crowded by the gate, she reined in her horse and leaned down, offering a bunch of leaflets to be handed round.

Johnson's face reddened and he pushed his way through the crowd.

'You're not wanted here. Clear off,' he shouted.

'This is a public road,' Beatrice said. 'We have every right to be here.'

'I won't have you disrupting my workers,' he blustered.

Anna thrust him aside. 'They are not *your* workers, Johnson. And have you forgotten this is a holiday?'

'The charabanc will be here soon to take them home – and this rabble is taking up all the road.'

'Don't be ridiculous.'

As soon as she'd spoken, Anna realized she had said the wrong thing. She had undermined the factory manager in front of everyone and it was a slight he would not forgive. She flinched as his hands clenched by his sides, relaxing as he turned away and called to one of the men.

'Get those crates and stack them over here by the gate. And you,' he said to Gracie, 'finish packing those boxes. The driver will want to get away.' He strode across the field, issuing orders to the men to dismantle the trestle tables and benches.

The suffragists had stopped chanting and were muttering among themselves. They looked shocked but, Anna reflected, they should be used to such treatment by now. At least there had been no violence today. She looked up at Bea, still mounted on her horse.

'I'm sorry about that,' she said.

'The man's a boor,' Bea replied. 'Does your father know how he treats those people?'

'He has no idea what he's really like.'

'It's time someone enlightened him then. Perhaps I'll call and have a word.'

She laughed and leaned down to pat the hunter's neck. 'Perhaps we should move on, though.' She straightened and turned her head, beckoning to the group of supporters.

'Onwards, ladies,' she cried.

As they formed up, Anna spotted Daniel at the rear. He smiled as he caught her eye, and dropped out of the group.

Before he could speak to her, Johnson appeared, glaring up at Lady Beatrice. 'You still here? Be off with you.' He slapped the horse on the rump, causing it to plunge and rear. As it careered off across the field, with Bea clinging to its neck, Anna gasped as a picture flashed through her mind. She had seen it all before, hands reaching out from the crowd to push Lily into the road. She remembered seeing Johnson lurking in the crowd around Lady Beatrice and wondering why he was there. She still didn't know why but she was sure she was right.

Anna turned on Johnson.

'What a stupid thing to do,' she snapped.

Sam rushed over.

'I'll try to catch them,' he cried, grabbing his bicycle.

Daniel followed at a run with Anna and Gracie stumbling behind him. They entered the copse and stopped short when they saw Sam bending over Bea's still form. The horse was nowhere to be seen.

Anna raised a hand to her mouth. 'Is she...?'

'Let me look,' Daniel said, thrusting Sam aside and kneeling beside Bea's crumpled body. He placed his hand on her forehead and she stirred.

'What happened?' she asked in a faint voice. 'He's usually so placid. Something must have frightened him.'

'I saw it,' Anna said. 'Johnson hit the horse, made him bolt.'

Bea struggled to sit up. 'Is Hector all right?'

'Don't worry about the horse. Let's make sure you haven't broken anything.' Daniel proceeded to examine Beatrice, nodding with satisfaction. 'You'll feel a bit bruised for a few days but no real damage. You were very lucky.'

Anna knelt on the ground beside her friend, placing an arm round her shoulders. 'I was so frightened when I saw you lying there. Thank goodness you aren't badly hurt.' She looked up. 'Where's Sam?'

'He's gone after the horse,' said Gracie.

'Well, even if he catches him, you won't be riding him home today, Your Ladyship,' said Daniel.

'We'll see she gets home safely,' Anna said. 'Gracie, would you go and see if Joe has arrived with the Daimler, please?'

Gracie nodded and ran off across the field to where the picnickers and suffragists were milling around, uncertain what to do. The charabanc had pulled up beside the gate and Johnson was chivvying the factory workers into it.

Anna and Daniel helped Beatrice to her feet and, with their arms around her, made their way across the bumpy turf.

The Daimler had pulled in behind the charabanc and Gracie was explaining to Joe what had happened. He jumped down and took Anna's place, helping Bea into the motor car.

'What about Hector?' Bea asked, her voice shaky. 'Is he all right?'

'Sam will catch him, Your Ladyship,' Gracie said.

Anna didn't know what to do. She felt she ought to accompany Bea back to the Manor and make sure she was really all right. But on the other hand, she felt responsible for her father's employees and that it was her duty to stay until everyone was safely on their way home.

As she hesitated, Johnson came over to her and said, 'You don't need to stay. Why don't you go with Her Ladyship?'

'I want to wait and see if Sam manages to catch the horse. Joe can take Her Ladyship home and come back for me.' She gestured to the charabanc driver who was waiting to drive off.

'Go along, Johnson,' she added. She couldn't wait for him to go so that she could tell Sam what she'd seen.

'If you're sure, miss.' He glanced behind him, his lips tightening as he spotted Sam leading the chestnut hunter towards them. 'You caught him, then?' he said. 'I wonder what made him bolt like that.'

'It's obvious to me,' Anna said, abandoning caution. 'You hit him.'

Sam's lips set in a tight line. 'And not just with his hand. Look at that.' He pointed to the hunter's flank which was streaming with blood. He glared at Johnson.

'This was done deliberately.'

'And there's blood on his hand,' Anna said.

'I cut myself picking up broken glass....'

'Don't lie,' Anna spat. 'You meant to harm Lady Beatrice.'

Anna realized she was right when a snarl of rage erupted from the factory manager and he sprang at Anna. 'You're just trying to discredit me. Think you're too good for me, don't you ...'

As he tried to claw at Anna's face, Daniel intervened with a punch to Johnson's jaw. He slumped against the five-barred gate, and all the bravado and bluster went out of him as Sam handed the horse's reins to Gracie and reached for his handcuffs.

Daniel's arms came round Anna and she leaned her head against his chest. She was trembling, but whether from the shock of Johnson's attack or the feeling of being in Daniel's arms, she wasn't really sure. Once he had made sure she was unharmed, he turned to Sam.

'What are we going to do with him?' he asked.

Sam waved to the charabanc driver to drive off. 'When Miss Anna's driver returns, we'll take him in to the police station.'

Gracie, who had been silent up to now, lunged at Johnson.

'You killed my sister,' she shouted. 'You came to her funeral, offered condolences and all the time ...'

Her face twisted in anger and she lashed out with her foot.

Anna took her arm and pulled her away. 'The law will deal with him,' she said.

Johnson found his voice. 'I'm sorry. I didn't mean ...'

'You might not have meant to harm Lily but what about Lady Beatrice? It *was* her you meant to kill, wasn't it?' Anna said.

'I needed the money, but he didn't pay up. Said I'd botched it. When I saw her sitting up on that horse all hoity-toity and looking down her nose, I thought, why not try again?' He looked at Anna. 'I was desperate. When your father started coming in to the factory again, I knew it was only a matter of time ...'

'Who was going to pay you?' Sam interrupted.

'Ponsonby-Smythe.'

'I knew it,' Anna whispered. 'It *was* his car I saw.'

'I don't think any of us should say any more,' Sam warned. 'Miss Anna, you'll be called as a witness when this gets to court.' He glanced up as the Daimler appeared over the brow of the hill. 'Here's your driver. The sooner we get him to the station the better.'

'And I'd better take Hector back to the Manor,' Daniel said. 'Lady Beatrice will be fretting about him.'

Anna was disappointed. She had hoped that Daniel would also accept a lift back to Midchester.

Trying to keep her voice neutral, she said, 'Is he badly hurt?'

'It's just a surface cut – enough to startle him and make him bolt though. But he seems none the worse for it. I'll ride him back to the manor and let Lady Beatrice know what's been happening.'

'I promised to call on her too. Daniel, could you explain, tell her I'll call tomorrow? And warn her about her cousin too. He may still try to harm her.'

'Why don't you come with me? I'll see you safely home afterwards.'

Anna's heart was thumping as Daniel helped her up onto Hector's back and mounted behind her. They waited until Joe had driven off with Gracie, Sam and the factory manager.

Daniel's arms came round her and he grasped the reins. It was only two miles to the Manor but Anna wished it had been twenty. The events of the past hour faded as she gave herself up to the sheer joy of being so close to the man she loved. His arms tightened around her and he leaned close to speak in her ear, a hint of laughter in his voice.

'Who would have dreamed when we started out this morning that we would end up like this?'

Anna turned her head, smiling. 'It's a good end to the day, though, isn't it?'

'I'm glad you agree.' He leaned towards her and his lips brushed hers, gently but firmly. 'I've been wanting to do that for a long time.'

'And I've been waiting,' she answered.

'I take it you and Johnson...?'

'I tried to tell you. It was my father's wish, not mine.'

'We've got a lot of talking to do,' Daniel said. 'But here we are at the Manor so it'll have to wait.'

As they reached the top of the drive, a groom rushed towards them. 'I heard there'd been an accident. Is he all right?'

The man seemed more concerned about the horse than his mistress, Anna thought as Daniel helped her down. They watched him lead Hector round to the stables, then walked up to the house. A maid showed them into the drawing room where Bea was lying on a chaise longue, a blanket over her legs.

When she saw them, she threw the coverlet back and tried to stand up.

'Stay there, Your Ladyship,' Daniel said. 'You've had a bad fall, you must rest.'

'I'm perfectly all right. Now – I need explanations.' She turned to Anna. 'Did that man deliberately cause Hector to bolt? And why....'

Daniel told her how Johnson had lost money at the races and Alfred had offered to pay his debts if he helped to get rid of Lady Beatrice. After his arrest, he had broken down completely and once he started talking, it had all come out.

'I knew Alfred was desperate for money and he was devastated when I turned down his proposal,' Bea said, shaking her head. 'My own cousin.' She sighed. 'I knew he was only interested in my fortune but ...'

'There's more,' Anna said.

'But why now? Lily died over a year ago. And, yes, Anna, I know you tried to convince me it wasn't an accident but I dismissed it. If anything I put it down to someone wanting to disrupt the rally, not....' Her voice broke as she realized how close she had come to being killed.

'I think today Johnson just saw an opportunity and grabbed it. You see, Alfred refused to pay him when the plot to kill you failed. But he still owed money to the bookies and he's been embezzling money from the factory in an effort to pay.'

'Has he confessed then?' Beatrice asked.

'Most of it,' Anna said. 'I found out about him cooking the books but I couldn't prove anything.' Her voice caught as she continued. 'I'm sure he was hoping that Father would die and he'd never be found out. When Father came back to work he knew it was only a matter of time before he was caught.'

'So he seized the chance to harm me, hoping Alfred would pay up?'

'It was his only chance to put the books straight before Father realized what was going on.'

'It was a foolish, impulsive act,' Daniel said. 'He couldn't have been thinking straight.'

The realization of her narrow escape seemed to hit Bea all of a sudden and she leaned back against the chaise longue, a hand over her eyes.

'I would have given Alfred the money if I'd known how desperate he was.'

Daniel took Bea's hand, feeling for her pulse. 'You must calm yourself, Your Ladyship. You've had a shock.'

Bea pushed him away. 'Where is Alfred?' She tried to stand. 'I must warn him.'

'No, Bea. You can't help him now. He'll be arrested soon. Sam was going to send someone.'

'But he's still my cousin. We grew up together ...' A tear rolled down her cheek. 'And poor Mother. How will she take all this?'

'It's out of our hands, Your Ladyship,' said Daniel.

Dusk had fallen and a maid came in to draw the curtains and light the lamps.

As she did so, a shadow passed by the window and a few moments later, they heard the sound of car starting up, the roar of an engine as it sped down the drive.

'Too late – he's gone,' Anna said. 'He must have heard us.'

'He'll be caught soon enough,' Daniel said, standing up. He turned to Anna. 'I think I ought to get you home. Mr Grayson will be worrying about you, especially if Joe has informed him about what's happened.'

CHAPTER TWENTY-SIX

ANNA AND DANIEL did not speak on the short drive back to Midchester, each engrossed in their own thoughts. Anna knew she should be pondering on how to break the news to her father that his trusted manager was not only a thief but a murderer. The shock might bring on another attack and she was grateful that Daniel would be with her. But uppermost in her mind, despite the shocking events of the past few hours, was the memory of Daniel's arms around her and his lips against her cheek.

Now that they were alone she'd hoped that he would tell her it hadn't just been an impulsive gesture. She stared at the back of the chauffeur's head – of course, they weren't really alone, although, true to his training, George had stared ahead, oblivious to their presence.

The Lanchester stopped in front of St Martin's House and he got out, opened the passenger door and helped Anna down. When Daniel stepped down as well, George asked, 'Shall I wait for you, sir?'

'No, thank you, George, I can walk from here. Besides, I may be a while.' Daniel glanced at Anna, smiling. 'I need to speak to your father – if it is convenient.'

Before she could reply, Millie opened the front door.

'Oh, there you are, miss. It's late. I was getting worried.' She caught sight of Daniel and gasped. 'Dr Peters – is anything wrong?'

'Not at all, Millie. The doctor escorted me home, that's all.' Anna invited Daniel in and turned to the maid. 'How has Father been today?'

'He's fine – back to his old self, I'd say, although he was sorry to miss the outing.'

'It's a good thing he wasn't there,' Anna said.

The maid's eyes widened but Anna put a hand on her arm. 'I'll tell you about it later, Millie. But now, we need to speak to Father. Is he in the study?'

William looked up from his newspaper when they walked in, a frown crossing his face at the sight of Anna's companion.

'Why are you here, Doctor?' he asked.

Daniel came into the room and held out his hand. 'This is a social call, Mr Grayson. I hope it's convenient.'

'I suppose so.' He turned to Anna. 'I've had supper – couldn't wait for you, although I expected you back long since. You'd better offer this young man some refreshment.'

Anna glanced at Daniel, who nodded.

'I'll go and speak to Cook,' she said, glad to leave Daniel to break the news of what had happened.

When she returned, William was leaning back in his chair, his hand to his chest.

'I don't believe it,' he whispered. 'Johnson? But why try to kill Lady Beatrice?'

Anna rushed to his side. 'Father, don't get upset. I know you've always trusted him, but I did try to warn you …'

Daniel leaned forwards in his chair. 'Perhaps I'd better start at the beginning. It's a long story.' He glanced at Anna. 'If you don't mind, I'll have to tell him everything – about why you were in Brighton …'

Anna sighed. 'I was planning to confess myself so, go on …'

'Confess what?' William snapped, sitting upright. 'What have you been up to, miss?' He glanced from one to the other. 'I trust there has been no impropriety.'

'Not at all, sir. It was pure chance that I was there too.' He paused. 'Please, sir, let me explain.'

William nodded and Daniel took a deep breath. 'You remember when one of your employees was run down by a car in Brighton last year?'

When he nodded again, Daniel continued. 'I was there – by chance, as I said – and so was your daughter. We were witnesses to what happened, but I'm afraid it wasn't an accident.'

Anna sat beside her father and took his hand as Daniel proceeded with his story. When he revealed that she had been involved with the suffragists, William gave an angry exclamation. She squeezed his hand and whispered, 'I'm sorry, Father – sorry I deceived you.'

She wasn't sorry for what she'd done; she only regretted the hurt she had caused him.

'Go on, Doctor,' William commanded.

It took a long time for the whole story to come out, how Sam Hawker as well as Daniel had had their suspicions, how Anna had been convinced that she had seen someone push Lily into the path of the car.

'I was sure it was Alfred's car, but he must have had an accomplice,' Anna said. 'I couldn't think who it could be but I had seen Johnson in the crowd. And when I discovered he was stealing from the firm I knew he was capable of anything.'

'But why didn't you tell me, Anna?' asked William, his face pale with shock.

'I didn't want to worry you and I didn't think you'd believe me without proof.'

'It was his action today that showed him in his true colours,' said Daniel. 'Sam saw him slap the horse on the rump, on purpose to make him bolt.'

'I'm finding it hard to take all this in,' William said, covering his eyes and sighing. 'I've been such a fool, trusting that man.'

'You weren't to know, Father.'

'Well, he's been arrested now and it won't be long before Ponsonby-Smythe is caught too,' Daniel said.

While they had been talking, Millie had come in with a tray and silently put it down on the table. She paused in the doorway, eyes wide as she caught the gist of their conversation. Anna caught her eye and waved her away but she had a feeling she was listening outside the door. She smiled inwardly as she got up to serve the coffee and sandwiches. Millie wasn't a gossip but her affection for her mistress meant that she had to be involved in anything that affected Anna's happiness and wellbeing.

William took a sip of his coffee and Anna was pleased to see that the colour had come back into his face. She was about to speak when he put his cup down and with a stern look, said, 'I'm disappointed in you, Anna. You knew how I felt about these women and their outrageous ideas. How could you deceive me like that?'

Anna almost reacted to his use of the word 'outrageous' but, as she opened her mouth to speak, Daniel gently shook his head. She swallowed her anger and said meekly, 'I've told you I'm sorry, Father.' To hide her expression, she leaned over to replace her cup and saucer on the tray.

'Very well, my dear, we'll say no more about it. I just hope you've learned your lesson and won't get mixed up in any more of this nonsense.'

Before she could reply, Daniel took her hand. 'I think I can set your mind at rest, sir. You see, I would very much like to marry your daughter. As a busy doctor's wife, I can assure you she would have no time for this "nonsense" as you call it.'

How dare he? Anna almost snatched her hand away, but his fingers tightened over hers and she thought she detected the suspicion of a wink.

William didn't answer for a few moments and Daniel, still firmly holding Anna's hand, asked, 'Well, sir?'

'You have my blessing, dear boy,' William said, shaking Daniel's hand. He stood up and went to the sideboard, picking up a decanter. 'I think this calls for a toast,' he said.

'But Father, Dr Brown said ...'

Daniel laughed. 'Don't forget, Anna, I am a doctor too. And I think a small glass in celebration won't do your father any harm at all.'

'Well said.' William raised his glass. 'Ring for Millie,' he said, 'and ask Cook to come in too. They must hear about this.'

When congratulations had been given and toasts drunk, Daniel declared that he must be on his way.

'I'll show you out, sir,' Millie said.

'No, let me,' Anna said with a smile.

In the shadow of the porch, Daniel took Anna in his arms and this time, the kiss was deep and passionate, the sort of kiss she had been longing for almost from the day she had first met him.

'A perfect end to the day,' he murmured, stroking her hair and finding her lips once more.

Anna wished it could go on forever, but at last he released her and, with a sigh, said, 'I really must go. I'll call again tomorrow when I've finished my rounds.'

She walked to the gate with him and watched as he strode away, her heart pounding and her legs weak. He paused at the corner, turned and raised his hand and she waved in farewell.

Inside the house, she leaned against the door for a moment to catch her breath. At this moment, the suffragist cause, the excitement of Johnson's arrest and the satisfaction that there would be justice for Lily, were all far from her mind as she contemplated the future with the man she loved.

Anna woke early the following morning and for a brief moment, she thought she might have been dreaming. But as the events of the previous day flooded back, she jumped out of bed, a smile on her lips and a song in her heart. At this moment, she didn't care that Johnson had been arrested or that her father might still be angry at her deception. The memory of Daniel's arms around her, the passionate kiss which was everything she'd ever dreamed of, drove everything else from her mind. He wanted to marry her – and Father had consented.

She dressed quickly, not bothering to ring for Millie, and ran downstairs. 'Good morning, Father. Lovely day, isn't it?' she said.

He had already breakfasted and was reading the newspaper.

'Is it?' His expression was grim and he rustled the pages of the paper.

'Is something wrong, Father?' she asked.

'You may well ask. Things have turned very bad in Europe – we shall be at war before the day is out.'

'War? I don't understand.' When she'd asked him to explain before, he had brushed her concerns aside. And now he did it again.

'You wouldn't understand, my dear.'

If only she'd taken more interest in what had been happening beyond the small town of Midchester. She could have read the newspapers. But lately she'd had other – more important, she thought – things on her mind. The future of the factory and its employees, as well as the threat to Bea's life, not to mention the suffrage cause, had occupied her thoughts to the exclusion of everything else. Well, almost everything, she thought with a smile. Thinking about Daniel had taken up a lot of her time as well.

'Will it really affect us at home, if war is declared?' she asked.

'See for yourself,' William said, thrusting the newspaper at her. 'I must get off to the factory, find out what Johnson's really been up to.'

'Can I help, Father?'

'I don't think so. You might come along later, after Daniel has called.'

'I'll be there.' Anna couldn't believe it. Was Father at last beginning to see that she might be of some assistance in running the factory?

He had not been gone long when the doorbell rang and Millie

ushered Daniel in. He scarcely waited for the maid to close the door before he swept Anna into his arms. It was some minutes before either of them could speak.

'I can't believe your father gave in so easily,' Daniel said. 'I thought I'd have to fight for you.'

Anna laughed. 'Would you really have fought?'

'To the death,' he said, laughing with her.

She sobered instantly at his words as she recalled her father's earlier words.

'Will you fight – when war's declared?' she asked.

'I don't know. I think I would be of more use as a doctor.'

'I agree. But what about me? What shall I do while I wait for you?'

'Believe me, Anna darling, there will be much for women to do. They will be needed here at home – nursing and such. Even possibly doing the work that the men usually do.'

'I hope you're right,' Anna said. 'I wonder what it will mean for Bea and her supporters? They can't go on campaigning while the country's at war. Still, if what you say is true, women will have a chance to prove themselves – when it's all over, perhaps those in power will be more inclined to listen to us.'

'They will,' Daniel said, confidently. 'Meanwhile, let's try to forget these gloomy thoughts. Today is meant to be a happy one.' He felt in his jacket pocket and brought out a small box. 'I hope you like it – it belonged to my mother.'

He opened it to reveal a ring set with garnets and opals.

'I'll buy you a diamond ring if you prefer,' he said, looking at her anxiously.

'No, this is perfect.' She gazed back, her eyes alight, and he placed the ring on her finger. She had scarcely believed this day would ever come.

The kiss that followed drove everything from her mind and she revelled in his nearness, the feel of his arms around her, the clean smell of his hair. Whatever the future held, she knew she could face it with Daniel beside her.

When at last he released her, she looked up into his eyes. 'I love you, Daniel. I think I have from the moment we met.'

'We've wasted so much time with these misunderstandings. Nothing will come between us now.'

'Not even the war?' she asked, her voice trembling a little.

'We'll face that when it comes,' he said.

That evening at midnight, Britain declared war on Germany – as William said when he read the news at breakfast the next morning, how could they leave Belgium at the mercy of such a mighty power? Anna could see that they'd had little choice. But her heart was heavy at the thought of what was to come, and she dared to hope that it really would all be over by Christmas, as the papers were predicting.

All she and Daniel could do was make the most of their time together, for who knew what the future would bring? She just thanked God that they had been given the chance to acknowledge their love for each other and gain her father's blessing in time.